The Voyage of Gethsarade

M. G. Claybrook

Also by M. G. Claybrook

YA Fiction

Mabby the Squirrel's Guide to Flying

Poetry

The Clarity of Fire

Short stories and novellas

Psychocide
The Miller and the Moon
Goldenfire and the Bad Luck Roman
The Legend of Elorus the Hesperian

THE VOYAGE OF GETHSARADE

*Copyright © 2019 **M. G. Claybrook***

All rights reserved.

Dallas, Texas

Cover art by Matthew Gene Claybrook.

ISBN: *9781-97349-083-8*

For Laura, who shares my feelings about unnecessary mouth noises and drivers in Texas.

Table of Contents

Prologue

Many things in this world plainly are when they should not be, despite the greatest of odds. Think nothing impossible! Some impossible things persist even against the inconsolate hurls of time ever vast, like the Sun's endless burning away at the gates of a long abandoned home. Sometimes they haunt your door like the ghost of a friend. And sometimes they sit in your arms and laugh while they tease your whiskers, and they kiss your worries goodnight like a half-told story, telling you worry no more.

Of all things that should never be, yet are, one should never expect to come upon a squirrel far, far out at sea, and not somehow lost beyond finding. In the wake of all things, he—whom some might say had a reputation and infamy to others—stood against all in the heart of a storm and wrote poetry.

There was a pup wrapped up tight, hanging in a small hammock in the front port-side corner of the aftcastle cabin. The rocking of the waves and the soft chatter of rain held him well asleep. But woeful as it was that a captain should take not only a female, his wife, to the sea despite the protests of the crew but also a babe, causing some of them to mutter that this caused their calamity. But such superstitions entertained the lower ranks, not him. Anywise, the pup slept most sound, as the rolling waves at night oft affect. He was concerned utmost with the apocalypse of squirrel-kind and how he might still prevent it.

The captain's tail swirled as he wrote furiously, left to right, then crossed a piece out and hurled every which way again. This strange one sat among an array of books gathered laboriously over a lifetime, some taken without permission as good collectors fitly do.

There were bookshelves along the walls of the creaking cabin. But in the tempest, the books in majority forsook them a while back and took their rest on the deck, now gathering in the seeping-in rain. But our subject had not left his seat to trample over them. The piece under production was of the most utter importance.

Of all the books from the shelves facing him across the evening light of the cabin clapping side to side in the waves, this incomplete chapter concerned him most utmostly in its half-scribbled state. Though his ship tossed and pitched, he held onto the table with one shaking paw and scribbled with the trembling other, eyes wide upon the paper in the dying half-light. His mottled paws had broken quill after quill, and they ranged like mendicant savages around the swooning desk.

"Sangareth!" A voice rang beyond the cabin wall where he heard running, steps that fought all the directions of the wind and rain and rolling in the dark. He could tell it was the voice of his beloved. Oh, why had she come?

"Sangareth!" She cried again, and he scribbled harder, for she knew precisely where he was.

Let her come, thought he, but sod it all, I shall do this.

Then the door broke open, sending pages flying all over the cabin, yet still he did not look up, but only strained his eyes and dug his nails in, for the candle was now out and distraction would not do.

Alya looked at him, hoping he would look up to see the tears streaming down her face, hoping she would not have to say what she had to say then, for she wished the words not to come out.

"They're upon us, my love."

But yonder hero stared only harder at the page. He slapped his paw down to hold the page in the eruption of wind. "Curse this storm!"

"You're writing now?" She cried, "Forget your books and weather. Of all our adventures endured, this one may do us in, and here you are, a squirrel of action, sitting there writing. Oh, whatever should I do with you?"

She took up the swaddled youngrel, awake and crying from the bluster. She tried to hush him by whispering, "There, there, my beautiful Gethsarade."

"Hush now, please!" He set his pen in its secure inkwell and came over to console her at the door.

"My dear, you are right, and we may be done in as well as I can tell, for they will hold no respect nor quarter for us. I cannot allow our story to go down into the depths, with no one, I mean our child, knowing what happened here. For the moment, Love, I put eyes on the dark ship I knew what to do. It's over, but not for him. Go, ready the lines to lower him to safety and do try not to be seen. I will complete this letter and get it into his raft. Then whosoever shall find him, bless them and keep them, and he shall find his home again on the day. The Great Nut forbid we should fail and lose all! I shall have none of this making our story one with a sad and senseless end."

He helped her take up the pup from his hammock. "Now, I beg, go!" And he continued to write of a treasure he had once fought to save, bewondered by all the world.

She bowed her head to him in acquiescence to the tones of defeat, despair, and yet hope in his voice, and then she disappeared.

As the sea closed the scuttle door behind her, he looked for a moment at it with so many thoughts racing through his mind, namely of want. Want for seeing his beloved for the last time, and yet also how strange he should seem. What things might a squirrel do in the face of impending calamity? He allowed himself to chuckle at the irony she pointed out. Of all the poems he made up in his head to charm her, and of all the times he had dreamed to sit down and write his tales, only now it turned out to be genuinely far more critical than he ever knew, the doing of such things.

He returned to the desk, made the last scribbles, and clapped shut the book just as Alya, his beloved, broke in once more and screamed into the flying, dark cabin, "They're here!" Those were her last words, he figured, to the muffled poundings of running on deck, swords and grappling hooks striking and dragging about.

He ran to the wall, but just before she could take the book from him, something whipped her out of the doorway and tossed her somewhere out of sight, probably knocked unconscious, alas! But the volume remained in his grasp still, as the screams and crashes became deafening. Then, just as quickly, they stopped, followed by a deathly silence concluded by a boom of cheers from voices he did not know.

In the silence, he had heard the muffled whimpers of his wife beyond the doorway out of his line of sight, to which he breathed a breath of relief to himself when there appeared a grotesque rat through the cheers. Then in came one or two of his horde, carrying lanterns and torches, offensive in their own rights, sheathing their bloodied swords.

But Sangareth kept his eyes on the leader. He bore the stench of sea rot and scales on top of rodent filth and vertigrae, a smell that offended the saltiest of nostrils, be sure.

Sangareth was repulsed at the sight, for the creature sported a massive head as ugly as could be. It was as the sight of a sea-demon with his lips rolled back and red teeth like a thousand rotten knives. And when the rat grinned his eyes, empty casks like a locust's molt, were only the uglier. Neither captain made any move for a moment or two, but at length, the short, fat, unwelcome one invited himself across Sangareth's threshold after realizing the owner of this vessel was not as prone to formalities as some of his other captures.

He took one unwelcomed look about the room and said, "Well, someone's lookin' for a good rib rackin'. Don't move. Let me guess that you're the captain of this ship?"

"What's it to you, bagger? Plague-sack! Filth!"

"Name's Barrogan Black." The rat's scurvy-swollen paw became a fist, and he then began to shake at his fury from the insult, but he held onto himself.

A rat in possession of composure. Intriguing, uncommon even, thought Sangareth.

"I don't care. We both know you haven't killed me yet because you want to see where the rest of my trade is, so let me just expedite this and tell you this ship is everything left of me. There is nothing to take from me you haven't got so just kill me, take your kind, and go die."

The rat said nothing.

"I said there's nothing here for you."

"Nothing here for me...?" the rat repeated absentmindedly. "Nothing here for me...meaning nothing here for me to know about bein' here, or nothing here for me but for someone else? Anyone at all, or anyone in particular, or just not me? Because if it were nothing, what would be the point of saying anything of the kind?"

Sangareth was in no mood, but the rat looked at him for a moment, smiled his bloody smile, and then turned once more to inspect the cabin.

"True, I see nothing of particular interest." He kicked a book and stepped on another.

To this, Sangareth took another jab. "Your appreciation for literature suggests an expansive understanding of the value of things."

"Dogs got no use for readin'." said the pirat, whose tone was approaching impatience. "They bite and scratch and play along to their masters."

"And mice piss and moan and eat their own–"

The rat never let him finish, for the breath went out of Sangareth when the pirat whirled around and stuck a knife in the captain's unexpectant side. He fell on a knee but did not complain.

"Eat what? What did you say?"

But the captain of the Tara Feen could not speak at the moment.

"Loss for words suddenly? Well, shame. I was enjoying our little fact-trade. What's this, then?"

The rat noticed the parchment in Sangareth's shaking claw and snatched it away. Sangareth struggled to breathe, kneeling on the deck as the pirat hmm'ed and hawed over the pages, ripping out the ones he saw as unfit and tossing them to the floor.

"Yeah, not so good. Mmm, that one's better. Oh, I like this one, very nice. Hoi-yo, the ink's still wet. Did you write this, bub, just now while we were comin' aboard yer ship? What could be so important that you would neglect your own schoon and boon to write poetry?"

He perused a little while more. "I see...I see. Hmm...Indeed, I see. Persimmonia...Upward...Earth and Sky. What?" The pirat touched his lips thoughtfully. "I say, you're good. So good I don't understand it at all."

"But the one meant to understand, at the right time, will. Just don't worry about it, fool. The book in no way concerns you."

"Oh, I'll be the judge of that, thank you much." He clapped his miry paw on the hero's back, and Sangareth fell to the floor. His tail writhed as inchoate moans emitted from his gut.

"You see, I see here talk of salvation for everyone, right?" said Barrogan Black, the rat.

Sangareth said nothing and staggered to his knees. Just let the rat talk, he thought.

"Now tell me if I'm wrong. Salvation for everyone comes after someone is needin' salvation from something. That something is usually war, and war is usually 'cause of somebody wanting something someone else's got. And that something has to be worth a'fightin' a war over, if there's a war to be saved from."

"I'm sorry, but could you please stab me again? If you could be so polite as to end my misery instead of making me listen to you talk?"

"Oh, well, then I'll keep going. As I was saying, do you know what pirats do? Mr.?"

"I'm not telling you."

He flipped to the front matter. "Ah, Mister Sangareth."

Sangareth rolled his eyes. Okay, the rat was smarter than he appeared, but hopefully was still not smart enough to shut up. The crew were about to burst at the seams for they, like all crews, loved a good roasting of the captain.

Sangareth thought, *keeping up the banter might buy Alya the time she needs, if she's still out there*. He began, however, to feel the lull of blood loss drawing him to unconsciousness, and he sank further to the floor, panting, and balling his fists to keep alert. The pirat kept pacing.

"So what pirats do, for those here who are unfamiliar (he waved his paw about, bringing chuckles from the rat crew). A pirat makes his trade by making the trade of others his own. A straightforward concept, now, the one thing more profitable for a pirat is to accomplish this task by proxy."

Sangareth looked at him as if to ask precisely where Black was going with all this, and just then one of the hench-rats leaned down and whispered, "We call it outsourcing."

"Thank you Donglefist. That will do. Now, outsourcing is getting someone else to do all the heavy-lifting of fighting battles and the like and letting us just get on to the work of stealing. If I had to guess, you know something about that, don't you? There is no better way to find such a fitting situation for an ambitious rat such as myself, than for you to point out for me exactly where to find two kings who recently finished tearing each other to bits. Then all I have to do is walk in, right when they are both too weak to do anything, and take whatever I want. You don't want to tell me anything? No matter, you've just told me everything I need to know."

He took the book.

"You seem to be on the way to finding a savior for your tribe or whatever you call yourselves. Well, I have bad news. You got me instead, and I will be your apocalypse."

Sangareth sank in apparent defeat. But just then he heard the hum of a line being suddenly let down and there was a faint splash outside at the waterline.

Barrogan motioned for someone to check out the noise, and moments later a slime-ball rat hauled Sangareth's wife through the doorway with her arms bound.

"No! My love, I'm so sorry, dear, I know you wanted to get the book to him, but I couldn't wait anymore. I had to! Mmm, hmm!" A rat clapped a paw over her mouth.

"It's all right, dear. I understand. Better the boy alive at all odds than a well-read corpse."

"What's going on here?" said Barrogan Black.

"What's going on, mister pirat, sir, is you've been had. All I had to do was keep you, like all your arrogant kind, talking, and bought all the time we needed to get the savior of our world out of your filthy clutches."

The pirat bolted out of the door, and two of the bigger rats grabbed the couple and brought them out and up to the aft deck. There in the wake was a lonely lifeboat, with nothing inside but a pack of provisions for two, and a small, swaddled little squirrel infant crying and frantically looking for its mother, but to no avail. His mother worried herself with what she could, and then she noticed the knife wound in her husband's side.

"You are wounded!"

"But oh joy that our little one should live," he whispered to Alya as she wept for him.

"I only regret I could not hold him one more time, and I could not see him get your message someday. But it is with him."

"What did you say?" Barrogan Black snapped. He put his knife to her throat.

"She said you are a buffoon if you think you will ever conquer us. You will lose and at his dealing, as faith commands!"

Sangareth, despite his weakened state, tried to stand up, but failed, and sank down next to his wife on her knees. She looked at the pirat with pity, then at Sangareth. "He will find us. I know it!" she whispered.

"Oh, really. Find you will he? Tell me, I've heard of a land of legend where rodents can fly. Is this place real? The land of 'deliverance' you speak of?"

"As real as I am here before you. Just as well for me to tell you for the likes of you will never find it."

"Oh, so you can fly! Both of you? Flying squirrels, truly?"

Sangareth's chest puffed, but his eyes held suspicious.

"Tell me, I'd like to see you do this trick. And if you can do it, I will let you live."

"You jest."

"I do not! No, just fly right out to that boat. Your precious little button lies waitin' for you, and I will turn course and ere you shall see no more harm come from me."

"I don't believe you."

"What's to lose, Captain, except your child if you fail. And what of your life? If you succeed, you can come back and someday find me and give me a run for my money. I mean your money. Ha!"

The legendary Sangareth and his wife, Alya, took the bargain, and they lighted off the stern of the ship once their own, a vessel of the most delicate construction from the most excellent place in all the world, her home of Hesperia. She had a high stern and a broad wake indeed.

"Are you sure we should just let them go, sah?" said the husky voice of one of his crew. But the pirat captain held up his paw to silence them for he knew plenty about flying squirrels. They were travelers though they were not so prevalent in other lands. They were mean animals, with a spirit like coal, and they loved to watch their enemies squirm and struggle like worms on a hook before they died.

Nevertheless, Barrogan's found this entertainment dry as he watched while holding on to the book and muttering to himself in a most uncharacteristic manner of broodfulness and curiosity, repeating repeatedly, "Message? What message?"

"The usual orders, boss?" said one of the filthy rats.

"No, keep this ship. Burn the other."

Over the side, one might have been able to strain the ear to hear those words as Sangareth fought against the waves and wounds to hold his dearest once last as they began to be taken under.

"It is all right my dear," he said as he struggled. "No matter, for our pup shall find safety and peace from all this now, thanks to you, and our story shall live. He shall live to find and save us all. Worry not, it is done."

And struggle they did on the way down, but not in a cowardly fashion. For though Sangareth and his lovely bride, Alya, took the rat's bet, they stepped up on the stern, looked out, and bowed their eyes to one another, knowing. The waves were far too far away for them to reach their weeping baby, as the infant's raft continued to toss its way under the vaulting procession of the stars.

Now flying squirrels can fly well as they are some of the most amazing creatures in all of nature. Although Sangareth and Alya fought the waves valiantly after going as far as they could, like any decent parents would do when faced with the impossible, on that day the waves were too much. Squirrels are simply not built for the sea.

The fair hero Sangareth was too weak from his wounds, and his wife would sooner die than leave the side of either of her beloveds. Thus, they committed themselves to the despair of the waves in the most horrific fashion, such was their demise that caused the very earth itself to cry out to the Great Nut in all its wisdom for justice. Even as the clouds cleared that night, darkness has come upon us.

—Excerpt from The Annals of Hesperiana, often called Wintersfall, after the Great Fire. Author uncertain. The book tells the stories and legends of the exiled General Sangareth. Some sources speculate the text to be the work of a surviving crew member of his lost ship, the Tara Feen.

After reading this text, the truth came together for Hesperia as we recovered the last of scraps from the Library Tree's remains. But this part of the story does not exist within those charred tombs. As I tell it, though the little one was too young to even know what was happening, they took his happiness from him.

To those horrid sounds of laughter from the evilest rat in all the seas, Gethsarade, the young pup, began his unwitting, and most unwanted search for his home against all odds.

There was a day he could not even remember, yet he knew growing up, for as long as he *could* remember, that something always called to him from the horizon far out among the waves—no matter wherever he was, beyond the sight of the evensun.

What we do not know about the tale of *Wintersfall*, the other story that started all this, is its ending goes beyond the prophesying of an ousted and deranged leader as some believe. Though the lovers' story ended too soon, in their wake another began.

Now, what I am about to relate to you is entirely conjecture and speculation. Dismiss everything if you like. However, being who we are, we should also consider above our typical rational need for typical evidence and ask what the odds are. In this case, one, does such a book exist with names written upon and in it? Two that, with days betwixt and in a far-off land, there should be discovered weeping on the shore a baby famished and weary, appearing to an elderly old hag with some kindness left in her long gray hair for the young types as the Great Nut had never graced her with a youngrel of her own.

Then also consider this: Of all of the odds to beat, the chances of a lost book's pages upon a lost ship and crew, there was a name, the same as the strange one, Gethsarade, written inside a bottle hidden in the same pup's swaddling, who was found inside a boat wedged upon the shore by a kind squirrel hag.

These circumstantial events were entirely unbeknownst to one another elsewise in the note there written—and this was told by her to her gifted pup by the spirits of the sea to him and alone—these words, "Please care for our Gethsarade, as you would the last of hopes..." written in haste, without the name of the author. I suppose knowing that name should have made things all much easier. But, as a good friend of mine once said, "All great journeys must come to a beginning." G. B.

1: A Brave New Squirrel

Thus, we begin our true tale. There was a sailor long ago. Some say he sailed the wide world, all the way round it, and he touched with his own paw every monument to the sky and became a legend among squirrel-kind. End to end, he connected a great golden circle within all the starry lines.

But wait, you might say, "Squirrels who are sailing is poppycock and unheard of." To which, I'd say you haven't heard the tale of Gethsarade.

But the consummate warrior of the seas you have heard of was not him. No, friends, he did nothing of the sort, as much as I might wish he had, but he had not yet done so when we met.

Though these two stories are like circles closing over each other, I'll tell you, though the other story is much better, with many astonishing and doggish scrapes and moments of captivating suspense, this tale, plot-wise, is a flop.

I still feel this story is one I must tell you, for now such things pass, and you must know them before we can understand all other starry things in their pure light. You could once go read about the Heroes of Elorus and the Sons of Sangareth in the Great Library of Commons Hollow, the legend of the Wintersfall. You now must ask your parents, but who knows what interpretation they'll render unto you? There is talk, I hear, of rebuilding.

I feel this story is the one that speaks, the one no one else can tell like I can as I was *there*. A splendid adventure, yea though we never knew him and didn't even know his name until the end of everything. You think you know someone, but it's not so unusual. We all come from such places and lives all so different right up next to each other, and thus we just can't judge someone until we know them completely, and we can never know them entirely before they entirely change. In contrast, good squirrels believe in well worked, long-term relationships and in thinking hard before jumping off into them. It's also why good squirrels don't like strangers.

This squirrel was in search of something, he would always say, but really he had a tendency for leaving things behind. When I met him, he wore a red kerchief around his neck and a petty officer's coat from some far place with all of its patches torn off. He wore some baggy pants, and his hat was floppy. He tucked his pants into boots up to his knees. Everyone noticed his sense of style was fairly bunkum.

He told me he was living in exile and had been once the leader of the liberation army of some place called 'de Algarve,' and he had spent his days in the world looking for adventure.

This all turned out to be entirely false, but we believed him at the time. When he told us this story, he often hitched up his belt and spit. Though, he only spat when he said that. Me not knowin' anything about the world, I supposed his rattling off quite a few names of places I hadn't heard of before seemed evidence enough for me. Frankly. knowing where he was from or anything about him wasn't terrifically important. But I digress.

From the look of him, there were never a worse look of defeat, and yet he still had this kind of strange majesty almost as if he were two beings, sometimes one and the next moment the other.

As he once told me, I'll tell you. The rest of the story I pieced together. He told me he lived in the City of Faro. This was a place stricken by war and all radical ideas always going round about the gates. Ask anyone there what squirrels did, and the answer was obvious. But ask them where they were from, and they'd tell you, "Why, we fish!" Yes, the world is a strange place beyond our walls. I ought to know as I'm from there.

Into such a life our hero drifted from calamity after being ripped from his parents' paws. Were our hero able to comprehend his

17

surroundings, he would have, in his infant form, watched himself float up over the horizon and into the view of a towering cliff. Not a frightening cliff, but more of a kind of dozy, limestone cliff that shone in the sun at the right time of day (in our time at sea, this was how he talked about it). Seagulls were often the loudest perturbance on a Sunday walk down the beach, where the waves were not crashy but sleepy or mopey as everyone got lazy under the endless oppress of mild breezes and basking sunlight.

Here, imagine a bent-over old squirrel kitter so crusty she could barely walk, talk, or swish. Her cheeks had been stuffed too long with too much numpet, shoulders trembled, and tail hair flicked wispy old and gray.

This might seem like a bad state, but the mind of an old hag might think, *Well, if I'm not getting any younger, any richer, or any prettier, I will make sure I live at least somewhere there is a nice beach I can walk down in the morning. That'll be nice.* You might think this is even worse: old, unsightly hags stalking perfectly good beaches like windblown carnival garbage and probably yelling at pups. But in the mind of a hag, she thought, *See how the bubbly waves greet my craggy claws. See how the tide lovingly washes my tail out so clean.* Then, there, you might think, *That is awful. What kind of belligerence must one absolutely inflict upon the world, bathing in public? Go to the toilet. Get some wipes.*

But now, the mind of a hag might think instead, *Oh, look at the beautyful sunrise, and now I'll smell all up and down like my wonderful friend, the sea, all day. Oh, joy! Say now, doesn't the horizon sparkle and glimmer and flash like the coming of Heaven?*

And still others might think, *What on earth, you old sot? The sea doesn't make flashes at you; instead, your insane brain does.* But in the mind of a smelly, slightly demented, yet tender old squirrel-hag, she'd think, *Oh, well, I suppose that's right. Thanks for reminding me. But I believe I see something in the water over there.*

It was Lady Rodriga, whose miserable life was unbeknownst to her any more, save at this moment when she experienced true joy. She received a miracle: a pup. She never had any of her own.

Looking in the tiny life raft, she also found a small bottle with a note inside, and she barely got the slippery thing out as her nubby fingers were so arthritic. The smudged and salt-worn paw scrawl showed only this, "...Gethsarade...last of hopes." She yelped in joy for he must have been the pup of an Italian prince, or something, and so right that her last hope was him. Surely, they would come looking for him and reward her handsomely. But then she gazed into his deep eyes and at the smile on his goo-goo lips, and then she thought, *perhaps they'll not come at all.*

The little pup grew up in a place called Algarve, only with without a father unlike all the other pups. He had a mother, he believed for a time, who needed more help to get around better than average. At times all she could do was keep him from killing himself when he climbed things and for what was beyond her, jumping off of things thinking he could fly.

"Now, dear, squirrels are rodents, and rodents don't fly."

Or at least none she had ever known or heard of outside of faraway fairy tales. And since Gethsarade arrived, she was all worldly and understood everything.

Still, his days were filled with the utmost joy, under the care of someone who knew all the tricks in the book for parenting, never mind her lack of practice, having talked and dreamed about a baby of her own all her life. She treated little Gethsarade as if he were the last chance she would get.

And he was.

When youngrels normally go to bed in Faro, they listen to the lullaby of their fathers gently plucking a guitar. But Gethsarade listened instead to the one he called his mother plucking to the best of her ability for him, as she made up the melodies, for his untrained ears only, to the songs she once heard. She could only read to him out of the few second-hand paw books they had, but his favorite from his first memory was the *Count of Mousey Christo.* So she read it to him over and over till he learned to dream of pirate days.

She often joked to Gethsarade that soon he would help her out of bed. To which the young Gethsarade would say, "Oh, Mama, you will never get old." Then, one day, she did, and they shed a tear of love together as he put back the sheets and read the *Count* to her.

Then she joked that he would one day help her eat. Gethsarade laughed like pups do, and said, "Oh, Ma, you will never get any older." Then one day, after a nasty fall, he cut and held her food up to her mouth, for she had become too weak to lift a tiny spoon. But to be honest, the swelling of her face made a permanent smile appear on one side, and though her condition was terrible still, they for a moment had a laugh at the silliness; their portrait, making faces at one another between giggles. Little Rodriga let a tear escape and fall to the table and young Gethsarade saw it. She laughed for him even when laughing for herself was too painful. And they once more wept by each other's side.

Then one night she joked a little bitterly that one day he would have to play the guitar her for her to sleep. Suddenly, he had to catch little Lucinda before it hit the floor. She could not even hold the guitar up on her knee any longer. He laughed and said, "I'll play for you now, Ma." Oddly, only that time he called her Ma, did she suddenly feel compelled to tell him something that stirred the heart of him, despite all the happiness of their simple life.

"Gethsarade, my love. You are now grown and strong, and I am growing too old for life. I must tell you something. I am not your mother. I am just a simple old hag who found you in a boat adrift on the sea."

"No, Mama," he said. "You're having another fit."

"No, I'm not. You mustn't call me Mama anymore, please. As much as I love the chance to take care of you and to see your beautiful face, I am only reminded the more and more you say that, and as I age, my fate belonged to someone else. I don't know how you came or why, but I now know this much. My boy, find it."

"Find what?"

"You must find out why you are here. I mean, what brought you to this place." She gave him the piece of cloth, onto which she had gone over the writing with embroidery: Gethsarade... last of hopes. "I thought it meant the last hope for me, a gift from above, but I realize something now. The message is about who you are, not who you are to me. Find who wrote this. When you do, you will find your destiny. Take courage and be brave."

"Okay, Mama."

He didn't quite understand her, however. One day not long after, Gethsarade, who had grown skilled at the guitar to play for his love, his her, sat and played the lullabies to his mama whose words he did not believe for a moment. He leaned over her smiling face as it had gone to rest. But as he gave her a goodnight kiss, he realized her fair, white fur had gone cold. With a last tear of love, he buried her by himself in a field, in a place only he knew, for they had no money for a decent burial and Gethsarade had only the guitar to earn a living. So, as the concerns of life took over, Gethsarade soon forgot about the words of his mama, the Lady Ridroga, leaving the song of the sea alone to play her the elegy of time.

This was the end of the time in Gethsarade's life that hadn't been so bad as the condition in which I found him, if I correctly sorted facts from tales. Before he was all the way full grown, he even felt the tug of life like strings at his fingertips. He told me this much in the long course of our voyage on the many watches we shared.

It came in the form of a longing to know who he really was or what he was meant to do. When he played, he watched himself grow full up, half that figure in the cracked mirror still disbelieved. The other spent nights imagining his parents had been adventurers, and all the battles and such they went through, the lands they conquered, and the wines they drank.

If what Lady Ridroga said was true, oh the comerades they must have had! All this he fantasized about while playing in run-down locales, and then going home to the old rent to imagine a better life that never came.

There was, despite his disbelief, something undeniably odd about the nonsensical plea she had made to him with her last ability to speak. He eventually found he was grateful for the chance to hear her last words. They had the strangest way of making him dream about things he never did before.

In Faro de Algarve, a cliff separates the town from the sea, so far above as to make their sea nearly inaccessible, except by rope or a great deal of travel up the coast and then back again even farther and uphill all the way. It's good to build a city this way, for a city can't be too easily attacked if it's some ways from a port and so only those with real business made the trip.

You might ask, why couldn't they just give a hop and fly on down? Well, believe it or not, there is a part of the world where all squirrels don't fly, and places where they can but rarely do so that only myths speak of them, just as Lady Ridroga believed. I swear this is as true as the light under a window.

In those parts, flying was unheard of. If someone lived there not knowing they could fly, he or she would carry on just the same, for there would be no one around to tell them to fly. No one could just go runnin' off cliffs, you see. The hard way was the only way.

It made one think of the amazing adventures just out beyond the horizon, as they might feel if one stood upon their very tippy toes, as they enjoyed creamy cheeses and lively songs so far above, perhaps no kind of cold could touch them.

These great imaginings often occurred on bright and cheery Sundays, with lots of homely pups and kits all around running and screaming in utter safety and a merry wingding to the soothing of the crish crash of waves far below. There, the lightest of breezes reminded the subjects of the world of the Algarve, or at least part of them, were full of far more happiness and good than anything else.

Gethsarade, however, possessed no such memory or experience save about his lost mama. In fact, he lived quite some ways down the hill on a lonely outcrop where the loveliness was far declined. He was a lonely chap, rather than a lovely one. He lived in the hovel Lady Ridroga left to him in the dirtiest, hoveliest side of town just down the road to the north, where hags lived, and any scoundrel might've still ventured without getting too good of an impression of the area. Those on the fairer side would only pay someone to fetch a thing or two rather than do it themselves. But the closer one gets to port, the less anyone could tell what might happen.

Sitting alone by himself in his little hovel and dreaming of a better life for season upon season with only the memory of Lady Ridroga and the dream of his real parents to comfort him, Gethsarade often heard the advice of the neighbors.

"You know, Gethparade, or whatever, it's all about attitude."

So eventually, he thought to himself, *Well, just what kind of attitude should I have?* So, when he heard them say to think positive, he asked the only appropriate question, "What is positiveness, exactly, if it's what I solemnly must think?" And then when he heard the candid advice that life is what you make it, he thought, *I decide*

22

what is good and bad, and I, therefore, alone, decide the destiny of Gethsarade!

Wait, so why should I take their advice, then? What do they know? If all their advice that their advice is stupid is stupid, then what am I doing listening to them about listening to myself? Bah!'

Then he went right back to dreaming, a thing he had become good at, rather than sorting out the philosophies of filberts and derpy-dos. In a world where he was an explorer like the amazing circumnavigator Flagellan, he could happen upon a magical destiny only he could possess, as well as fulfill. He dreamt of a world in which he led armies that followed him for the purity of his heart and dedication to the cause. A world in which he was a passionate lover and a music star. Because why can't you have everything if only in your dreams?

Then one day, he started writing down little bits of music on top of the old melodies. And then he put more little bits of music on top that he strung together into a song or two, without knowing what they were all about. A riff there, a strum and an arpeggio or a fiddley-diddle in that spot, a little quiet bit, then a loud shouty bit, and before he knew it, he had a full-blown musical on his paws.

But what to make the music about? This problem seemed like the very best opportunity to take all the wonderful advice he received and make a story about a squirrel commander who just kept winning and whose attitude was always right. This kind of thing makes the absolute best kind of story.

And so, the harrowing tale of the revolutionary Vincent Poppaldi was born, from which Gethsarade was sure to win the favor (and money) of all as he planned to retire as a millionaire at the top of the hill, having become everything he ever dreamed.

Rich that is! A fine plan, yes!

In his most disheveled fashion, Gethsarade lived as a budding musician playing the tunes of war leader and commander Vincent Poppaldi, whose achievements were of the most epic caliber—and entirely fictitious.

Gethsarade once told me all righteous revolts begin the same way—by not bein' paid. And his troubles began at the restaurant of Arnando Desi Baudelio Antonio Duarto Bonto de Joaoie whose

23

Frenchiness was forgiven, for he made the most excellent fish sausage in all the Algarve. Everyone loved old Bonto for this, except for Gethsarade, who hated fish parts for supper almost as much as he hated looking at the sea for what about it needed explaining.

Mind you, it wasn't the first time he had not been paid, but it definitely was the first time he decided to start trouble about it. This small aspect of life was one of many that made Gethsarade wonder from time to time if the Fates really intended him to be a part of this place, to which the usual response was, "Just be positive, then it'll get better Mister Guess-Parade, or Ghettoshark, or Gethsardine, or whatever your name is."

Because, ugh,, can you even think of such a disgusting thing as fish sausage? What was there to be positive about? That night, someone offered him a piece of this revolting vittle, with little explanation as he was tuning his guitar behind the curtain at Bonto's Bend.

He stopped, for it so distracted him. "No, I cannot eat that before I sing, friend," motioning to his delicate throat. "Or any other time."

However, it was all he could do but to make his revolt known with gestures and motions of sickness, as the server muttered something to him and went back into the kitchen. What Gethsarade did not know, however, was the waiter's muttering was, in fact, a proclamation he had just refused payment for his services as the night's entertainment. The waiter immediately reported this to the manager who was very pleased about the whole idea.

The curtain lifted as he was still tuning, and he sat up feeling a little cheated, for they did not properly announce him.

"Welcome! Ladies and Gentlevermin! Come one come all!" He waited for a dramatic effect, but the crowd just sort of looked about and remained seated.

"Get ready to experience a night of wonder and enchantment, as little Lucinda and I (he waved his paws around the guitar) recount to you the story of *The Five and a Half Hour War!*"

"Never heard of it!" someone yelled rudely from the back. Another shouted, "A short song, for a short war, I'm sure. Yes, please!"

Gethsarade went on unfazed. "Well, let me tell you then. It's a harrowing journey, revealed to you with the magic of music!" Someone from the back shouted to get on with it. He turned away from the audience to begin for another dramatic effect and to tune his last string. It didn't work.

He turned back around slowly, strumming a fast but gentle rasgueado trying to stave off the out-of-tune top string.

"*Mi caramba.* Not this again," said one out in the crowd. Someone else whistled. "Hey! Ain't yew got nuthin' else to play?"

"Aye, *mi bebo*," said one squirrel at the back who had just discovered his wine glass was empty and began smashing his head on the table in inconsolable grief. Gethsarade withheld from drawing conclusions.

"Can't you-ah do any requests?" said another squirrel, whose drunken face barely hung onto his skull as he sat shaking his head. He threw a grape for good measure, which just missed Gethsarade's head.

"Well, I suppose I could try." The audience cut him off with requests for the Moliere and so on, which he despised. Someone said, "Hey, give us a little spice, a little *cortejo,* eh?"

"No, I don't think I know any of those. Might still be under copyright, so…." The crowd met him with a "Get on with it."

He held up a dignified paw. "I know, I know. Let me think of something here, I know." And after a few quiet strums, the mob calmed and strained to listen. He sang, "Numa casa portuguesa fica bem pão e vinho sobre a mesa...," a lyric that rendered something like "Everyone here is broke as jacknuts, but at least we've got each other!" And that was all he got out, for the audience would have none of it.

"Ach! Ack, no, now eetsa too-a sad!" the forlorn expat in the back said and threw another grape, which splattered all over Gethsarade's face. He restrained himself. The cook, a moron by the name of Signor Cervello, appeared offstage in the corner and he knew Gethsarade was done. He tried one happier song, and a string broke on his guitar. He attempted to work around it as he also tried to pretend this top string was not flapping about like a drunken grandmama at Parchisi.

They nigh on rioted. "Look, hold on. It's not my fault! You're ruining my act! Just give me a minute," said Gethsarade as he fought to wrap the hopelessly broken string around its post. Then he felt the hook.

Not again, he thought. It tugged so hard he almost choked, but he tried to hold fast. And let me tell you, friends, there is nothing sadder than the sight of a minstrel trying to stay on stage when he's got full on grapes and such flying at him.

"Get Ramon out here!" They chanted, "Ramon! Ramon! Ramon!" But Gethsarade was desperate. This was the only gig in town he hadn't ruined. "No!" he shouted and tugged as hard as he could on the hook and caused the big oaf cat to fall off balance, and the next moment the cook was standing next to Gethsarade in his greasy undershirt and apron right there on the stage, with a deer in lantern-lights look on his face.

Gethsarade motioned to the crowd and back to the cook and said, "Everyone, Signor Coppa Cevello!" which in Gethsarade's corner of the map was rendered euphemistically as "Mister Big Butt-Face." Someone clapped only twice, but most held silent as the cook leaned over Gethsarade and said, "I speak a little Italian," in perfect Italian. And then he raised his arm to bash Gethsarade straight in the head.

Moments later, Gethsarade stumbled out of the back door of the restaurant, with his beat-up guitar and no pence. He dusted himself off. "Bonto! Bonto! Don't I at least get paid?" he shouted as he rapped as hard as he could on the door.

The owner poked his head out. "I'm sorry, but we tried to pay you, and you said you didn't want it."

"What do you mean? You mean before the show? Oh, come on, this is just criminal! You expect someone to take payment in fish sausage?" he nearly choked on the last words.

"Everyone else liked it, you don't like it? It's better than money. A full belly is the best thing in the whole world!"

Gethsarade forced back another heave. "Okay, now," he retorted, holding up his finger. "There are a lot of things better than money. Like ripping mad guitar skills," He ran a riff the length of the neck without taking his eyes off of Bonto, or skipping a word, "or being rich enough to not need money, or play guitar in diners. But I need money, Bonto, not fish. This isn't fair."

"Look, Gethsurgery." Bonto could never pronounce his name, so he just ended with a slur of gibberish. "We tried to take care of you, but they like Ramon here."

"That simpleton only knows three chords! I worked on this set of mine for years! It's good; it's more than good, it's a masterpiece. And you know what?" He pointed a thumb at his chest. "I don't sing with my tongue hanging out."

"Yes, I know you don't, and it is a masterpiece every time you play it. Night after night. Ramon, he writes a new song every morning, and he comes and plays it here every night."

"Yes, yes, I know. I believe he titled his last song, 'Ramon tem calcas,'" which for those of us who never danced upon the shores of Porto, means, 'I [Ramon] have nice trousers.' And this comparison to Gethsarade's superior artistry was the source of his contention all about town wherever he had played. To be sure, some of Ramon's other famous hits included, 'Oh, Oh, Oh, Chinchilla Oh,' 'Livin' La Hanta Loca.' So, obviously, his bane was every bit justified.

"But it was funny, right? Ha!" Bonto laughed so hard the hump on the back of his stooped neck wobbled up and down, but he saw the despair in Gethsarade's eyes, and he straightened up, for he was a gobbley badger.

"I have helped you every way I know how, Gethsardine. And I'm sorry, but I have a ristorante to run. Best of luck to you." He was about to close the door, but he stopped, and said, "Hey, buddy, why don't you retrace your steps a little, you know? Find out what you want. It'll all work out, just think positive." Bonto closed the back door, and there you had it.

Gethsarade stepped up to the door to make another protest. But then he overheard Bonto talking to the head cook who spoke a little fluent Italian, who said, "...so glad that chapter is over. Hopefully, he just never comes back. I never want to hear his name again. Oy, Mami, such a disgusting Italian name. Is it Italian? I don't know. But I'll tell you, if I ever hear the name Gethslurpee again, it will be too soon."

"Yeah, boss. Way to let 'im down easy."

"Now maybe we can get out there and get back some customers. 'Diner,' he said. Pff! The nerve."

"Sounds good to me, boss."

Gethsarade stepped away from the door and considered bursting in and fighting for his dignity once more, but instead, he hung his head and sat down on the steps. Lucinda made a little depressed "boomp" sound as Gethsarade set her down onto the cobblestone alley under the argent moon.

The thing he hated most was, Bonto was right. "You know what I really want? Some food." he said out loud to himself as he clutched his growling stomach.

So, after much consideration, he retraced his steps to around the front of the diner.

Moments later, Gethsarade ran as hard as he could with the fat-cat cook wielding two feline-sized butcher's knives, lumbering over the crowd, yelling, "Thief, criminal! Stop him!" He ran toward the seaside bazaar with two plates full of apple tarts stuffed down his trouser pockets.

Cats are slow, big, beasts, especially when working their ways through gobs of squirrels and mice and groundhogs and badgers all darting about. Gethsarade worked far ahead in the night air and the bustle. *Time to find a hiding place,* he thought. There were barrels all full of apples and such. There was a Help Wanted sign for work at the north piers. No good, those are usually military. Then he heard the cat's blunderous stomping and thought quickly.

Cervello, the cook, stopped for a moment to catch his breath, realizing he had lost sight of Gethsarade. But just on the other side of the counter of an empty booth, there was an empty barrel, and Gethsarade jumped in.

Ha! He'll never find me in here, thought Gethsarade. This was just as Cervello spied a brown puff protruding conspicuously through a loose apple barrel. He tore off the lid with rude force, sending it flying into a wall that received it clear through. Cervello looked down inside. Gethsarade grinned back innocently. "Oh my, silly tail," he said. "Let's play again, double or nothing, what say?"

Cervello, to Gethsarade's surprise, considered it for a moment, but then shook it off and he was then immediately ripped from the barrel and sent flying through the nearest window into the home of an old curmudgeonly kitter, and he landed directly on her couch. She dropped her knitting at the commotion, but her face lit with an exquisite joy at the sight of him with his guitar.

"Buggah, ain't this a treat! Play me a song and gimme a kiss! It's not every day this happens now, is it?" She clapped her paws and wagged her scraggly tail. Gethsarade obediently played, more out of an attempt to stall than anything, but it relieved him to see Cervello's overweight mass barrel into the room and begin making muck about the old jab's things. This displeased her. Cervello grabbed Gethsarade by the neck and moved to strike. This was interrupted by his tail being put in a cramp, and the old squirrel set about making dough out of it with a rolling pin.

"Don't you dare, you big oaf! Get out and let me enjoy my big day. Out, out, you sodding lout!" The cat got on his knees and begged the old kit to let go of his tail, but she held fast and pounded away.

"Very nice, thank you. I must be going. Ta-ta. Thanks for the fun." Gethsarade slung his guitar over his shoulder and strolled out after grabbing a biscuit while the old kitter pounded away. "Ay, *porca*, won't anyone ever want to hear me play?"

Altogether relieved, he made his way away from the commotion back down the street to his house.

He pulled his faithful Lucinda from over his shoulder and played while he walked, letting himself relax a little.

"Maybe Bonto was right. I should write something new. I should write something even better than before, and then no one will deny Gethsarade is the greatest guitarist in the Algarve, nay in the world!"

He picked at his instrument and imagined a tune he might like to play sometime, perhaps a new one was in order. Perhaps he would employ an arpeggio here, a rasgueado there, a little falseta, and he watched more than listened as his fingers danced about the neck of the guitar. *Perfect,* he thought, *this will dazzle and dizzy them.*

After a few moments, he was zipping all about on the guitar neck. Those on either side of the street peered at him, only to look right back down again upon seeing young Gethsarade had come, probably to ask for some money by playing some melody no one could understand.

Soon he realized the whole street, growing darkly in the waxing moonlight, was as empty as his stomach. "Aye, Mami, why doesn't anyone want to hear me play?" He reached absently to pluck his guitar some more, and then wearily let it down again, shrumped his shoulders, went home, and shut the door.

His tiny hovel was about halfway to the sea upon the peninsula. It curled outward from the western shore and wrapped around the south bay whence he came. The little gray board structure had a leaky roof, and spears of sunlight always invaded the walls unwanted. He scampered about, making sure there was no landlord in sight. The landlord had wanted payment by afternoon. Satisfied no one was there to invade his repose, he snatched the last morsels of the mashed-up apple tart he took during his escapade.

Ugh, I am so alone, he day-dreamt to himself. *If I had just a little bella, I wouldn't care for all the poverty I had to slog through, all the empty tip cups on earth couldn't make me sad.*

He set his guitar down on the floor by his straw bed. "I'm sorry, little Lucinda. You're enough for me. I didn't mean it. It's just…you're a guitar, you know? And I'm a squirrel. How can this work forever? Just someone to…you know, take my ugly 'Italian' name." He shook his head and sighed again. "It's not Italian. No, Lucinda, ragazza, I don't know what it means, but it's not Italian.

"I told you, I was adopted. Shipwreck, I think Mama said. Oh, I'll be all right…If only these fools knew." He saw his reflection in a dirty shard on the dresser without drawers that he used to hang his drying. "If only they knew what I know, seen what I've seen, but I, alas, live no common life, dear girl." Then he thought in the moonlight for a moment more, and said with a sigh, "Ah, who am I kidding. My life couldn't be more common."

He stared silently at the guitar for a moment. Then he picked it up and dusted off the scrapes of dirt and mud, realizing he was getting in deep with an inanimate object. He placed the guitar back

30

on the towel he kept for it on the floor, and went to sleep, humming the song he had written all those seasons ago, *Vive la Risorgimento.* He absentmindedly reached over and strummed one last time, letting the strings ring out across the room, and he patted the strings so only the sound of the echoes of the strings resounded in Lucinda's diatonic voice.

He remembered the one other comfort in his life sitting beside his straw bed on the floor and propped up by the sagging wall: a faded portrait of the old lady-squirrel who raised him. Alas, for even she had not lived to see what the squirrel had become. *All the better,* he thought and turned in. She wouldn't be too proud.

"Do you know what I wish, Lucinda? I wish I could fly. What? No, squirrels can't fly; we're rodents, like Mama said. Flying is magic. Because when have you seen one do so? It's a tavern myth, like when they get drunk and talk about war owls and enormous turtles. No. Just go to sleep. This is nonsense, and you're a guitar, and I'm talking to you. So, goodnight."

The next morning, he woke softly, wiped his eyes, and placed his guitar around his back out of sheer habit. Foregoing breakfast as usual for there was none, he went out to play once again for tips till he dropped or someone chased out of wherever. He tuned the top string, mourned at how he would pay for a new high E string, and, he felt a growl in his stomach, so his morning went from normal to bad. It went from bad to terrible when he realized again he had just been kicked out of the last place in town with a corner to play in. And boy, he burned that bridge hard.

He closed his front door without looking up and unlatched the gate outside to leave. It creaked ever so gently. But just as the latch hit the stop, he heard the familiar gruffy growl of his landlord from the bottom of the hill. Down the way was not only that, but the equally furious grimace of Cervello, the cook, cradling his tail, which was more like a paddle, then. It appeared they had been talking.

His landlord shouted, "Rent, boy!"

Cervello shouted, "And biscuits! Better cough them up, or we're not putting up with the likes of you in this town no more."

So Gethsarade ran, and he ran the other way, with his poor guitar hanging by its twine from his shoulder, flapping behind him in the wind, as he fought the sleepies from his eyes, and the wobblies from his legs.

They chased and chased and chased. Just as the two pursuers were gaining on him, Gethsarade came around a curve on the road by the ocean to the north, and he saw a small pier he had often spied through the boards of a backwall up on the hill, as he caught the sound of the bells.

He often guessed the owner used it for private expeditions of some sort, but the sight he beheld after finally going down there stopped him, but only for a moment.

There in the morning sun was a golden ship, the tallest, most richly adorned he had ever seen, and as he took it all in, there at the entrance to the docks he saw his escape, a sign:

Help wanted - no experience necessary - greatish pay - pretty okay benefits - overtime available - paid travel - advancement opportunities widely available - accelerate your life on the high seas on board the magnificent ship, the Tara Feen: The Rising Star of the West.

— Message sponsored by Her Majesty's Royal Imperial Navy.

Taking off again just before the two overweight blunderers behind him nearly got him by the tail, he ran from the both of them down to a port on the other side of the hill that turned out to be the pier of the Tara Feen. No better place to hide from getting beaten up than in public.

The registrar saw him too late, and Gethsarade shouted that he was with the band as he whizzed past waving his guitar, and the registrar on the pier said, "Okay, okay." Then he thought, *Oy, hold there. There ain't no band!*

But Gethsarade was down the pier by then. As the registrar was just about to ring the emergency bell, the other two pursuers got to the table and stopped, having caused all sorts of commotion. Neither was better than having a stray musician on board: one a badger, which was just bad right out and the other a cat trying to board a ship fitted for squirreldom. No one ought to put up with that kind of plumbing backup.

"Get your paw down out of my face, wretch!" cried Mr. Cervello, but the guard took none of it and proceeded with whacking Gethsarade's pursuers most judiciously with a shilellagh.

Gethsarade boarded of the ship with a sigh of relief and without a ticket just as the ship began to throw its lines to leave the pier. Yet, still on the plank, he scrambled over the side and smiled back, as the cat could only look on in anger. He laughed, waving a goodbye salutation, "Salud! I'll be seeing you, old friend, perhaps when you learn about fair labor! Ha!" He took a bite of a biscuit he had stolen. "And my colon thanks you!" he shouted.

The big cat threw his knives into the hull on both sides of Gethsarade, while screwing up his Himalayan face at him. This gave Gethsarade a brief pause. He turned around again and shouted, "And tell your boss, it's pronounced Geth-sah-rahd!"

Then the cat threw his paws up in the air in a gesture of frustrated defeat. "Ah, good riddance! And your music sucks!"

Gethsarade turned around, "You wouldn't know good music if it punched you in the face."

This he said, only immediately to turn around and be met with a large, muscular squirrel in black who said, "Registration?" Gethsarade stopped chuckling at once and searched his pockets. As he stalled for an excuse, the guard grunted. Gethsarade grabbed his instrument from behind and held it up by the headstock, however seeing as it had taken quite a battling in the scuff, it was now missing a few strings, so it sounded like utter garbage as he swayed his hips and strummed and offered the guard a song.

"Gitarra? Ha-ha. Oh yes, nice." The guard then promptly punched him in the face and threw him overboard.

It just so happened Gethsarade caught the rudder sail as the ship passed by him, and he hung onto it all the way out of the port, unseen.

"Il motivo per cui mi hai lasciato qui come questo?" he said up to the sky after the whole pier laughed at him being dragged out to sea. This was a statement that roughly meant, "What the heck am I doing with my life?"

Nevertheless, he held on to the ship's rudder, using his poor guitar as a floatation device, choking and sputtering and pawing at the water. Eventually, he clambered up to the poop deck and hid beneath a couple piles of definitely fresh high-transit storage. This he accomplished on account of the cat size knives lodged in the ship's side by a certain Mr. Cervello. "Aye, Vincent, mi poppo. Nascondere e nascondersi di nuovo." This roughly means, "Perhaps I could have just taken the fish sausage." He said this remorsefully as he tucked himself in, doing his best to mask his breath in the frigid sea air. He thought, *I really, really should have taken the fish sausage.*

Gethsarade slept and dreamt soundly under the storage tarpaulin, despite the rocking and rolling, for Lucinda provided an exceptional comfort in the crook of her hip. He dreamed of the great character he had used to compose his tales over the seasons.

He got the name Vincent from a bar fight he had witnessed. It all began with the acquisition of one young squirrel's labor portion over a shipment of saltpeter. Gethsarade didn't know why anyone would be angry over salt, or who Peter was, but the fight was a sound throttling. The victor, an Italian jefe with muscles like wood, stood tall after dealing a good many wallops. He made a meat pie out of the other's face and received much doggardly applause, smiling and waving while his opponent twitched on the floor.

While all of this would ordinarily be traumatizing for a teenager, for him, it was another day playing at the bar. This was exceptional entertainment to seafarers, especially when they suspected unfair dealings were under paw and to which they were all privy.

The cheers, the jollity, and furious swishing of tails inspired Gethsarade. He even got to shake the paw of the victor and discovered his name was Vincent. The hero was born.

'Poppaldi' came from the sound in his ears he got when he heard Ramon al Cuates sing his first hit, "Me mordí, ahora necesito comer mi cabello," which woodenly translates to, "I bit myself, now I need to eat my own hair." It was a song about a love story between a young pup and his favorite bandoline. The sound may have been a small stroke, but no matter. A big hit to the sailing squirrel types. He never understood why.

He did understand one thing granted to him by the experience: the value of *confidence* from the illustrious Vincent and Ramon. More specifically, the value of what most meant by *confidence*, which was acting like one knows what one is doing even when one doesn't. Strive for the former, though most seem to get by with the latter. Everyone else is no one else. With these thoughts, Gethsarade dreamed of faraway lands to pretend to conquer and fame to lavish, while bravely hiding like a cave marmot on a ship under a pile of sea rubbish.

2: Pirats!

How anyone slept on a ship was beyond Gethsarade when he lived high on the hillside in his rental in south Faro. Back then, he often counted the time by the bells rung over the foredecks as they rang on the hour by twos. He wondered if he would ever get a proper sleep cycle going. The bells of a ship were loud enough for everyone to hear, even deep in the belly or high on a hill. He had learned long ago, one could tell by the number of times they rang, always in even numbers: when it was four o'clock at 16 bells in the afternoon, six at 18, eight at 20, and so on. However, even being on perhaps the very ship that often awakened him and kept him up night after night all those seasons, he found he was ugly-sleeping again.

As the waves rocked and rolled in such gentle, cradling motions on the sea, he realized what those old salts were saying in the tavern when they talked of being driven mad by the waves at day and drunk by them at night. He saw a lot of ugly-sleeping in his future. A fun little fact, ships are unceasingly without relief from the weather, and there are no fires for warmth. *How will I get out of this one?* he thought, shivering. *Confidence, ol' boy...confidence.*

Still, it was a terrible pain lying in the same position. For whenever he tried to adjust himself more comfortably, someone new would invariably march in for a squat. He had hidden by the hole going down to the head. It had been the first convenient place to hide having crawled up the back end of the ship. *What a mirthful design,* he thought as he all but choked on the fumes once more, and finally after a long while cajoled himself back to sleep.

In the middle of his dream, a thudsome fat squirrel awoke him coming through the aft-storage and down the ladder into the poopdeck, as he heard it appropriately called by listening. He heard a bump, and the whole ship rocked for a moment from side to side. As the voices came closer, he made sure he tucked his tail this time and held his breath.

"Psst. Oy. Are you down there, Joff?" he heard.

"Yes, Gottfred, sah. How did you know it was me?"

"Mostly by the smell, good soire."

"How do you know what kind of smell is attached to me, sah?"

"Oy figgered it out when I heard you tell me name, Joff."

"That don't make no sense, Gottfred sah."

"It makes perfect sense. Don't believe me just ask me. Anyway, no mind; wazzat you?"

"Was what me, sah?"

"The bump in the night. 'Twas a right frightful bump."

"Heavens, sah, I don't weigh so much so's to rock the howle ship!"

"Just mak'n sure, Joff. 'Is excellent service you do for the ship, keepin' the keel together, boyo, down there in the cell block," said what seemed to be one of the aft watches roving just feet from Gethsarade's hiding hole, and some on-hearers giggled.

"When I get out of this 'ole sah, I'm going to nnnng (floop) set you straight, I'm telling you right now! And anyway, first mate said be on the lookout for pirats. So, shouldn't you be watchin' yer watchy stuff, instead of peepin' down here at my li'l doojers?" The heavy one in the toilet shuffled, keys jangled, and boots banged the deck.

"No, sah, you're a beauty-full old boy, I assure you, but Captain says we got to grease the anchor."

"Yeh, and what's that supposed to mean? Aaagh-glorbl-blarbl!" Gethsarade detected splashing, glooping, and gasping sounds through the laughter. Then, oddly, the laughing stopped. Then all the noise from the ship stopped. He could tell from the fact the laughing had stopped so suddenly, the bump in the night had been something waryful, and they should have paid attention like the fat one who was now passed out down in the hole had been saying.

He listened to the cold, salty night air, which had been working diligently to degrade those elements less equipped for maritime rigors as it well does, and the most delicate of all those being those cat-gut strings. Especially when those strings were considerably worn. Upon the realization someone's bare feet were shifting right near his head, feet that didn't sound like a squirrel with proper business, he cradled Lucinda and patted the neck ever so gently so as not to make any noise. However, this was all the pressure necessary to make an end of two of the four remaining strings, which sounded a pop and a ping.

He did not dare move or breathe, but waited, and waited, and waited. *There now,* he thought, *no one out there heard a thing.* So he relaxed his shoulders and let out a breath, which was precisely what the greasy headed mug with his ear on the other side of the itchy-wool tarpaulin was waiting for.

Without ado, the scurvy rat threw back the tarpaulin, and rudely ripped Gethsarade, fighting uselessly, from his hiding place. He tucked Gethsarade's head under an arm and stole him away with little to no concern for his delicate instrument, which caught and pulled sullenly on the tarpaulin and then hit the deck with many pangs of protest.

The unusually large rat took him to the main deck where there was a gaggle of rats all drinking and carrying on, and he heard one with a booming voice whom he could only assume to be the captain or first mate shouting, "Looks like it'll be a bloody sky tonight boys. What say? It's a party every night and drink all the rum till it's gone, you say? Good idea! And when we get where we're goin' we'll all be rich!" much laughter and so on.

"Oy, sah," said the greasy rat, whose armpit was also greasy, as he gave Gethsarade over with one paw, struggling even still. In the middle of protesting, having enough of gloppy poopoo-grease and sticky rat sleaze for a lifetime, Gethsarade demanded they put him down.

"Oh, you'll be put down all right," said the pirat, putting Gethsarade on the deck and licking his chops, then he turned to a shadow. "Oy found this load of understock at the poop deck a' this flyin' pig. Pickin on a geetar, he was."

Now, the trouble with rats, besides the problem of living up to their namesake, is the lack of standards. As in size. If one were to shriek, "I just saw a rat," this wasn't altogether worrisome. One has to be more specific. For instance, domestic house rats are only a little bigger than waist high to a squirrel and that's big for its type. They can still be trouble in big numbers, though. Then there were the rats that could eat a whole squirrel for breakfast with toast and jam. Most of the rats standing before Gethsarade in the torch-lit night were of the former, save of the one that had nabbed him and a few others.

"Much obliged, Yank. Now, go away" was the only other voice Gethsarade heard, but he could not see who owned the words.

"Who's there?" said Gethsarade, left standing alone in front of them peered into the shadowy corner, but he could see nothing along the floorboards. Yet slowly there appeared a pair of glowing, jaundiced eyes and red teeth—and that's all he could see, and all whisperings fell.

He sought about dusting himself and complaining. "You know, I think no one could treat me worse if I was a prisoner aboard this vessel, but seeing as I'm a... a fine upstanding squirrel, I know my rights! I want an answer for this travesty. I'll see someone hanged! This no way to treat the...noble..." he spoke no more, as a pair of eyes flashed in annoyance at his playing the claim to aristocracy, none of which he had. The eyes peered at him, now red as the apple-rum moon. "So, you must be the captain."

"What? I thought you would be...never mind. Why, what makes you think so?" asked Gethsarade.

The eyes of the figure in the dark rose. "Because only a captain of the scobberlotchin' Imperial Navy values his life so far above any other he would hide like a peever. And further yet act like a whiney little wog when he doesn't get his way! You would hide in pauper's garb, t' boot. So like you cowards."

Gethsarade felt his throat shrink as the pair of eyes rose above his head higher and higher. "Fair enough. You're eh, um. You're not a squirrel, are you now?"

"No. I'm not. I'm not at all. Quite the opposite," said the voice. "I am...."

"You are...?" Gethsarade waited.

"A big...."

"Handsomely large, I see." Gethsarade's arms went from akimbo to dangling loose in disbelief.

"Giant…" the eyes loomed higher still.

"A well-bred chap, sir." Gethsarade yet could not hide the shaking of his boots and bated breath, for the eyes stood easily 10 squirrel-feet to his five point two.

"Massive…" the overwrought eyes paused again.

Gethsarade all but cried out in despair. "You're not a cat, are you? I'm just about done with cats, and I promise I'll leave if I've upset your cat-ness at all, I swear."

"Far worse than a cat, land bait. Ha, ha, ha." The laughter shook Gethsarade to his fingernails, and he cowered down and covered his head. "Oh! Don't hurt me, only don't hurt me. I'll never be a captain or play guitar again. Please!"

The eyes were locked onto Gethsarade again. The beast finally poked his massive head out of the shadows, revealing the fattest, most repulsive visage Gethsarade had ever seen.

"I am the Rat-Captain Barrogan Black," the pirat said in a voice as gruff as an old shoe. Giggles made their way about. As Gethsarade was trying to figure out how a rat could be so huge, in a hare's hair's time, the figure had hopped down off of the giant pile of booty he had climbed up on for effect out of the light of the moon and emerged from the shadows on the deck. He stood a good head and a half under Gethsarade. He got away with his little illusion since his massive head approached the size of his entire body.

"Oh, whew, " said Gethsarade and, *"Mi coppa!"* said he the next. But he barely got a gasp of relief for the sake of his person under threat of being made into extra-large rat pellets before the highly roundish rat had a rapier at his throat. Gethsarade marked this bloke to be considerably dirtier than he imagined a respectable captain and noted the rat's teeth were even redder in the light. "Oh. A rat. What kind of decent squirrel ship's captain isn't a squirrel?"

"A decent pirat captain's what kind. And not just any old pirate. A rat pirate is a pi-rat, and that's no decent thing at all. Course, bein' decent blokes ain't the prerowgaytive of the piratin' like. Like I said, quite the opposite." He nodded around to his crew, who had gathered, gibbering and snickering.

"Pi-rats!" gasped Gethsarade, who knew, as anyone who knew anything in a harbor town in old Faro de Algarve knew: pi-rats are a good deal worse than pirates of the regular old kind, mostly just because they were rats right along with being pirates.

"Yessah. And do you know what a decent squirrel cappy-tan's punishment is for bein' a stow on a pirat ship? 'Scuse me, a fancy, noble stow." the captain bowed mockingly. The others giggled.

"Well, if it's quite the opposite of a decent captain's then, then you'll keel haul me and make me into chum and feed me to the squids," said Gethsarade, gathering his confidence.

The pirat captain smiled. "Too much work. Again, sah, different."

"Oh. I thought you might say so. Well, then you'll let me go now and feed me rum and bacon till we reach land. All right, I suppose I shall accept my lot." He held up his paws in submission. To his surprise, everyone nodded as if this reasoning was complete rational thought. Then the pirat captain shook it off and became all the more enraged.

"No! I mean quite the opposite as in…."

"Ginger beer and giblets? Fine, I can make do."

"No! You insect!" the pirat pressed the blade into Gethsarade's throat, so he dared not make breath nor sound lest he lose his fool head.

"WE eat YOU!"

This sent the crowd into a furious uproar of salivating cheers. "Now take him down till we're all nice and hungry. It will be a fine meal tonight, boys!" They yelled a lot more for a while, and they whisked Gethsarade below as he shouted, "But sir, are we not of a kind? Is it not fratricide of a sort? I beg you to reconsider!"

"Stop!"

The captain stopped the procession just before they pressed through the crowd and below deck, and looked deeply, inquisitively into Gethsarade's eyes.

"Just a moment, though. Just in case it does be you is some boo-gee-oy-zee…." Gethsarade rolled his eyes at the captain's terrible diction for who couldn't say *bourgeoisie*?

"...Then who is you exactly? Because if it were up to me an' me alone, I'd say you looks a mite familiah." They pulled him about and teased him.

For the first time in his life, no one in the crowd knew who he was, and none had heard his song before—a new audience!

"Well, if you must know, heh, heh," he stalled for a moment, and thought, *you know, perhaps it is time I gave myself a little promotion if it won't come on its own,* and so he thought not long for a name that he had known and whom others would know—even as he should surely knew better than they.

He could think quickly of no name other than the commander in the army of the days in which he still held a memory of some fresh and youthful hopes, alas, be they even in the throes of an imaginary war.

"All right!" He held his paws up in concession, quelling the crowd.

"I'll play my paw. My name...is Vincent Poppaldi, leader of the Army of the Risorgimento. Now, pay your respects."

They all drew back in fear for a moment. But then just laughed, "Well, we better just kill him then since he be leadin' revolts all over the place." They laughed and laughed.

"Well, you know, leader, is a very loose term and all."

More giggles.

"Oy, I think I'm havin' a revolt right now, in me pants."

"Quell the uprising!" they shouted, as the last one to speak ran off to the head.

"You'll regret your quippy...quips, giggle pants! You...pi-rat!" said Gethsarade.

"Oh! A mouth like a beehive, it's got stings, it does!"

Still more giggles.

"No, I just realized calling you anything other than precisely what you are would be a compliment." Gethsarade felt proud and feeling he had set that one up well.

"Oh!" went some onlookers.

"You bet," said one of the more surly ones, who then took a deep bow.

"You better not or you shall force me to exact the consequences. I also do not look well on gambling."

The pirats got a little curious and a hush fell over them as they wondered what in the blueberry buttons he was talking about and what squirrel thinks he can threaten a rat?

In that moment of silence, I could not tell you what mechanism inside Gethsarade must have broken, but suddenly he got another idea and said in a low tone, "There are many in my regimental command awaiting my arrival where this ship is going. They shall hate the disappointment if I show up before them dead. There will be dire consequences."

Gethsarade had no intention of making it all the way to anywhere with these folks, and he would only play by ear, as musicians are wont to do.

"I'm not just any captain. Ever heard of the five-and-a-half-hour war—the *Risorgimento*? Well, I led their army."

"Hay! Oy've heard a' that thing! 'Atsa myth. I heard that story made up by some washed up fiddle playah."

"F-f-f-f...fiddle!" Gethsarade felt for a moment as if someone doused him with cold water over the head and briefly forgot himself.

"I assure you it was no fiddler, sir, for no one could just make up such a fantastic tale!"

They all nodded concession.

"Great! How much did you hear of this? I must know so I may weed out for you the truth versus legend!"

They all stared blankly at him.

"We ain't heard none. Everyone just laughs about the fiddle player part and then moves on."

Gethsarade grit his teeth audibly.

"No matter." It mattered.

"You are familiar, at least, so I will teach you the truth!" And with a little hop, he was in his performing mode.

"Come one, come all, listen close, and you will find what may seem too familiar to you from the hallowed annals of time."

Smashes of laughter cut him off for Barrogan Black had clipped the back of Gethsarade's belt with his sword. While Gethsarade was speaking, his baggy pants slipped to the floor.

"Not too hallowed them annals is, now is they?" said Barrogan.

"I'll have none of this! I'll have none of this!" Gethsarade shouted without avail, then went into himself as they laughed, swearing under his breath,

"Porca, Lucinda, no one EVER wants to hear me play!" But he was actually more relieved than embarrassed he'd thought to put on underpants the other morning. He had learned to come prepared for pantsings as a stage musician.

"Oh, no!" The captain of the pirats stopped, trembled, and shook in fear, which made Gethsarade pleased his ploy seemed to work for a moment.

"What will we do now? The commander here will take us all back to shore and make us...powder his nose! For fear!"

The dissolution could have handled a brass pot.

"We'll be subjected to torture. If we don't give him back right away, he'll make us listen to his diverse political views!"

"Aha, and we'll be forced to drink breakfast tea with his army and have feelings!"

One of them was laughing so hard, he literally bent over, punched the air, and farted.

"But it'll be fiery hot tea, so it will burn our tongues. The horror of it all!" They all clawed at their mouths and wailed in mock pain and completely genuine cramps.

"Totes horrif!," one cried. The captain got the last of his squeaky rat giggles out and came back over to Gethsarade while wiping the tears and trying to control his stomach.

"Oh, it hurts, it hurts, lad. You've given me a good laugh. You know what, I think I like you. Do you know why we've taken your ship?"

"Well, I have no idea, to be honest," as he was.

"We are going to find a golden city, and we need this ship to do it."

"How's what?"

"I suspected such ignorance. Well, we will kill you anyway, so why not make you understand your own patheticness in full. Your admirals never told you why this ship exists. So they employed on it obviously the most groveling, and therefore unquestioning, captain in the whole fleet. I understand survival of the fittest and such. On this ship, there is a key to the greatest treasure in all the world. The key to a city, a golden city. Some call it Hesperia, full of riches, and squirrels so advanced they have taught themselves how to fly unassisted. I have hunted this treasure since I heard about it years ago, but alas we lost the ship! But then, we got it back!"

"Good for you."

"But then...we lost it again."

"Oh, the sadness."

"Don't mock me! We got it back one more time and more times after that, say, about three, I think. It's difficult to fight a ship when it's built for squirrels, and your crew consists of tiny rats. But this last time, we definitely got it right. We will find the key on this ship, then find the city in the new land, and we shall take what is rightfully ours!"

"Say, what makes it rightfully yours if you *need* to take it?"

"It's rightfully ours because we *can* take it!"

"I see," he didn't.

"Then, when we take the treasure, we shall fund an army to take over the whole trade circle for ourselves, and we will control the world's riches on all sides! We will! Ha, ha!" they all cheered.

"Then all those fat, weak, rich rodents out there who ever messed with Barrogan Black because of his unfortunate stature shall bow to him instead!"

Gethsarade had to hide a laugh as Barrogan Black apparently did not see the irony in the notion that those with money are fat and weak. In contrast, he was obese and was a tiny winey being in relationship to his massive head. But his giant jaws gave him a clear advantage.

"Something funny, pollywog?" Barrogan said as he pointed his rapier back at Gethsarade's throat.

"Why, not at all. But my, it sounds like a grand 'ole scheme. Mind too terribly if I tag along?"

"You're off it," said Black, surprised this grand strategist of the Revolution would be so willing to alter loyalties so quickly.

"No, I think it's splendid, honestly. You're obviously a rat who knows what he wants along with how to get it. I would be right obliged to learn a thing or two from a rat like you. Perhaps we have something to learn from one another."

Barrogan looked around, then back at him. "Is yew really Vincent Poppaldi?"

"I am. If you don't believe me, just ask me." said Gethsarade. He was, however, more relieved than surprised to find they believed him for some crazy reason.

"Now, Mr. Black, Captain, Sir. Are you going to let me in on this treasure you're going after so I can use my superior strategizing know-how to help you get it, for a nominal fee or what?"

Barrogan Black eyed him, with all the cleverness and suspicion a pirat could eye someone with.

"Bah! Yew all see 'ere, this one. He's got his head on straight as an arrah!" He accompanied his speech with waving his rapier about pontifically.

"I wish I could find a one a' yew had his kind of sense. Sounds like an honest dog. Yup. But after all…." He suddenly jerked back, and just as Gethsarade thought he was making the right waves, he found the rapier at his throat once again.

"Sensibility and honesty and such ain't the predisposition of the piratin' like."

Gethsarade gasped. "You're kidding?" he said and immediately regretted having the mouth he had, always talking before thinking.

"Oh, believe it." The captain said, "And believe this. The only thing I's hates more than squirrels is musicians! Throw him in the bilges!" he said to uproarious cheers, and down went Gethsarade into the dank and dirty dark.

3: The Big Break

The rat threw Gethsarade into the onboard jail with the imperial cargo of the Tara Feen and other such characters to be eaten or worked to death at some point.

"Oy, Cammandah!" the rat-jailer saluted Gethsarade, popping his heels together, and then went back to his corner on the other side of the bilges, chuckling. He plopped down and did not hesitate to roll over and drop face-first into a comatic sleep.

Gethsarade observed his chains in the silence, broken only by the jailer's rampant distant snoring off in the ribs of the boat or the rush of the midnight waves. There along the walls were masses of creatures he could barely make out. Mostly they were so compacted into the shadows, it was hard to tell if he was even looking at a shadow or whatever formless pile of ill-happenlings were there.

"Hello?" he called out, but then realized he could be grateful of the chains and barriers held between them; still, he listened. Few moved, and more seldom did he spy an eye or two daring to surmise him only to disappear on pain someone had discovered them a-peering. And oh! The stench.

He gave up his neighborliness and retreated to the farthest corner, climbed up into a rafter in his cell, and curled up.

"Aye, matey," someone said. Gethsarade ignored it, seeing as he was not now, nor ever would be, anyone's *matey*.

"Aye, aye," a voice said. Gethsarade heard the individual of interest pawing his way up and snorted as the figure reached an arm inside his cell and poked him in the ribs.

"Aye!"

"Leave me alone," said Gethsarade.

"Aye, what's your name, sod?"

"Get away from me, clump." Gethsarade snapped back.

"What did he call you? Didn't he say Cammandah? Are you the captain? What's he mean by Cammandah?"

"What's it to you if I am or if I'm not?" He turned over and propped himself up on his paws. There was an arm inside his cage, all right, which at his turning around opened into a pawshake gesture, barely visible.

"Leave me alone."

"This over here's my friend, Tiburtine. He's a sorcerer or at least he calls himself one. I'm a sorcerer, too, by such accounts, with a crack o' the cup and dice. Heh." The figure showed his tricks, rolling the dice about and in between his fingers, making them disappear from inside the cup and then seem to appear in the other paw.

"For getting money out of others' pockets, I am a right wizard."

"Hey, I'm a magician, too." They perked up at Gethsarade's reply. "I can make the both of you shut up." He plopped back down in his cell and faced the wall. He stared at his paws, wishing he could just stretch his nails across those strings once more, but remembering that someone was probably making toothpicks out of his beautiful companion.

"He's a sour pup, ain't he?" said the bigger one, going back to their game. He shifted an indiscriminate pawful of torn-off and scribbled on scraps of rucksack

"Eh, yew got a colt's tooth, bub?" he asked the other in some wager.

"You bet I do," he produced three. "I'll see yours and raise you a sack of old ribbons!"

"Call!"

The older, larger one slammed a heavy paw down, and the other put out his cards on the snapped plank they were using as a tabe.

Out of curiosity, Gethsarade peeked at what game they were attempting to play.

"It's complicated bub, and you wouldn't understand." The big one said this in Gethsarade's direction, but he paid no mind.

"Yup," said Tiburt with his chin up in the air.

"He probably can't. His head's probably too full up of commanderly stuff to get anything like this," said the larger one.

"I bet you I can do one better. Watch," said the one called Tiburt, snickering.

"What's goin' on down there? Shattap!" yelled the jailer. This, however, only made the lot of them think of more to converse about.

Gethsarade propped himself on one elbow. "So what sailors don't know the name of the captain they're sailing under?"

The two loquacious new compatriots eyed one another, and then him. "We ain't sailors, mate," said the big one.

"Then what are you?"

"We're...." The other one interrupted, grateful for the chance of a proper introduction. "Tiburtine Tabbit, at your most excellent service! Magician understudy to the powerful (and famous) Mousetradamus!"

"You can call him Tiburt or Tibby," said the other one.

"How'd you get here?" asked Gethsarade.

"Well, Tiburt's not evil, friend. They sold him into slavery on account of having been an entertainer."

"That bad?"

"Oh, no! He is an incredible jongleur by trade. At one point, they caught him giving smooches to a lady-squirrel of a very wealthy baron after a show. She thought he gave a very impressive routine." And about this Tiburt said, "I kissed a squirrel."

"You kissed a squirrel?" Gethsarade asked, incredulous for such an act would land someone on a slave ship, and Tiburt emphatically replied, "Yeah, and I liked it!"

"I'm Gy," said the big one.

"Aye, he's Gy," said Tiburt.

"I'm just bad luck. Stole a loaf of bread-type stuff," said Gy.

"Not such light paws, I guess? I was about to ask you to show me a thing or two, but never mind." Gethsarade scoffed, contemplating whether they were telling him any bit of the truth.

"And you might be…?" said the one named Gy.

"I am the great Vincent Poppaldi," he said with bravado, and he suddenly felt the compulsion to hitch his pants up and spit through the bars. This he did, and the happen-ling his loogie landed on barely noticed, rather accepted this gift as the course of life. It faded back into the bowels of the ship. Gethsarade felt a pang of remorse, for bound to whatever fate this soul, he should not like to make it worse. He resisted the urge to hold out his paw and apologize, and so appearing as a squirrel of weakness, worrying about useless rodents with no name and what at all.

"Never heard of him," said Gy.

"Well, I have!" said Tiburt.

"What? I mean, of course," said Gethsarade.

"You, sir, are famous!"

"I know."

"Your story is told far and wide."

"It should be."

"What story? I never heard of you in my life. How do you know about him, Tibbs?" said Gy.

"Well, I don't personally, but it sounds like it's true."

"Well, then I shall tell you. It began the way all righteous revolutions begin—by not being paid. I have traveled the world, fought wars upon wars, and...." Gethsarade found his bravado fading, realizing he was now officially abroad in the world, and it was not to be cracked up one bit. In fact, his life was still rubbish.

"Oh, it doesn't matter. I've, you know, been around. Sea-faring captain and everything."

"Well, how do we know you didn't just lie about who you are to the jailer beforepaw, and besides, how did you get stuck down here if you is such a big shot?"

"Didn't you hear the jailer?"

Gy eyed the unenthusiastic leader but kept it to himself that he didn't believe Gethsarade at all. Tiburt, however, looked on with boundless revelation and rapture at the soter of his caption, convinced entirely. This was only slightly odd, for Tiburt having introduced himself, being with much ado a sorcerer and fortune teller, Gethsarade expected he would know better. But he just didn't feel like playing anymore at the moment.

"So, um, Captain, sir. Uh...are you going to escape and get us all out of here?"

"No. I will die and probably be eaten. Goodnight."

Not much happened for a while afterwards, for they had all felt bad. The others exchanged banter at a depressed rate.

Gethsarade didn't think the little one could take him quickly. The little fat one was a question of leverage, but the big one could probably throw him across the cell with one paw. The little fat one, Gethsarade noted in the shifting shafts of moonlight, was a very odd squirrel, having the facial resemblances not unlike a rat. But a squirrel he was, and for a rat's tail he would be as bare as the evening; his, however, was fluffy as a sesame cake, all but the bandaged part from surely some brave scuffle.

He was asking many annoying questions to lift the spirits, but the big one interjected.

"I'll be honest with you. I'm feeling just a mite crummy in the particular circumstance. Don't see much point in talking my brains blue."

"What do you think they plan to do with us?" said Tiburt.

"Well, I would wager they're preparing to eat me, seeing as they said that very thing." Gethsarade surveyed his stench-ridden corner.

"Oy dunno. They're keeping us alive when with all the food we're gonna eat by the time we hit shore, it would be better to just throw us over, truth. Unless...."

"Unless what? Out with it!"

"Unless they's plannin' to sell us as slaves."

The little fat one gasped. "Uh, hum. Slaves it'll be. Or worse."

"Ma-donna! What would be worse than slavery?" said Gethsarade, clapping the back of his paw to his forehead.

"Other than just being eaten right off? I dunno. But I know it's not gonna get bettah. They was riggin' out topsails and comin' about to starboard even while they were takin' us down below. It can only mean one thing."

51

"I don't know what you mean by all these stars-boards and comings-about unless you're talking about the billybubs and the bees, friend, and I'm inclined to believe thou art the least educated on billybubs, you ugly sod," said Gethsarade.

"I mean we're going north to Wisterland. We're gonna be traded to a proper slave ship, where they don't survive the majority they take on the way to the West. It's worth it to them 'cause out there word is they go pay top pence and go through the likes of us like buttah. Likelihood says we'll meet our end there. Unless…."

"No, no. Just stop unlessing. I don't want to hear any more unlesses from you. It never comes out well."

"I was goin' to say unless we get out of here right now," said Gy.

"But how do we do that?" said the other two.

"Pipe down insects!" shouted the guard.

Gy got to thinking. "I got an idea," he said and peeked his head out of the bars. "Allo! Jailer! Who wants to play a game?"

"What game are YOU playing at? Bringing the ward over?" said Gethsarade.

"No game I assure you. Play along," said Gy.

"Eek!"

The guard came out of his coma with a snort, and he got up, annoyed they interrupted his beauty sleep.

"What do you want, lich? Can't you see I'm getting ready for dinner?" he said while eyeing Gethsarade and licking his chops.

"Yes, got to be prepared. Seeing the well-prepared and vigilant kind you are, sir, I don't suppose you'd be interested in a bit of cerebro-genic quizzicularial stimulation." The guard looked at Gy almost as if the words just made him sleepier.

"I don't understand what you're sayin' maggot."

Gy motioned him closer as if he would whisper something to him. "Don't mind my friend over there. He thinks of his self as some kind of spell-caster."

"A witch!"

The jailer reeled back in his boots and then stepped to get his keys out and unlock the door.

"I will take you to see the captain and have you right hanged post-haste. No witches allowed!"

"Well, how do you know I'm a witch?" asked Tiburt.

"Didn't he say so?" said the guard.

"Hold on, mate, need none of that," said Gy, but just as soon as the jailer had inched the cell door open and ordered the lot against the wall, Tiburt, having scooped up his two paws full of water, hopped madly from foot to foot and dancing in a circle, shouting.

> Light as a father, frayed of the bark,
> Get'st behind me, thou General Bore!
> Dogs of a feather, stiff as the dark
> Pirouette up to Heaven's lore!
>
> Hurdy Gurdy, Hooty Birdy!
> A palindrome, a stuff of stars.
> Two ships, a circle in a line,
> Now look, the Jailer's behind bars!

The jailer started at them again. Tiburt went into another fit.

"Woowoo-woowoo-woowoo, MAGIC!"

And he stopped, reaching quickly down and dashing bilge water in the jailer's face while making spirit fingers, and nothing magical happened at all, except the jailer became supernaturally angry.

Immediately, Gy knocked him unconscious and grabbed the keys, having been able to move on the jailer unnoticed due to Tiburt's distraction.

"'Bout time; I was running out of things to say!"

"What were you saying anyway?"

"Oh, I don't know. If I understood it, it probably wouldn't be a superb prophecy, would it?"

"But if you don't understand it, how can you say it's a prophecy?" said Gy.

"You wouldn't understand. No matter. I think it is important to point out this was a galleon ship earlier in the day."

"Which means…ah! Thank you, Tibby ol' boy!" Gethsarade waited to be included in the conversation. "There is an armory is what he means. A bigg'n," said Gy.

"Well then we're lost. The rats had to have got to it by now," said Gethsarade.

"You see them holding any new swords or just the same old pirat stuff? I'll wager they either cannot find it, don't know about it, or can't get in, or they would have already."

"Sounds sound. But what if you're wrong?"

"If I'm wrong, we'll not escape the fate set for us worse than death, which should be motivation enough."

"Hm. A little dramatic."

"But true!" said Tiburt, and Gethsarade just shrugged.

"Okay well, I will be eaten otherwise, so might as well try."

"Right."

"Right."

"But if by some slim chance we actually escape with our lives, what do we do?"

"Well, we take this ship and all the treasure in it! The reason these galleons have such vast armories is, they carry an even vaster hoard of gold! Somewhere. Then we go take the treasure they keep talking about, too."

"All I see here are broken folks, no money at all."

The masses laid on the deck with nothing behind their eyes. "Not even an ounce of fight or flight."

"Maybe they weren't always this way." said Gethsarade.

"No matter, they must learn of themselves once more before they can hope for freedom. They will probably only trip us up. But we'll help if we can succeed. Just the way of things." They turned from the silent darkness, writhing in languidity.

Gethsarade hoped without knowing why, were these squirrels so broken they looked not even upon salvation's herald, were not the squirrels who had purchased the vessel, or were they simply the most previous victims of the imperialist crew come before himself? *It would mean something,* he thought, *as yet I dare not explore, for my heart.*

"Hey, ain't you going to let me out? I don't want to be pirat-food either, you know."

"Do we let him out, Gy?"

"He's a good one. He just don't know it yet." Tiburt, without further question, opened Gethsarade's cage and he walked out and they finally shook paws.

"So how do we find the armory?" asked Gethsarade.

"Well, the jailer has the only keys to the jail, probably for security reasons, it seems."

"Yes."

"So I'll wager the warden is somewhere they haven't found him yet."

"Oh! Because I know where it is, uh, no I don't, what?" interjected Gethsarade, who instantly regretted saying anything, for he would probably end up the one to try and acquire the keys.

"How did you get this perfectly convenient knowledge?"

"Oh, just an accident."

"Or magic, hee-hee," said Tiburt.

"Sure."

So they disguised poor Gethsarade by sticking him into the pirat's boots and shirt covered in and out with rat sweat and sea dirt. He flicked off something like either vomit or some strange foreign cheese, or both. They took the sash from around the jailer's waist, for all good pirats sport a sash, naturally.

Everything the pirat was wearing was old and nasty, and Tiburt commented, "One might think these boys haven't been doin' so well of late. Been a while since they could afford a port fee, I'd surmise. Tough life."

Gethsarade interjected fast, "Yeah, well life's tough all around." And just as he was about to go, Tiburt stopped him and, gathering up a load of bilge grease, slicked down Gethsarade's tail with the viscous black slime, so one wouldn't even know its former puffy, cloudlike squirrel glory.

"Ew, agh! What's that?"

"You've got to look the part," said Tiburt.

"I've most likely got lice now, bloody rat. If I didn't know better, I'd say you enjoyed that."

"Yeah, whatever," snapped Tiburt.

"Hurry!"

The jailer was waking, and they had to bonk him again.

Gethsarade had a thought on his way out, bending down and wrested the ankles of one slave free with the keys. The soul gave a test glance for disturbing his quantum, and returned to stasis.

"See, broken. Chained for so long he can't even walk unassisted without injuring himself. Until he can teach himself to stand under his own power, he's no use to us. It's all right. It has to be okay that we're doing what we can, Captain."

Gethsarade shook his head, and they turned away.

"I was just thinking, wouldn't it be better if we all went?"

"Maybe not. If one of us dies, the others have a chance. But we need stealth now, power later."

"Thanks for your concern."

"Sorry, we just met."

And Gethsarade was off.

"There he goes." said Gy.

Several moments went by.

"He won't come back," said Tiburt.

"Yes, he will," said Gy.

"How do you know?"

"Because he's good. Though he might not know it yet. Good ones always need a while to come round. I thought you liked him."

"I don't know. Now, I think he's a little gruff. I think he will do what he acts like he'll do and act for himself. Just wait, you sent the wrong one of us. He's not coming back and we're never getting out of here. You should have trusted me."

Just then Gethsarade popped his head round, and once inside and a little smellier for wear, he jangled the keys to their noses.

"Good work, Captain," said Gy.

"I knew you'd come back," said Tiburtine.

"I heard you."

Tiburt said nothing further about it.

"Well," said Tiburt instead. "All great journeys come to a beginning!"

56

This was quite confusing to Gy and Gethsarade. They turned and left in search of the way out, stepping over the unconscious pirat jailer, who blubbered and sucked his thumb, while they closed the door and locked it.

"Now," whispered Gy, "the armory on these kinds of ships is usually close to the crew's quarters, and no doubt the next watch will still try to get some shuteye. We must get through with no noise to the other side."

They followed him to the end of the bilge, where a single dog hatch to the next deck up was the only way in or out, right up the center of the ship's belly, the only path to the armory from there straight on through the main berthing. Gy held up a fist. They stopped. Apneatic, broken and grisly rat snores filled the air.

"They might move with the graceful repose of a hippo's butt, but they will hear the halfest breath of a weevil's foof, boys. Don't make a sound. Once we get to the weapons, our egress will be wrought of blood and bone. Hesitate not from this moment, and we stick together. Let no one pass between us or to the side. Ready?"

Gy spoke low and quietly to the two of them creeping up to the door of the hold.

"Commandah, they'll know now instantly you're with us, so you stay back. You're valuable. They'll leap on you otherwise, and you'll be the first to go. This way it's a fair fight."

"I feel like I've waited for this moment all my life, a real adventure!" said Gethsarade, who at the time was still pretending to be a commander for the fun, and so seemed like quite a curious thing to say to the others. Gethsarade was more or less quietly thrilled at being valuable for the first time in his life. They steeled themselves, rapiers poised for their escape into glory.

So it went, as they made their best at a quiet parade. That is, they made it about as far as two feet from the door and found themselves amidst the sleeping cabin where there in the candlelight they saw a pair of pirats looking right at them. Gy and Tib looked at each other, but Gethsarade hung back, being more of a lover and a sneaker than a fighter.

The two charged ahead, swords brandished and, in a blink, the moonlight was snuffed out. The air hung with a bustling and a bumbling and a rumpling and a crumpling commotion. Then Gethsarade, Gy, and Tiburtine found themselves with who knows how many rusty pirat swords all pointed at their necks.

"Well, that worked perfectly," said Gethsarade, hoping to play the masquerade card. But someone knocked the stinky pirat hat off his head instead, and his big pointy squirrel ears shone in the only light from the moon, coming through the porthole. Then...bonk.

"Got yourself some recruits now, have ye Commandah?"

Gethsarade said nothing as he barely made out the mocking words of the pirat captain while rising out of his groggy unconsciousness. They were being held in ropes before Barrogan Black. Not because he was brave, but mostly because he had forgotten all about his ploy, as point of sword would affect.

"Did I mention I hate musicians?" said Barrogan Black, leaning in so close the sour whiskey that laced his breath made Gethsarade retch. He noticed just then Tiburt and Gy were gone, and so much for adventure.

4: The Truest Dream

Sometime later....

"Psst."

Gy said nothing, which Tiburt found disturbing, so he said, psst again. To which Gy rolled his eyes and replied, "Don't psst me, Tiburt, we're the only ones up here."

"So what do you think will happen to the captain? Do you think he'll make it?" Gy's jaw shifted, and he abruptly said nothing.

Both of them got from the bottom of the ship to the top, only by being hung from the yardarm, all without taking up a single deck space.

All the more, something of Tiburt's poked him in the kidney. He nursed not one cramp, and the crusty fishnet kept getting in his mouth. "I bet he slipped through the crowd unnoticed what with the incredible disguise we gave him," said Gy, half-sarcastically.

They had all been bonked and dragged off, but Barrogan Black had taken a special interest in Gethsarade, who, having the keys, had managed the escape. Gy had turned out right, but for the wrong reasons. Now the rats would feed them to the albatross, while Gethsarade would probably be given some fate even worse.

"I don't like the odds," said Tiburt.

"Seriously? We gave him clothes too short and too big, and we covered him with slop. There's no way he wouldn't pass through them unnoticed," said Gy.

"You're being unrealistic."

"You say I'm bein'! Look, I think you think pirats think alot more than they do. Perhaps as much as you, but think about it. There's nothing in the life of an outlaw but to be a thing out of place. He would only be a sore thumb if he had everything lookin' exactly right like a pirat thinks he should. Remember what happens when one accuses me of overthinking?"

They heard and listened to the commotion below them, quite an uproar for out of the crowd waddled Gethsarade bound tail to tooth, perched upon a plank, blindfolded, and pleading with the audience while they laughed and jeered.

"Do you think he can swim?" asked Tiburt.

"We'll see if the old dog's got some tricks in him yet. I bet you he'll get us out of here."

Meanwhile…

Underneath the sails and lines, young Gethsarade possessed far less faith. For he stood to endure a far more immediate and harrowing fate, attempting to reason with scoundrels for his life while his awful life did that annoying flashing before his eyes.

"You guys, this is just a waste, you know? I have so much to give, so why don't you let me come with you? We had a good thing going, you know, I mean, doesn't every ship employ a musician, you know like those old shanties? I can learn. I can!"

"Bob. Tomato." Captain Black motioned with his sword, and Gethsarade was hit full in the face by a red, half-rotten blob that knocked him backwards, further down the plank. It stopped him from a pathetic attempt at rousing the spirit of "the troops" with a calling cadence he had learned from a bandolier he had once jammed with, (but only once, for the bandolier was much better than he and therefore bad for business). At least, he finally smelled better.

"We would eat you, but that's a lot of trouble, and now I just want to watch you die. Now walk, little dog!" barked Barrogan Black as he poked his rapier into Gethsarade's back, forcing him to scoot out to the end of the plank. Gethsarade was badly blindfolded, difficult as it is to secure a blindfold around the head of a squirrel, but he could see straight down through his partially uncovered left eye.

Down below him, if it didn't beat all walking down a plank, there was a shadow moving beneath the sapphire waters surrounding the squirrel-sized ship. It floated leisurely by until it rolled up and saw Gethsarade looking right down at it. And if one's fate hadn't been poorly decided enough, it smiled at him. But not the "Oh, great, dinnertime" sort of smile one would reasonably expect. It was as if the underwater mass, which Gethsarade had figured to be a shark by this point, had smiled like a juvenile as if to think, *Oh, playtime with a new toy!* Gethsarade realized he was not just shark food, but shark food about to be very rudely jockeyed about instead of properly eaten. So it was then his senses overloaded, and he passed out.

He woke up suddenly and screamed, "Oh no, I'm dying. I'm lost in the wild. I'm going to die all filled with teeth, and bloody and gross, oh no (gasp). Save me!" But then he realized if he could scream, then he was not dead and, in fact, was not even very much hurt. He felt rather as if he had awoken from a beautiful pre-bedtime nap, one of his favorite things. Being very much surprised at this, he discovered himself to be on strange ground. It held no dirt or shrubbery and was rock solid, bearing the iridescent, striated inlay-work of some exotic emeraldine heartwood. The world's tiniest little island was just big enough for a squirrel-butt, right in the middle of the vast ocean. He thought, *Now what are the odds of that?* He patted himself to check for blood, but there was only seawater, a little kelp, and some drool. It was still nighttime, and he had been ugly-sleeping with the back of his head in the water.

In his moment of respite, he noticed two things. One, the night was most beautiful, and he questioned his hatred of the sea, notwithstanding. Second, the ship's aft fog lantern shone just about to drop over the horizon's end.

Just then a skip-stone blubbed up to the surface just off to his right, which made Gethsarade blink, and it noticed him. The stone brought itself entirely out of the water and showed itself to be the eye some kind of horn-beaked lizard devil creature, and it looked open-mouthed at Gethsarade, who did the same right back to it. He asked the devil creature, "Am I going to die now?"

"Ew ayoo?" It said, then dipped his head in the water. There was some rocking type of commotion. Both turtles poked their heads up out of the water and turned to look at him. Gethsarade, realizing they both were turtles and not devil creatures, was too wrapped up in the moment of his relief to notice the scale of his offenses. It nudged the turtle Gethsarade was on, which slowly opened its mouth and said, "May I ask politely what the 'ell yew is dewing?"

"Well, I'm not sure," said Gethsarade, dismissing the turtle's pedantics. "I was about the business of being eaten, I thought. Do you have any notion as to how I got here?"

The turtle did not answer. Gethsarade waited and then asked him, "Do you see that ship over there? You know, the only thing around above water?"

The turtle did not answer for a moment still more, and said, "Let's suppose for argument's sake, you was at your squirrel home up in a tree somewheres, and...."

"Up in a tree? What squirrel lives in a tree? In de Algarve, we sleep in very nice houses, and...."

"Well, just let me finish. You're bein' rude."

"But I don't...!"

"But yew wuz, BUT YEW WUZ...livin' it up, see, and suddenly I came in your house and decided I was goin' to take a nap, see, it's not funny, a turtle could live in a tree if he wanted too, it's not funny. And having done so, I goes to you and ask...."

Gethsarade held his paws up defensively, trying to stop the barrage, "No, you see, sir, it's just not like that. I'm...."

But the turtle continued undaunted, "No, no listen, s'pose I gose up to you and says, 'I have to sleep 'ere,' just because there isn't anywhere else, as if that was any kind of argument at all. That's what you're getting at right. Well I can only assume by your lack of reasonable objection, so moving forward, no, don't change the subject, listen. So you says, 'what are you doing here?' being perfectly reasonable and polite, and I say, 'Well, I just want to get out of here, you see.' And now you can't help but think I'm just a freeloader and an unappreciative one to bunt it all, now wouldn't you feel the same way? Hum? Hum?"

The flabbergasted Gethsarade said, "Sir, I am not sure how I got here, and I just want to get back over to where I came from. I mean, land-wise. Really, that's all."

The turtle stared at him for a moment, and then the other turtle poked his head up and whispered, "It's not worth it, Bill. Let's just go."

Bill erupted, "Well, buh-bhuh-buhbuh-buh I can't go anywhere if he's going to be there. Wouldn't be any point, as he's takin' up residence on top of my house. Where can I go? To answer your question, you must have flown here, mister squirrel, sir, obviously seeing as you are a squirrel and you are perfectly dry, as anyone with proficiency in nautical sciences can tell. Of course, you mammals all think the sea is full of nothin'. It comes as a great shock to be in someone else's space, too shocked to even kick around the thought of an apology, sure, with your dirty feet. You had to know you flew here since you flew here, so don't act like you didn't."

The other one spit in sarcastic agreement. "And your deficiency of insight into the matters of turtlery alone is highly telling. Now, sir, just put yourself in my shell. I mean not literally, of course, but just put yourself in my place for a moment and imagine how you would feel if someone felt like they could just come over to where you live and use up all your resources and ain't no one goin' to get a word awise to say about it."

"Now, shut up. Can you just listen to me!" Gethsarade shouted.

They looked at each other. "A privileged one awroight!"

"Now you're just being rude, get off, vagrant!" Bill, the turtle, tipped over, and Gethsarade went splashing into the water, gurgling and such.

So it was he had narrowly and inexplicably avoided the shark, only to be assaulted by logical turtles.

"Oy, thanks, mate. Hope you get where you're going sometime soon. Slow and steady ain't going to work out too well this time, will it? Nope!"

Gethsarade tread water for a while, thinking of how to get back to the ship, or whatever he would do about all this. *I can fly?* He just floated for a while, unsure what to do, but after a while, he gave up seeing the notion of squirrels flying as craziness. *What does a sea turtle know about squirrels? They think they can fly. Heh,* Gethsarade laughed, *only birds can fly, and that's only because*

63

feathers are made of magic. And so obviously I would need wings. So not much. Pah! But wait, he had to be right in some sense because, well, facts facts. *And here I am. And why on earth does everyone suddenly think squirrels live in trees?*

"Psst." Gethsarade heard but saw nothing. Then he heard, "psst" again. There below his chin was a relatively innocent looking bubble. It came to almost touch him and sat there for a moment. Then it popped and out came the sound of another "psst." This being most perplexing, he looked down into the water only to see the same shark's giant eye he had seen before.

"Ah, bugganuts! Not the shark now!" Gethsarade started shouting in various dialects of expletives and splashing his arms in hopeless fury. The shark began to move up, and Gethsarade felt the water rising and him with it, till the water's surface broke. The silver eye came up out of the water and locked on him. Then the rest of the beast came out, rolled around for a moment, and then finally came to a stop after next to killing Gethsarade several times with his thrashing.

It breathed to him, "I'm not a shark."

Confusion is one of the more calming emotions when brought on suddenly. "Um. No? You are, I'm afraid," said Gethsarade.

"No, I'm not."

"What makes you think you're not a shark?"

"Uh, I don't know. Sharks don't like me."

"That doesn't mean you're not a shark."

"It doesn't mean I am."

They both paused.

"Look, you look like your shark friends?"

"Mostly."

"What do you mean, mostly?"

"Uh, I just don't like to say anything for certain, you know. Making broad statements isn't very inclusive."

"Well...anyway, you look mostly like your shark friends, which means for all intents and purposes. You're a shark." Gethsarade couldn't even figure out why he was bothering to argue this most self-deprecating point. But these kinds of errors can't be overlooked in the wide, wide world, you see.

"For certain." The one whom all but he would be in agreement was a shark at this point raised the area of rubbery skin that would typically comprise an eyebrow were it not the area above the eye on a shark, and the nature of this non-eyebrow raising was very sarcastic.

"Okay, for almost, but not completely, certain. And anyway, I am a third-party, objective source. I can tell you, you are a shark," said Gethsarade.

"Have you ever seen a shark in person?"

"Well, no. This is my first sea voyage."

"Well, what do you know? What are you?"

"I…I'm a squirrel, sir."

"Do your squirrel friends like you?"

"Well, not much but that's beside…."

"Then how do you know you're a squirrel?" the shark said matter of factly raising his eyebrow-area thing.

"Because…because…Phmmph oh, golly good fracking gaaah!" He slapped himself.

"There is no cause for substitutionary language," proclaimed the shark.

"You! How do you know you DON'T mostly look like a shark if you don't know what every shark in the entire universe looks exactly like? Huh? Hm." Gethsarade crossed his arms and turned away with his eyes closed.

"Well, that's easy. I know I'm probably not a shark because I know no shark will look exactly like me…. So the more sharks you see, you see, the more empirical proof you will find I am totally unique." The shark smiled and wiggled, letting the drops that clung to his rubbery skin sparkle in the moonlight.

Gethsarade couldn't even handle it anymore. He pulled his hair and yelled at the sky. "But you said, shark, you see? You said shark, your shark friends are sharks."

"Stop being so pedantic."

"Is it the sea? Is it the loneliness? The isolation? Am I doomed to this fate?" He turned to the shark again and eyed him. "I simply don't know what to do with you."

"See? Now we're getting somewhere." The shark smiled.

"He-he. I like you." he said, "What's your name?"

Gethsarade almost answered, but then he thought about it, and said, "If you must know, you can tell your friends you have met the one and only Vincent Poppaldi, world-class guitarrosso y generale de Risorgimento."

"He-he. No, you're not."

"What? How do you know?"

"Because there are tons of squirrels, and the likelihood is therefore very high that you are not Vin...Vin Chen...you know, what you said."

"Gah!" said poor Gethsarade, pinching the bridge of his nose with both paws full force.

"Well, since you demand legitimacy of opinion at the cost of all basis of thought, who do you say I am?" said Gethsarade, having discovered the point in anger at which one becomes apathetic.

"I think," the shark paused, then looked scared.

Gethsarade said, "What?"

The shark jumped, "No way! No way, dude! You're a shark! Don't bite me! Mercy!"

The shark rolled and flopped around, trying to get away from Gethsarade who floated there annoyed, when another shark came up, quietly like a shark should, out of the water. And the shark was entirely and exactly like the shark next to it.

"Hey guys, what's going on?" it said, attracted by the sudden thrashing—like a shark.

"Oh, wow, what kind of animal are you?" said the shark who had up to the present been talking to a squirrel, which is about the oddest thing one could imagine had it not been for the actual conversation.

"I'm...a shark," said the new shark, at that point highly confused at the situation of a large identity confused predatory animal frantically avoiding a tiny, sopping rodent. "Um, what are you?"

"Wow, you're a shark?" said the other identity-confused shark who began enthusiastically examining himself. "Lemme see, fins, and…gills…and teeth." he gasped, "You're like, exactly like me! And you're a shark! Wow, oh wow, you are EXACTLY like me, in every way, that is so cool. It's like whatever you are, that's what I am cause it's like we were, like, meant to be together! Hey! This must mean I'm a shark like you! Wow! You learn something new every day! And here I was wondering if I was a squirrel."

The new shark peered at him. "How do you not know you are not something you are not?" And Gethsarade motioned towards it in silent agreement.

"Lemme just get a good look at myself," the first shark swam several swift circles around the second shark and suddenly popped his head up again and said mostly as enthusiastic as before, "You're not exactly like me."

To this, the new shark whose voice did perfectly resemble the first's happily replied, "Nope. I'm a girl shark."

"Wow, you're beautiful. Will you go out with me?"

To which the other replied, "Of course, how could we not?"

"Oh, and while we're at it, what's your name?"

"I'm Atraxia."

"What a cute name for a girl."

"I agree! Wow, we agree on everything! Dating is cool! I love you so much!"

"Me, too!"

Then they both turned to Gethsarade and said together, "Thank you so much for helping us find one another in this crazy, mixed-up world. Love like ours is so rare. We owe you, dear friend Vincent for all time. We are here for you at your service, indebted to you forever."

"What? I didn't do anythi…well, you know what? You see a ship? Over there."

"On the horizon?'

"Yes, the only one. Can you get me over there?"

"Sure! Out of curiosity, why?"

"Lend me your ears, friends." And they leaned in. However, he looked for the sharks' ears and then gave up.

67

"Where are your ears?"

"What's an ear?" said the confused one.

Gethsarade shook his head. "Anyway, I'd like to tell you a story."

After recounting his tale, for which he regrettably possessed no instrument to gild it in proper glory, the sharks gleefully gave chase to the galleon, catching up to it stealthily and in record time.

According to plan, they approached from the ship's stern so the lookout would not spot them in the wake.

"Steady, steady, aim right for the couple of choppers poking out. I need to get those, and I'll be back in a moment."

The choppers he referred to were the humongous butcher knives once belonging to Mr. Cervello the butcher-cat. They were still stuck in the ship's hull from their special moment, for which Gethsarade tipped his pirat hat and quietly gave thanks as he went up, but first he stole up into the tarpaulin and grabbed the old rope that secured the refuse, releasing the tarpaulin over the side.

"Oops. No matter." Just then, he noticed they had thrown his guitar back into the refuse pile, so he grabbed it and slung it over his shoulder. He went back down by the line, wrested the two knives out of the wood with some difficulty, for they were buried almost hilt deep, and tied them to his waist. Then he let himself all the way down, back onto the first shark's nose.

"Well, that was fun. What now? And what are the knives for?"

Gethsarade thought for a moment. "They're for justice."

"Okay. What's the guitar for then?"

"For the poetic." He grinned. "Now. Ever gone ship-tipping before?" he whispered.

"Why, yes." Said his shark friends.

"Why?" said Atraxia.

"I thank you exceedingly for your help, Lady Atraxia. And what is your name good shark, sir?"

The male shark thought for a second. "Oh, yes, I have a name as well! It's Arfaxad! Amazing things, names. You cannot hold them, yet never lose them." he said formally. They both bowed, which in water, and performed by something with no eyelids, looked a lot more like they were just suddenly going a-looking for something.

"Wow, Arfaxad, such a cool name."

"Agreed."

"We agree about EVERYTHING!"

"COOL!"

"SHHH! Good, you're meant for each other." Gethsarade said. He was used to their bantering now. And so, he tipped his hat to them and said, "But I suppose I shall need some help with the next part, and that be all. Just a nudge. A very, very hard nudge. But I need you to wait until I give the signal, understood?"

"Mm-hm. So, what's *your* name?" asked Atraxia as Gethsarade leaped up onto the rudder.

Gethsarade leaned back, "Vincent."

The first shark chuckled to himself and nudged Atraxia, "He's not. He-he. I mean, what are the odds?" He shook his head, and at that point, Atraxia began to question the structural integrity of her new relationship.

The rats drank and partied late into the night celebrating their victory and new ship thrice or so again. But it was not to last. For once things had got nice and pitch black, and they were slovenly basted with grog, they might have otherwise been alert and able to see a loop of line slip quietly over a turnbuckle, then slip back down into the dark. The forlorn Gy's and Tiburt's spirits might have been lifted to see their latecomer friend appear, hanging, rappelled off the side by the waist and, with a count to three, give a wave back to the sea.

Boom!

The rats cried out, for the ship shook to its keel and moaned like a bedridden old maid rolling onto her side. As it creaked and groaned to its starboard, many a barrel of grog and spice went into the sea. As for the rats, the intrepid Gethsarade stood right side up and secured them all as they clung sideways onto the many bollards and lines. He strolled up to the center where all could see him.

"He is risen!" they cried. They threw down their swords to surrender.

Someone said, "But no one ever comes back from walking the plank!"

"Perhaps it's possible I'm just the only one dumb enough to come back," said Gethsarade. To this, the crew gave it a thought, and nodded and muttered in agreement. Definitely had to give him that one.

Then Captain Black yelled. "No, you idiots! That musician just survived, somehow. Pick up your swords."

Then Gethsarade gave another wave. The ship arc'd further, now sideways. All of the rats' remaining swords fell into the sea as the rats gave them up to favor the lifelines.

Gethsarade said, "Let me help you. Where's the rope holding you all up?"

The poor, shaking rats were all strung out on the mast and scattered ropes as Barrogan waved at them to stop. The dumbest one in the crowd pointed straight to the rope next to Gethsarade's left.

"Thanks! Now, salud, salvey brutes, and auf wiedersehen! Puedes bañarte en breve y beber la misma agua!" This was a phrase meaning, "You must now drink your own bathwater, for you stink by all means." Gethsarade saluted, unsheathed the knives, and, in a scissoring motion, clipped the rope right in twide, and Barrogan fell to the water screaming against the lot, "You idiots!" The pirats, all drunk, could not hold on anymore, one nor all.

"Please, yon squirrel master, throw us a line! We don't want to die. Are we not of a kind?" shouted one rat in the water.

Gethsarade laughed and shook his shoulders as if he were some mighty conqueror, and he said, "Why should I do that?" Their screams of terror were so horrific that Gethsarade swung at another rope and let down the lifeboat, and they all climbed aboard, shimmying their tails and looking laughable. Gethsarade was not a monster, yet still, despite this kindness, Barrogan Black's last words to him were, "We'll get you Poppaldi! We'll get you yet!"

Gethsarade shot a thumbs up to the two sharks who let the ship back down into the water right side up and held her till she was stable. Then Arfaxad and Atraxia found the massive pile of rats all struggling and fighting to get on top of one another in the sea. This elated them with great elation. But a few of the rats took notice of them, and then a few more, and then they all fell silent at the shark-shaped shadows many times the size of a squirrel-galleon, looming over them and grinning with all their might.

"Hello, new friends!" They both said at once, but to their disappointment, they were only met with screams of the most unimaginable and annoying levels of rodent terror.

"We don't like loud noises, friends! It hurts our not-ears."

"Yeah," said Arfaxad in his approximation of sounding tough, "which we just learned of." And that was that, and what happened to the pirats beyond then was of no concern to Gethsarade.

"Goodbye my good toothy friends and thank you from the bottom of my heart. I shall not forget you and, if I see you again, it shall probably be very awkward!"

They swam off, happily, carrying off the sounds of many screaming rats while talking to one another. "I hope we get to have that much fun again soon," said Atraxia.

"Anything, as long as it's with you, my dear."

"You duplicate me," kissy-kiss.

Now, this whole time Gy and Tiburt were safely dangling, entirely captive, on the yardarm. Earlier while Gethsarade slobbered on the deck, the rats tied them up in nets and played pinata to tenderize them, for they were on the breakfast menu. Gethsarade let them down unbothered by the rabblery.

"Well, that turned out well," said Tiburt.

"Now we make up the whole crew," said Gy, nursing his bruises. "Let's hope for smooth sailing, wherever we're going."

"Roger." Tiburt didn't know what *roger* meant, but it seemed appropriate.

"So, what do we do now, Captain?"

Gethsarade realized suddenly he much liked the sound of the word *Captain*.

"Well, I'm not sure, but I know what Captain Black said to his crew when they were up here making a racket. Wherever they were going, he planned to make them all stinking rich."

"Well, they were already stinking. Why enrich one's stink?"

"Well, being richly stinking and stinking rich is a critical distinction of stinkiness. I believe he meant the latter. From context," said Gy.

"Quite," They said.

"But how do we find the stinky riches?" said Tiburt.

"Well, maybe."

And they went to the captain's quarters where they searched and searched. "What would they look like?"

"Well, I know lots of stories of when these types of things happen," said Gethsarade.

"And?" said Gy.

"Well, generally, the crew looks at a piece of paper with drawings on it, with x's and dots and squiggly lines going everywhere."

"You mean a map?"

"What? Oh, yes, yes, a…map. Once they look at this thing called a map for a while, then they go and dig around while holding this thing that points to the treasure or something."

"An azimuth compass?" interjected Gy again.

"Yes. And I think the map must give them an idea of what to dig for, by telling the um...hazy-mutt...where to point."

Tiburt gasped, "Magic?"

Gy's eyebrows were quite high by this time, for he knew neither of those things did exactly either of those things. "Few sea voyages under your belt, Mister Commandah?"

"Well, my battles were mostly by land, you see."

"Aye," Gy rolled with it. "Then you seem to say you would require the services of a coxswain."

"Don't sass me."

"Aye, sir. Would you like someone to steer the helm?"

Gethsarade eyed him closely for a moment. "...yes…yes, I think that would be good."

"Good then, on our way. Come, Tibbs, I'll show you how to find the stars."

"Stars! What a find! An incredible thing. I love astrology! I think I love the sea!" said Tiburt, and out they went.

Yet after some searching, they came upon the same problem Barrogan Black had and that disallowed him from ever finding the key to the treasure of the City of Elorus.

Gethsarade sighed in frustration. "There must be a map. That's how you find buried treasure, right?" he asked.

"Well, yes and no. Maybe the map has been made to look like something else," said Tiburt. "Or there is no such thing as buried treasure."

"No?" asked Gethsarade curiously.

"No. All you'll find is a fate of another," said Tiburt.

"Well, very interesting. So, let me get this straight. You believe in magic, but not money?" Tiburt met Gethsarade's giggles with a stern, obstinate, yet altogether silent glare.

"Wherever he put it, you must think intuitively. The book says somewhere he will never find his destination until he can find himself first," Tiburt said.

He browsed silently through its tattered and torn pages, ripped into many pieces, it seemed, from much more cavalier perusal and long frustration. Then he came to this, which he read out loud:

How to Find Thy Truest Dream

Where a terminal moonlit pillar
A geyser's upward golden stream
Is Elorus's angled message-sender
Averse, a blinding, blinding beam.

This alone can bring you to me
When Heaven's tracers darken sky,
Hold up what bindeth two together
And let it make the Goldwing Fly.

At Wintersfall heroes return,
Persimmonia at Almondale,
Until you find the city's key
only then shall peace prevail.

On the day Elorus comes,
A warning to thee faith and fate,
Wilt thou city's hidden doors discern

Or bear alike thy father's fate?

And look unto the luminous light
Shining in thine glimm'ry eye
Resting 'top the hillven world
And at bottom-most of the sky.

For true depths you'll never sound
As then can thine true heart suffice
Until thine own true soul be found
A right and proper sacrifice.

For how to find thine truest dream
Like the bogmeat, best not try,
Until thy wind returnest to thee
Then bow to thee shall earth and sky.

And he couldn't help but notice the poem seemed to call to him, as if it knew him so deeply, so intimately like no one could. Also, whoever this was that shared his distaste for fish was good in his book.

"What's it say?" asked Tiburt

Gethsarade came to his senses. "Oh, I don't know, some blobbity bleching about true love, woo. Don't care. Moving on." Gethsarade tossed the book, and Tiburt grabbed it.

"Don't you see? The words are your map! It has to be this book." said Tiburt.

"Why do you suppose?" said Gethsarade.

"Because it was the only one he used." Tiburt waved his paw to the plethora of books upon the shelves, all dusty and hardly touched, but only one bore the smell and the stains of ratful negligence on it.

"And as you can tell, he used it quite a lot."

"How do you know the book is a map? I mean, couldn't it just be like the book says, there is a key hidden somewhere, and we just can't find it, likely seems to be the case."

"Think about it. He searched high and low on this ship and never found it. In fact, the only thing he's found is this book. So, whether there is a key, it is not here, and we must move forward with only the book. Whether I'm right doesn't matter. The conclusion will still be the same."

"You know, Tiburt, you certainly know rats well. You're quite a smart squirrel when you want to be." said Gy.

"Well, seein' as reading books and such ain't the predisposition of the piratin' life," said Gethsarade, imitating their voices, he held the book up, and a considerable number of notes and things fell out. He flipped open to the last page where anything was written and looked at the poem again.

At Wintersfall shall heroes return,
Persimmonia and Almondale.
Until you find your city's key
Only then shall peace prevail.

"Great Grendel's Cabbages," he said as he pointed to a page of the book: "The map is a book. The book is a map!"

He turned it over to the cover. It read: "Wintersfall. It's late summer."

Tiburt and the captain shared a moment, breathing in the evening air. "It's getting cold."

"Two things at one time. Magic!"

Gethsarade smiled. "Yes, Tibbs. Magic!"

5: City of Gold

Months went by.

Such were the times came when the ocean made one put things into perspective. The Continental Passage, the trade route used by sailors all over to the New World and back, and mists rising over the warm waters can confuse and cause trouble of the soul in the doldrums.

One may wonder if *he* shall ever emerge. Such things first-timers called pollywogs are in no position to know about, and the obviousness of this put Gy, an old salt by comparison to Gethsarade, or should we say, the Captain-Commander, in such a tension that the Tara Feen could hardly contain it. It had been well-nigh a season without a foxbutt's hint of land or breath of wind.

Gethsarade, on the contrary, sat in the scullery eating tack and examining poetry.

The quarters were full of fantastic arches. Yet the moldings reflected the battles of the gods and goddesses, nymphs, and giants of the north. There were a few carvings, all done up the posts, rudimentary yet of striking faces with the most extreme expressions. Some bore wings and sharp teeth, serpent tongues, hollowed eyes from worlds unknown.

The captain ran a finger along one of the many posts and trims all about the galley cabin. The plates were the only things tarnished, but still finely made. He declared himself in a state of utter shock, for even after all their time in the ribs of the Tara Feen, all the silver-colored metal around him was indeed silver and, rather than brass. The fittings and railings all about the bulwarks, even the common areas and everyday things, were entirely made of the finest gold.

Gy banged open the door, all a-sweat. "Heavens, Captain, these masts are so far apart! Most squirrel ships I've seen have the masts close together so they can swing from one to the other, but we've got to climb all the way down and then back up again just to get around lest we splat on the deck."

"True, I've never seen the like or capacity for speed anywhere. 'Tis the most solid construction and larger than the largest from where I'm from. If I didn't know better, I'd say it sported sides of iron, barring some things that just can't float. I'd literally kill to get a gust of wind, though!" said Gethsarade.

"Agreed. Ne'er saw its like. In fact, it's not just the finest boat I ever observed, but the goldenest thing. But how does one build a ship so stunning, so complete, and yet not know to hang the catchy-nets down behind the sails and such things? Such a basic thing, everyone knows a squirrel can't jump 10 body lengths—that's practically flying! Why no fancywork on these brass bars, so they don't go green in the sea air? A rich squirrel who knew nothing of proper sailing built this pig, I think."

Gethsarade shrugged. "Right, and yet…," he never took his eyes off of the ceiling of the captain's quarters. "Such richness, it was almost as if these squirrels weren't the kind to bother with small ships or distances. Yet, all the same, I could swear this ship knows me. Knows us. You know?"

"No. Ships, sir, know nothing."

Gethsarade sniffed but did not reply.

Just then there was a knock at the door. A gaunt figure none recognized at first, but recognized all the same, stood holding himself up against the jamb with one paw, and trembling at the knees, head bowed poorly, and staring at the deck. He barely whispered to announce his presence.

"May it much please the masters, we pityful happenlings humbly request our daily rations. Seems we've had nary half a bean for some time, and, forgive me, Sah, and it's no one's fault but ours.

But we're a mite 'fraid we might have a bite of trouble makin' rows for the masters, most, m-most respectfully, masters…" he trailed off.

Gy's arms went akimbo. "What do we do about the happenlings when anybody mentions them?"

"Well," Gethsarade said, "we could just take them wherever we are going and I don't know…."

Gy rose, "And what?"

"Sell…?"

"Don't even think about muttering another word."

"Pardon me, good sirs," interjected the dark-haired one at the door. "But just so's we're clear, it wouldn't be no trouble on us, promise, if you's was to do that, as it wouldn't be no mind at all. There's no dime for us to see in any of our lives, but, of course, we'll be seein' two hots and a flop, don't mind any none. No, sirs, no…," he bowed pert near to the ground.

"Hear that, Vincent? He's practically beggin' for his life."

"No, he didn't. He said he wouldn't mind it at all. What's your name, dark one?"

"Scurrid, Master."

"And if you was a tye-rannical and all too typical sea-cappytan, you would hear them words and do just the opposite, keep 'em on board a bit longer, just for the meanness, just to keep them in line? Think about it. He sees you. Right through he does. Perceptive. He knows you won't. Will you?"

Gethsarade sighed. "No…all right, fine. But what are we going to do about feeding them?"

"Something is what."

Scurrid's eyes went wide with hope, but he did not look up from the deck.

"What do you care about them?"

"I don't, personally. I care about squirrels like me being treated like they're not. It's a matter of principle."

"Agreed, I think," said Tiburt, coming in from his watch. "In any case, I have been looking at the charts, and the closest thing to land at this point is now in the direction of where we are going, at least all probabilities being equally so, since we have officially traveled off the map."

"Great Rojar's ghost. When did we go off map?" asked Gy.

"I think it was somewhere between the time we stopped steering the boat and the other time we neglected to record the alidade readings," said Tiburt, removing his sweat-logged hat and bowing his head.

"Well, which one of you sorry dogs neglected to do that?" Said the Captain-General, whom it seemed was beginning to get comfortable in his position.

"Well, sir," said Gy.

"Well, you should have reminded me. I'm far too busy, you know, to be doing that all the time." He puffed his chest, but his eyes got dodgy, and Gy swooned, leaning into Tiburt's ear and whispering something, and then Tiburt just nodded and left.

"What did you tell him?"

"I told him you must uphold an image, but what you said was your version of an apology and that you appreciate everything he has done to help you. This reminds me that we are helping you, which means we are under your employ and that means the matter of remuneration has been a conversation pushed far too far out of mind."

"What do you mean?"

"I mean, respectfully, sah, you don't get to sodding yell at us as you ain't payin'. We's friends, but not that good a-friends. This work is hard, and we want to know what we're getting out of it, with you sitting here staring at paintings and bein' the captain."

"Well, to be honest, I don't know how to pay you, seeing as there is no bounty or booty to divide among us."

"I know. I'm asking what your plan is to get it." It had not occurred to the captain-general that pirates don't just go around being pirates for the love of piracy.

"I've been going through the books here. I'll be honest. I don't quite know what I'm looking at."

"Well, lemme look at them" Gy got impatient. He rushed to the spread of files on Gethsarade's desk and looked through them, quickly realizing they were full of unexamined documents probably concerning things potentially profitable, and one old used-up book.

"What do you have there?" he said, hiding his indignation.

"Oh, it's some old book, some story."

"Well, let us take a look-see," said Gy impatiently, "It has no publication date. This is paw-bound."

"Yeah, it's like a bunch of old legends. Wasn't even traditionally published. Must be crap. Let's go look at something else."

"It says something here about a City of Gold with a giant golden nut as big as an owl. You know what this means?"

"They have big storage facilities?"

"No! Where there's smoke, there's fire, and likewise where there's gold, there's rich fools with money to lose."

"And…?"

"We're gonna go become rich fools, too."

"But why do I want to be a fool?"

"No, I'm saying you need to go where the money is if you want to make more of it. We need to find this city. Come on, we don't need another Tiburt!"

"I kid. But this idea is in a fairy-tale book."

"Don't you see this is real? Whoever owns this ship was writing this book! A place where they used gold to make their rail-irons, and enormous jewels for ice in their drinks! These are not fairy tales but rather history. Someone wanted someone else to find this book. Why would they lie, especially if they meant for only one squirrel to figure it all out?"

"About flying squirrels? Ridiculous. They don't exist. Only birds can fly because they have feathers and feathers are magic."

"What? How do you know? Just because there ain't nothin' like them where you're from doesn't mean they're not real somewhere else. Clearly the treasure exists. Maybe flying can, too."

"I don't know. This just doesn't seem real. This writing is just so dramatic like one of those penny pubs. Some bohemian nonsense— one of those popular but ultimately terrible authors of their day. A golden city of flying squirrels— it's incredulous. You know, like *The Count of Mousey Christo*. Great story, you know. But hundreds of pages of mindless, over-embellished droning to take up the space on page on page, and on and on. Verily, I am presently nonplussed and bestuck to discern what cretinous, circumlocutory prolix would perform such threats of literary violence and herniations upon the good populations of the world, anywhere. I say, much less is done to the good art and to the dismay of all, they should seek even a pinched penny's worth of remuneration over such a conflagratory affair! Furthermore, and in addition...."

"Please, stop, it hurts," said Gy, who was suddenly having trouble holding himself up.

"Apologies," said Gethsarade.

Gy regained himself. "But does terrible writing alone mean it's not true?"

"Well, I mean, probably."

"Actually, I believe this could be true. I mean why not? And we've got nothing else to do. Why not go find out if we can go get rich?"

"Rich...." said Gethsarade. But the poem's declaration troubled him.

"Well, who here has a better idea? May I remind you we are near out of grog and joe."

So Gethsarade agreed.

Whatever is troubling me, I'm sure I wouldn't miss whatever it is once I have everything I ever wanted, the Captain thought.

"All right, I'm convinced, whether right or not. On we go."

"There's a true believer. To Paradise!" declared Gy.

Just then the one who had introduced himself as Scurrid shuffled his feet, then thought maybe better, then looked side to side, just enough for Gy to catch him and then down again.

"Right," said Gy, "Rations, then. There's food to keep them alive till port at the least, even if in the next week. I'll scrounge up something, but we need to find land."

"Thank you, masters, thank you kindly," said Scurrid, and he promptly disappeared back to the hold.

"Good, off you go," Gethsarade pretended to give approval, and Gy pretended he needed it and was gone. Tiburt had found him again and followed him out, asking Gy what to do now. He had taken it upon himself to loosen all the sheep's heads.

"Heavens, why did you do that?"

"I felt bad for them."

"Now we've got to tighten them up again. Then, we'll go up top and look for land."

They left Gethsarade, or should we say the Captain-Commander, to collapse into the awfully comfortable chair, settling somewhat into his new life as the captain of a ship, and whose ship it was before he couldn't tell you to save his life.

Whoever owned this must have been incredible. But enough to keep away the pirats? Clearly not. Ha. The ship bore the marks of having been far from a craft-squirrel or caretaker from some time.

Like me, he thought. *Just like me. Maybe that's why it seems to set off such a strange set of feelings. Hey, I got rid of them pirats. Perhaps I could be better. Maybe this life was meant for me. Ha! It would seem the fates have seen fit to tend this ship over to paws more capable. Maybe this is what I was born for.*

He thought on all this as he looked up at the painting overlooking his bed that had been chipped away in the sea air. The picture matched, in some ways, the adornment on the book's cover, only it had a gorgeous landscape. Still the light was there and shone bright where at the bottom of the picture, with a massive river in the middle. They were ushering the river upward into the distance to two circles of gorgeously adorned monuments that directed their lights and lighthouses toward the mountain's curved top, where there hung a light. It was confusing, but brilliant. *Such a beautiful ship born for me.*

The time passed quickly—for a while. Three days later, the sailors were out of food and ready to kill each other.

It was easy for Gethsarade to know when Tiburt was on watch.

Ding, ding! The bell rang and then again.

Gy went climbing up and called up from halfway.

"Tibbs, is it land? Do you see land?"

Tiburt looked down and stared for a moment. "I don't know."

Gy wiped his face. "How many times do I need to tell you, Tiburt, you don't need to; no, you can't ring the bell if you don't see any land. Was I not clear?"

"Well, I wasn't sure, you see."

"How are you not sure if you don't see land or not?"

"Well, it's really fuzzy."

"That's because it's not land!"

"I just don't want to miss anything," said Tiburt, growing frantic.

"Tib, I love your spirit. I love the spirit of your spirit. But we need to sleep."

"Well, how can I know it's not land if it's far away? Never saw when it was fuzzy before, only up close."

"It's not a matter of…wait. What do you mean by fuzzy?"

"Well, I know it's probably not land if as you say, it's not you know, clearly land like when I, for instance, just see some kind of big glowey area. Obviously, land does not glow but I was wondering how clearly you meant exactly because if you looked over here, you would see–" But Gy's shouting interrupted Tiburt.

Gy turned and spied a stone wall 10 times the height of the ship's mast, port side, as it came forth from the thick fog.

The rocking of the ship brought a considerable protrusion from the wall close enough to force Gy to dodge it as it nearly smashed into the mast and came close to sending it crumbling into the deadly rocks beneath the hull.

"Great fat, Jee-how-sa! Tiburt, tha's LAND! Ring! Ring the bell. Oh, The captain won't believe it. Get down and get on the lines, hurry, we're going to crash!"

Gy scampered up, and Tiburt hurried down, as Gy yelled commands. "And remind me later to hurt you a lot!"

It had proven of little use to ring the bell, however, Gethsarade had come out of the cabin up to the aftcastle for air, for he had not slept. He was studying a book.

He stirred his little dirty cup filled with stale tea. He stretched and squinted upward towards the mast, chuckling to himself as Gy and Tiburt were going at it. He breathed in the mist, which brought relief from the sea's eternality, a gift best wakened up to after the best kind of sleep—the kind on a boat.

Their shouting grew so frantically and so suddenly, he stopped squinting and looked up again with an emergent inquisitiveness to see them now pointing and shouting.

He followed Tiburt's point to the bow, when a boulder nearly met his face instead. He threw his watery grog on the deck, ducking as the rock grazed his ears.

So he was well aware the moment Gy's head was almost taken off by the same jetty, and this was the source of all dismay. His chest felt tied tight like twine. Through the course of night, it appeared, they had come up the way of a massive river and were sailing down its narrowing path until they came unto a steep bend that carved its way about a looming mountain, almost mocking them, as they beheld the momentary future and the dismal extent of its mercies.

Gethsarade barely had time to shout some worthless, unintelligible commands and rocked on the deck, scarcely dodging mooring gear kabumping and skatunking across the unswept boards as the Tara Feen sheered off the wall sidelong.

Gy immediately came swinging down by the line to Gethsarade's side and checked to make sure his master was all right.

"I'm fine Gy, thank you. Are you all right?"

They had come around a rocky promontory into the southern tip of a small bay, but the curve of the shoreline was so steep there was no way to avoid it. Gy had no time to answer as they ran to fight the wheel to veer the ship a few degrees away. The struggle to hold the helm at its maximum turning radius yielded too little, and they looked on in horror as more rocks inched slowly and unstoppably closer to straking the ship's waterline, surely to ripping it clear and wide.

"Brace for impact!" Gy yelled, and they jumped to the deck. Tiburt had already strapped himself in. Gethsarade dug his claws into the line bit he clung to. He closed his eyes and grit his teeth.

In moments of inevitability each second is like a prayer to heaven. It arrests one's involuntary faculties, breathing, sweating, and even heartbeat for an eternal, cursed moment. Then there is the dreaded instant when the soul itself feels inclined to deny until it no longer can.

Not only was this happening, but all that was to come about after. They were not only irrevocably the impending victims of a shipwreck, but also soon to be a new feast for whatever strange curses, blights, or worse, natives, occupied this strange new land. Before this point, no poor sod in the visible past had the misfortune to break his hull upon its gray, sand-less, virgin boundaries.

Just as Gethsarade fought his ribs to expand and take in breath once more. In a moment of hesitation before the break of chaos, he opened his misfortunate eyes and was met with an explosion of stone and wood.

He threw himself back and away and just missed the impact by a pygmy's hide. Still, he was knocked unconscious by the subsequent clashing of debris and ship.

When he miraculously revived Gy was holding him, bloody and bruised the three of them all, but alive, gasping on the nightmare shore and in each other's' arms.

The ship crashed straight on into the rock wall and lodged on a natural jetty, which protruded with ghastly rudeness into the hull. It held, unable to move the ship off the rocks from thereon. The Happenlings, Scurrid and all, escaped through a hole torn in the vessel's side and disappeared free into the misty coast.

"Look!" exclaimed Tiburt, pointing to a massive structure not far off to the north and up to a little path that jutted out of the trees, high above them, so it was visible from anywhere in the bay.

There stood a rock, jutting upward in the light of the waxing moon of morning, an awesome, red granite-like structure up the path such as no ordinary squirrel could build. It seemed to be placed intentionally but so long ago the vines and waters of time had overgrown and undercut its structure by the river and the waves. They quickly realized these structures surrounded the bay.

"Where are we?" asked Tiburt.

"I don't know." Gy replied.

They looked about the stone masses, noting their size, each pillar comprising a height of 10 of the tallest of them. The tallest, 20, which they found themselves the closest to at the mouth of the bay.

"Clearly, it was intended as some ritual place," said Gethsarade.

"Or point to one," said Tiburt.

"What do you mean?"

"Where a terminal moonlit pillar...."

"Do you think this could be the pillar?"

"I don't know, but look here," they came around to the leeward side.

"This pillar has a marking on it."

Beneath the weathering showed an illustration carved into the relief of the rock still visible.

"It almost looks like some kind of cave carving," Gethsarade turned to the two.

"Are we sure this isn't some kind of grounds for squirrel sacrifices or cutting out still-beating hearts?"

"Who do you suppose Elorus is? Some kind of mythical figure?" asked Tiburt, who had locked in and was critically examining the structure.

"I don't know. Probably the king or queen or whatever of this magical Squirrelton, or whatever this place is called."

"Ugh, an awful name. But don't you see this structure is here for a reason, and it's probably the one spoken of in the book, meant to lead seekers to its destination. The book spoke of the rocks. It's fate, not accident. It must be," said Tiburt.

"All right, I'll grant it's a huge coincidence, but all this magic stuff is just foo-foo for explaining what we can't control."

"I refuse outright," said Tiburt. "This is fate! Fate!"

"Fate! This is fate. Ha!" spoke Gethsarade. "Who dares this after many moments rolling on a parting ship and then lying where we lay, coughing and sputtering, and clearing our spinning and throbbing brains? You say, fate?'"

"Ne'er I say it, but I believe it to be the work of a greater power. Or at least a great power, either way. To think of it as chance is the enemy of the industrious and the philosophy of the lazy headed, I think," said Tiburt.

"I think you overthink," said Gy.

Gethsarade just rubbed his head.

"But my point is, if this were the wreak of some holy power, we should think it to be a matter of mere perspective, if it pass. We should celebrate this new evisce as it shall surely bring good tidings if we keep the right attitude."

"So, I can make this thing good by asking the gods to make it so in my head first, and then it shall come to so be in normalcy and in fact?"

"Why yes, methinks."

"You don't talk to many sharks, do you?"

Tiburt stood confused.

"Never mind. This is nonsense. I'll go find some firewood, then maybe we'll survive the night," said Gethsarade.

"Didn't you hear the poem?" said Gy. "You practically memorized it, Captain":

"Where a terminal moonlit pillar
A geyser's upward golden stream
Is Elorus' angled message sender
Averse, a blinding, blinding beam."

"I think it means for us to get up top of this thing. Captain, we came here to do this. Whatever meaning there is to this, we will only find it up there."

Gethsarade looked up to the top. "How? There is no place to put a paw anywhere. It's too tall. No land-borne thing could ever get up there."

They looked up. It seemed impossible. The structure might as well have been an impassable citadel. And further, up on the platform, there was another yet smaller pillar, where there were paw-holds. But they were vertical, so no airborne creature with feathers could hold on to them, for there was nowhere to put a beak hold and climb. There, perhaps a bat might get on, but it could not climb up any further, for the pillar was so smooth the tiny hindlegs of a bat could never do but scratch away endlessly at the niches.

"One needs the gift of flight to reach the platform and prowess of ground battle to reach beyond. It's so backwards. What could do this?"

"I know—a flying squirrel," said Tiburt.

Gethsarade was about to address Tiburt's foolishness about myths and magic with admonitions of probability, but even he realized skepticism for skepticism's sake was becoming self-defeating.

"Perhaps they exist, rodents flying without wings, sure, but none are in our party, or I think we would know it."

87

None had an answer.

"I say we look for the nearest town or natives or something. Maybe they could even tell us more about the...thing. I say we can come back to this later, but for now, we need to do some exploring."

"Sounds like a plan. Onward, boss. Maybe we'll find the place he was talking about some other way," said Gy.

"Very well," said Gethsarade, who felt mixed as if he wasn't the one leading this expedition and yet was invigorated all at once. A half-measure of foreboding weighed down the hummingbird in his belly. *Nonsense,* he thought, *best to mind the path because if I don't find this treasure, this nice Gy might kill me.*

But as they turned around, they again encountered sharp pointy things at their throats. This time it was squirrels, but strangely they wore inadequate clothing, many disheveled and covered with mud and berry paint.

"Oh, I get it! They're savages! Oh, I've never seen them before—how fun!" said Tiburt.

"Tiburt. Shut. Up," said Gy.

"Oqunaquk, kokobabanikka suk. Ce, imbajhikatl!" said he who looked a chief.

"Sounds nice," said Gethsarade.

"You know what he's saying?" said Gy.

"No. but I'm pretty sure it means they're about to kill and eat us."

"No!" shouted Tiburt. "I got this, guys."

Everyone tensed.

"Whatever you're about to do, try don't first," said Gy.

"Boo! Ha! Hundungaut! Humbumbabanono."

"Tiburt, you can't speak their language."

"Well, there he went, and Lord help them."

"Hicky picky tricky do! Singa linga lookyloo!" Tiburt danced about in a fashion that made the natives oddly entranced, to the surprise of Gethsarade and Gy. Everyone relaxed a moment and forgot all about their weapons.

"Honky Wonky Dangalang, a wacky stacky finga fang!"

"We're going to die," said the Captain.

"Yeah, no way round it now."

But suddenly, as Tiburt gyrated and pounced around, clapping at the sky, and then pointing at his toes and so on, the tribe squirrels all slowly put down their spears and then, amazingly, chuckled. Then they began wailing with laughter, the most terrifying kind of guttural laugh. But laughter it was, and Gethsarade and Gy slowly relaxed and let out a sigh of relief.

"Kuwagwira iwo, adzasokoneza tulo mitu yopenga ta milungu ndi kubweretsa bingu pa ife," said one in slightly more dressy headwear.

"What did he say?" asked Gy, as if Gethsarade would know, as Tiburt stopped his cavorting and held up his paws as if to say, *See? I told you so.*

"I don't know, but it sounded happy. So, I'm happy."

6: To Otterdam

The natives received them warmly.

"So, Mister Captain, all things considered, how are you feeling?" said Tiburt, as they were hanging around before dinner.

"Well, I'm not sure. To be honest, I could be better, but if I think for a moment, I can only wonder how much better could I be? I read somewhere about looking at the bright side of things, you know, trying to imagine what it could mean in the moment if this indubitably were the best of all possible worlds. I mean, think about it. There's always a bright side, right?"

"Pardon me with all pardoning good masters, all, but if we could focus on the matter at paw, I believe the bright side at the moment to be getting brighter all the time, if you will. It's so bright I feel as if I were being turned about slowly on a rotisserie over the top of it! My sides are so bright they're about to be bloody well falling off! So, can we stop getting cooked and get out of here already!" said Gy.

You see, squirrels are talented and clever as many know. But it happened these native squirrels for all their cleverness were unfortunately not literate, and there was no one around to teach them the virtue of words, whereupon they could decipher the meaning of the text carved upon the rocks at the base of the beach. However, they discovered how to make and sling a rope, which allowed them another clever use of rock, which was to roast dinner.

Now, to explain the situation from the natives' point of view, it might be best to point out something first: natives worship their native gods and consider the needs of said gods to be above all.

The god of the Nicky-Nacky tribe, for various reasons believed by the natives, was a ravenous god all the time. And the preferred diet of this god seemed to be foreigners, especially crazy ones. Some were the quiet crazy type who walked around waving strange, thick rectangles made of skin in the air threateningly, which bound loads and loads of what seemed to be dried leaves sewn into open them at one side. The skins contained usually nonsensical scratchings and gibberish they did not understand, nor did it seem like any foreigners did either. Then they would smile and try to sell them to the natives. It seemed craziest to the tribal squirrels, particularly because it was such an obvious waste of the most indubitably perfect of all possible bottom-wiping materials devisable. While those crazies were best slow roasted with lots of spice, the ones that did all sorts of wacky dancy things to entertain the natives into not murdering them, why, those were the tastiest. When they realized their gods would dine on their best meal in years, maybe ever, it was too much for them to contain their joy at the favor they were sure to receive from the divine.

So, when the chief first spoke, it had been to say something like, "Hello, nice to meet you, we'd love to trade with you. Have you any tea? Or better yet, hotcakes? We love those. Or even crepes. We love crepes." And when the laughter began during Tiburt's dance, the next thing the chief said was, "Well, boys, let's get these nutballs up over the fire, ASAP."

The ingeniousness of the tribe was notable, for the giant stone pillar, possibly erected by someone unknown ages ago served not as a monument but as the most useful thing to a tribe worshipping a hungry god. Its protrusion at the top served as a rotisserie arm, and from it they suspended a rope able to lift a delicious meal of any conceivable size high above a fire where it could smoke like nothing else.

And they conversed with one another in their native tongue saying things like, "Are you sure this will please the gods? Their ship had a whole crew, and we only have three. This is not a big meal." Someone answered this with, "Nah, it's the crazy they like, and this little fat one's got enough crazy for a whole country."

"I think they're praying!" said Gy. They shouted the phrases, "...Noah-ga horan bee athoran, shanna garreteya..." over and over again almost like a rosary and pitching themselves about, barely paying their dinner any attention in the furor.

"Yeah, they probably thought Tib's dance was evidence we were all delirious, so better to kill us so as not to catch it. Good job, Tibby."

"My tail! My precious tail! Help!" shouted Tiburt.

"I don't think anyone's going to help, Tiburt, and I do think your tail is the least of your problems!" said Gy, trying to fan off the flames with his feet, causing a little wobble in the rope line. This gave Gethsarade an idea, who had just quietly discovered he could get an arm free.

Gethsarade loosened himself from one rope and then another.

"What are ya doin'?" asked Tiburt, but Gethsarade shushed him, and Gy concurred. Gethsarade climbed up to the top of the rope quick as he could, heaved himself on the platform, and commenced swinging the two of his tied-up compatriots below like a pendulum from the top out over the water just as their tails were about to be singed off.

However, this motion got them noticed, and the natives, tails high and alert by then, had set to letting down the rope straight into the fire, to which Tiburt made his protest very known, which brought the full attention of all along the beachhead.

Gethsarade, having developed brand new line-handling skills from his first mate, trapped the line with his foot and, taking one end, looped it around the post with much effort, but then they could not be let down unless Gethsarade allowed it.

This only made the natives angrier, so they climbed on one another and made passing jumps over the fire, trying to slash Tiburt and Gy to bits and make them fall, all the while clamoring wildly, louder and louder, yelping and whooping.

It was tremendous work for Gethsarade, who could only pull them up one loop at a time, to prevent losing any progress.

"Is there any way you could move a little faster, you know, right quick?" shouted Gy.

"Is there any way you could lose some weight right quick?" shouted the Captain.

Then to their joy and luck, the ropes suddenly fell away, for one of the natives had gotten up to just swinging close enough to reach, but he swung and missed them both at the height of his pass. Luckily, they held on to the rope! The natives hadn't counted on this apparently, and the two of them, sweating like sea biscuits, scurried up the rope to safety next to the captain who helped them up to the top.

"Nice work, Cap," said Tiburt, patting his precious tail.

"Yes, thank you," said Gethsarade.

"I can call you Cap, right?"

"No."

"But G...."

"Nah."

"Okay."

It was at that point, however, at once relieved of the prior situation, an arrow immediately rescinded their respite stealthily clipping Gethsarade's sash and, sending his baggy, barely buttoned shirt to the sea.

"Okay, this is not an improvement. I did not anticipate arrows."

"Well, could you do that next time?"

So went the story of how Gethsarade, Gy, and Tiburt all danced to the music of Death's dart, dodging this way and that way, and subsequently inventing snap-dancing, the Android, and the Hydraulic Boolagoo all at the same time. They are still studied by our masters to this day.

"Ow! This has got to go somewhere," said Gy without missing a beat.

"I think I just lost one o' me doojers."

"I've got an idea."

"Make it quick."

As soon as Gethsarade got a free second, he stepped forward, putting his arms high and shouting, "Okay, stop! We surrender!"

Everyone stopped.

"That's your plan?" said both Gy and Tiburt.

But to everyone's surprise, they looked up to the Captain, his shadow in the high moonlight overtaking the sight, and they all ceased to fire their bows, bowing low to the ground, all of them.

Slowly, but surely, they all backed off of the beach and out of sight, bowing in fear and holding their paws out in submission all the way.

"What just happened?"

"I don't know...that was only the beginning of the plan."

"Eh, what else were you going to do?"

"...Nothing." Gethsarade looked at the water.

"Okay."

After some time of them not returning, the threesome, still disbelieving, turned their attention to other matters.

"Well, here we are. I suppose it is possible," said Gy.

They looked about over the lagoon, taking in all its sights, and also examining the platform much more closely.

"What is possible, as you say?" asked Gethsarade.

"Anything."

"Captain, look, I see up there, a little peephole," said Gy.

"I don't like peepholes. I've seen in too many of them," said Tiburt.

"I don't think it's like that, Tib."

"This inscription here...." Tiburt wiped the dust off of a carving in the relief almost exactly like the one below.

"This one is pointing up the other way. I think you've got to follow the lines. It's Heaven's tracers on a darkened sky."

"Hardly. Any idea what for?"

"I don't know. We may simply find us another mystery, for destiny evades us even as we seek it."

"Seems to me the only ones ever going to know how to find this place, this destiny, is those who have already been there. And those who know about it don't seem to be too fond of talking about it."

"Yeah, it's like if it truly is real, anyone who goes there never leaves."

"Or won't say."

"But one thing is true, the natives believe it. Didn't you hear them shouting noach-gahoran, bee-a-thor-an, Shanna garret, Noghorn, Beethorn, Sangareth? That's from the book."

"I don't think so. I heard something different." But Gethsarade knew he had run out of steam.

"But they believed. So, whether it's real, it's real enough, and we are in the right place. Look through the glass. Just see what you will see, and if it doesn't confirm everything, then we can go home, and all of this is just crazy happenstance and coincidence," said Tiburt.

"I agree with Tiburt. Maybe in native-ese, but the happenstance of so many syllables could match up just so goes up exponentially until it would take ever so much more than a miracle for one to whisper those names, kowtowing in utter cowery, and it be all in the name of nonsense. We are strictly in the real realm here whatever the meaning," said Gy.

"Fine, all right. if If you absolutely think so, I'll go up. I'll look at whatever is up there, and then we can all go home, or wherever."

Gethsarade went up, looked inside the peephole, matched up to the right lines after a little finding, and almost immediately came down.

"All right, I'm sold. Let's find this city. Ready, all?" said the Captain, no longer questioning and on a mission. A squirrel changed, it seemed.

Gy stood looking at the two of them while Gethsarade went for the rope. Tiburt just looked up at him and boiled over with barely the breath to say, "Magic!" and then skittered after the captain.

They used the rope to make their way down, set the rope in the fire so no one could find what they had done, and recovered the book lying open on the beach with strangely a few insignificant pages torn out but otherwise no further damage.

Later in the evening and unbeknownst to them, out on the distant waters, poking up just over the horizon was another captain and crew with no ship besides the small dinghy they all piled into on top of one another like a tumor. Some straggled along the side, taking turns swimming, while others rotated paddling with their tiny paws and tails.

They had followed the ship's path and passed the wreckage. Though the ship still floated, they realized it had seen its last day.

"No bother, mates, we have arrived. This right here is the promised land. Look."

Gethsarade pointed to what had been quite an adventure getting to the highest most point in the bay to see from inside over the treetops and to the top of a mountain on the distant horizon. There glowed the golden light of the blazing fires brighter a thousand-fold from where they held, "Averse a blinding, blinding beam!" It glowed increasingly brighter in the evening light, a golden hue over the treetops, but then it suddenly went out.

When the blackness dropped over them, a cheer went up so loud that Gethsarade and his tiny lot heard it, even so far on their way on up into the deep hills of the forest.

"What do you suppose that could be?" Gethsarade asked, turning back. They shrugged. Maybe the natives found some better dinner. They went on the path illuminated by the crystal eye he saw burning in the high moonlight. Gethsarade now clutched the book in his paws, realizing during the night he'd best not let it go.

Down at the shoreline, the rats paddled and waddled their little boat up to the edge of the beach until its keel pushed up and stopped.

"How do we beat them to the treasure, Captain?" asked one of the crew, unleashing the others.

"Easy, we don't. We just catch up and then we'll get those scamps to talk," said Captain Black, clutching his sword tightly, ready for blood as the crew's mouths opened in droolly, ravenous grins.

"There are no secrets in this world, boys, at least none not worth finding out, and then taking for one's self."

"Looks like rocks at the bottom, sir. Three fathoms and climbing."

"We'll get our revenge yet, boys, and then we'll be able to afford a golden ship for each of us."

Upshore, Gethsarade wondered to himself at the sight of the light through the keyhole though he would not tell either of the others what he had seen. It was clear from the figure on the rock that the slanted pillar was Elora's angled message sender, strangely pointing the way to, not from, the blinding beam.

But he had to realize, by being the sender, it was leading the way and he was the one being guided. What message was he to bring? He had thought he was just looking for treasure or something else. Now, it seemed there would be something at stake, and a message to send meant a squirrel or two perhaps to meet when he got there. This he did not like.

As they walked, he also wondered aloud how the book came into the filthy claws of the pirat captain.

"Obviously he robbed someone, but, well, who did he rob?" the captain asked the crew.

"What do you think of this?" he said and pulled out the book.

"This brought me, brought us, here. I don't know who wrote it, and I don't understand it, but it keeps telling me what will happen beforepaw, and it almost seems like it fell out of the sky into my lap like it was meant for me. I feel the book meant me to bring it to someone, but who? How can this even be real?"

At this, they wondered.

"And if it were so hard to find the top of this mountain, if it were visible from the treetops and one could just fly one to the other, it definitely fits the narrative that flying squirrels exist."

"Aye, but we can't. I remember this book warns of war owls patrolling this forest and not allowing anyone to steal up higher than the tops. It is their realm, and they will snatch us up if someone catches us outside the boundaries of the city. The squirrel who wrote this seemed to believe owls are a problem."

"Ah, well, all great journeys begin with a search for paradise, and end with stopping where you are and making one instead."

"Tiburt, are you suggesting we give up?"

"No, I'm just reflecting on the fact we are looking for something and don't yet know what it is, so how can we know we've found it yet or not? And to think we shall arrive at a true paradise when we find it? Bah, an idealized representation at best, which would be still shabby compared to the imagination's fancy if you ask me. I recall a philosopher who wrote he had searched the world east to west for the treasure of all treasures until only once he gave up did he find it right in front of his face. Only then did he despair of what such a thing would be in his own mind and see the world for what it was."

"And what was in front of his face?"

"Well, probably words at the *moment*, since he was writing the things down."

"Don't be coy."

"I'm not. It's my point, actually. Maybe a treasure isn't always gold. A map can be a book. An apostle can be a lord. Maybe you've arrived and just don't know it yet."

"Tiburt, what are you saying?"

"I just think we should leave what we are looking for open to interpretation or we'll surely miss it."

"I understand, but there is something to be said of the certainty of terms."

"Oh, now we have the true believer in our midst," said Gy, and they chuckled.

It was, however, that remark that caused the two of them to pause, at which point they rushed to the precise wording of the book.

"For yes, I think, we should look to precisely the language, as any good poet would wish us to explore his meanest wording and find our fortune thus not within its conclusion, but within its many steps," said Tiburt.

"Cripes, will you just get on, old dog?" said Gy.

"Gah, I don't know," said the captain general. "It says Persimmonia and Almondale, the streets leading to whatever door we are supposed to knock on when we get there. I don't see any streets yet."

"Sir, you keep saying Almond Al and I'm hearing something different. Perhaps the poet, ever so subtle he be, is playing with the words. I see a place, an Almond-Dale," Gy interjected.

"I see, I see. It could be. But perhaps this is just a copy or scribal variation, as you know how the copying of sacred things goes over and over. Perhaps the scholar meant to write a double slash here, where he in the half-light accidentally made only one on top of the other. So, it could be another letter, perhaps Almond Avenue. The meaning would suggest with revolutionary certainty it is a street we seek, not a person," said Tiburt.

"Wow. Yes, and I might agree with you despite the failing stupendously many guesses you've built your certainty upon," said the Captain.

"But just consider it."

"I think the safest thing to say here is we don't know. Right? We are losing daylight, so perhaps we could talk while still going hereon."

"Of course. Wait, you don't think Black's figured this out, do you? How could he even know how to read?" said Gy.

"Well, he believed there was a handsome treasure, right? And he seemed to know where he was going like the way I told you he spoke?" said the Captain.

"Yeah just as you said, he seems to know, which don't mean he knows. It only means you think he knows more than he might. The look of seeming to know is the product of you not knowing any more than him. Look, you remember how he spoke of Almond Al as if he was going somewhere, as if Almond Al was a place and not a name? It's clearly a name. At least to me. We all saw Barrogan's demise. He's long a dirge deep in a shark's belly," said Gy.

"I think we all know rats are better in the water. Best not to underestimate such a vile pest for, at sea, they can make a boat out of their own backs. I'm just trying to say you can't know. If anything one must need is to default on the side of safety. We cannot say anything or alert anyone, I move," said the Captain.

After some serious consideration, Gy admitted he simply wanted to get on to the being rich part of the plan and had no mind to make things unnecessarily complicated in between.

Upon the captain's reasoning, it was evident things were unduly complicated, and the safe thing would be to go the roundabout ways. How sad the logic that occurred was neither the business of you or I to understand any more than one might task one's self to intimate the mechanics of shaping the clouds.

One thing stirred Gethsarade's mind more often than the rest about the poem. He had, upon Tiburt's prompting, thought on the meaning of the narrowly intended text and upon the phrase at night. He should have prepared himself to make a proper sacrifice. He wondered oft what such a thing would mean and perused how perhaps he should desire not to become close to anyone he was too genuinely concerned about.

A little while later, they came first upon some stone steps, quarried from nearby hills, but by intelligent paws and they led up over some roots, somewhat broken up. After a tree or two, they realized they had come upon the first shapings of a road.

"Wahoo! Civilization!" cried Tiburt.

They picked up speed and, after a while, the road widened so they could travel abreast, and then after another while, they walked double arm's length and did not take up half of it.

"Big road this is."

"I vote one of us takes a tree and checks for distance from the mountain before we proceed to make sure we haven't veered."

Tiburt shot up an arm enthusiastically. "I want to go, pick me!" which the captain did, slightly less than enthusiastically, and Tiburt ran up the nearest tree and was right back down in a beat.

"Alas, friends, it would seem we are no closer to the mountain than when we had begun. In fact, it has only grown larger."

The other two stared at him and shook their heads for a moment and then went on.

It was right they had done so, for not long after, they found themselves at a gate to a rather large city. The gates were made of wood—chewed logs, shaped, stacked, and hammered into place all without the use of nails. There were old structures and new ones atop them, almost as if the site were once abandoned and then reconstructed for other purposes.

Some buildings, able to be seen over the wall surrounding the city, were made of river clay and others of stone and wood. Other parts of the wall were orderly and neat, whereas other parts were crumbling and easily compromised, made of an amalgam of materials, almost as if the inhabitants had only taken up residence in the place with no real idea how to keep it up.

They went around curiously and found the city ran right over the river they had been following, a little way down from where it turned, and at its apparent narrowest point for some ways in both directions. Yet, despite all of this being half-shod, the city was on a scale none of them had ever seen—a formidable barrier to the mountain.

"Well, the only way to get to the mountain looks like through the narrow gate," Said Gy.

They agreed and knocked with resignation upon the pitched doors of the city gates. The door opened slowly, just a tad, and a huge, cockeyed head peeked out that was the size of Gethsarade's whole self.

"State your business."

"Thank you, sir. I was wondering if you might know the way...." Gethsarade stopped, as the otter opened the door all the way, stepped out, and looked at them menacingly, with squinted eyes. Then suddenly his eyes opened wide. "You're not from round here, are you?"

"Why, no. We're just passing through, honestly." Said the captain.

"Okay. Makes sense. The only groundlings around we know of don't dress well and they are not friendly. Have to be careful, you know. Can't just let anyone in." He waved for them to enter.

"Really? We can come in?"

"Yeah, why not?"

"I mean, didn't you just say one can never be too careful, and then you're just going to turn around and let us in your city without asking our names? And what do you mean by *groundlings*?"

"Oh, hey, it's not like that. I was just talking about you bein' groundlings. You're just strangers, you see. It's the ones we know about; they're the real threat. Tru-huh-hust me, you've got nothing on them."

"And these groundlings, they're what you call...?"

"Why, squirrels that can't fly. They're so rare. The ones that can are all over and seldom come down from the mountains or the trees and yet when they do, something's afoot in the air. Today, though, there seem to be a lot of groundlings popping up. Any well, in you go."

"Okay, I guess," said Gethsarade, who was actually and wholly conflustulated at what just came out of the otter's mouth. And in they went, for the lack of a better option.

Otterdam was a massive city, the kind to put things in perspective. Gethsarade had only known his one squirrel town way back in the Old World. It was quite a revelation to see how insignificant were the lives and concerns of squirrels. There were horses and pigs and gerbils, normally animals that just kept to themselves in their own type, but not there.

"Welcome to Otterdam, the Gateway to the Forest. My name's Rimbald. I'm an otter."

"My name's G-uh, Vincent. I'm a captain. These here are my crew. Tiburtine, there, and Gy."

Gy tipped his imaginary cap, but Tiburt was off in Imagine-land.

"Pleased."

"Also."

"No doubt. So, what brings you here?"

"We are looking for treasure."

"Aren't we all."

"What?"

"I mean, figuratively. Oh, you're looking for actual treasure, like, tinkle, tinkle, doubloon sprinkle?"

"Yes, there is a legend about a city high upon a mountain where the world's greatest treasure is to be found and we intend to find it."

"Wow, there's a new one."

"Why do you mean?"

"I don't know of any lost gold around here. But hey, I'd love to help you find it, ha! You're fine to look around and see. There's the market over there. Might be someone over there willing to help you out on your journey or relieve you of whatever gold you might have, one or the other.

"Either way, stay on the main road, and you'll always know how to get in or out the easy way. And one other thing. You'll want to duck out if you hear trumpets. You'll soon meet our mayor, Telmarus. He runs the place, but he doesn't much like squirrels for reasons. Good luck! And if you need anything, just call Rimbald!"

The gates-otter gestured a salutation and went back to his corner and, after sitting down, his face gained about 10 years or so, resuming what had to be its normal state of total and utter boredom.

"We'll let you know," said Gethsarade, looking back at the other two, Gy eyed him back knowingly, but Tiburt was distracted by something up ahead.

"Captain Poppaldi, sir," Gy interjected, "I think we should stay on task."

"No harm in staking out the place. Besides, we might find a few allies here like that nice Rimbald back there. Never can tell what you might run into. We may need backup with whatever is on the mountain."

"Good plan, boss." Gy did not think it was a good plan.

"Where's Tiburt?"

It turned out the bazaar had poor Tiburt by the nose. Venturing in, they found him by a table of fish at a short booth run by a squirrel and his squirrel crew. Tiburt was acting as if he was shopping for spices and singing to himself, but he was actually watching the booth owner intently.

"Good job Tibs. Fish for information from the natives. Get it?" the Captain ribbed him, but Tiburt paid no mind.

"Fishing, fishing for fish, fishy, fishy, shiffy, feeshey, fishy fishee," Tiburt sang without a care in the world when suddenly he stopped mid-verse.

Gethsarade, who had been taking care not to hear Tiburt's bad notes, was alarmed at the sudden silence. He raised his eyes to

Tiburt's face. Gethsarade was staring unreservedly at the squirrel who appeared to be quite busy with the activity of haggling a gabble of snail-shell flasks.

Tiburt moved closer and watched, inquiring most remarkably. Gethsarade and Gy looked at Tiburt and asked him in hushed tones, "Tibbs? What's the matter?"

"Psh," he waved at them to be silent. "I haven't seen this level of haggling skill since I was back home in my country land. Yes, my friend, that's the step. Now insults and belliggery."

He paused. Then he leaned into the two of them quietly. "This fellow knows the ways of the east. He knows the magic."

"The magic?" the two of them cried aloud.

"Yes, the magic of working out a great bargain."

At this, Gy stifled a laugh, but Gethsarade became upset, "For in all my days," he whispered aside to Gy, "I have met no one who believed so arrestedly in kinds of sorcery so subtle they don't even appear to be magic at all. In fact, one would swear it, in fact, is not magic in any sense simply to exchange words. I grow tired of this."

But Gy fought him back from assailing Tiburt's logic, lest he interrupt the poor dog's concentration. "Hold on, I've seen that look in his eye before, Cap."

"This one is good. Too good." said Tiburt, and though Gy and Gethsarade tried to stop him, they moved too late as Tiburt was the sort to be deceptively slow any time in which he desired to be fast.

Tiburt moved silently through the crowd so not even an audience of squirrels could notice one so uncommon. Indeed, they didn't and, in a flash, Tiburt had moved upon the haggler, smacked off his hat, and started into him as an impostor to the gush and guffaw of all around. Now their cover would surely be blown.

"A rat, this one! Rat!" How Tiburt could spot such a thing was beyond Gethsarade, and everyone else in the crowd for the rat was passing himself off impeccably.

Then all at once, they saw all Tiburt had seen.

The crowd was aghast with astonishment, yet they were still lost on the significance of Tiburt's accusation.

"Yes! He is! A rat! A rat! I'm a horse. He's a badger. Over there's a pelican. You got something against rats?" they shouted.

"No, not at all, but I mean he's...a rat! A rat!"

Gy had been looking around and saw heads ducking out around corners. "Ho, Captain, sah. We're being watched on all sides. We need to leave." Gy said this as he grabbed Tiburt, who had not faltered from his indignant tirade over the deception of the rat impostor.

Of course, Tiburt did not realize the full implication of the rat's presence and went on into a positive declaration that the rat-squirrels' skills still lacked finesse, and there was much work to do.

But just then, Gethsarade only barely saw an ax swinging straight at his head, which came down on the cages. The other rat, one they recognized on the ship as Bob, had swung the ax so hard it sank straight through the table and the cages crashed on the ground all around, completely disrupting the busy square, and not least the impact knocked loose the rat's taped-on tail. It went up into the air and flopped down next to his rat tail, now clearly visible as made of the fine tufts of some poor rabbit.

Suddenly, the disguises all seemed obvious. There wasn't a squirrel around but the three of them: Gy, Tib, and the captain.

Thereby completely distracted, Tiburt was caught up in a moment of confusion and wonder when he was snatched up by Gy and sent on a flight for life by the scruff of his neck.

"Unpaw me, instantaneously!"

"All right, but you better run and don't get left behind!"

"Why?" said Tiburt as he got to catching up.

"Because we been had! Come on!"

They looked about and on both sides. They were being followed through the vendors' alleys, and the rats were closing in and drawing their swords.

Barrogan Black emerged, yelling, "Thieves! Somebody help!" to rouse the townsfolk after the trio. They went right for it and soon the whole town was huffing after a few little squirrels with prejudice issues. Off from somewhere, they thought through the hubbub that they heard the bap-ba-pa-pa-pap of trumpets.

"Oy, some birds to carry us off would be super-helpful right now, I do say!"

"Well, suppose we tilted the odds in our favor?" yelled back the captain.

"How do we do that, General?" asked Tiburt.

For a second, Gethsarade waited, for at the confusion's height, he forgot who he wasn't, and then realized the one being called general was him. Then he said in a hurry so as not appear as if he were making it up entirely as he went, "They can't catch up to us if they can't get beside us."

"Uh, what?"

"We, uh, well just follow me."

The next moment, he jumped and clambered high up onto a booth. While plan-less as he was, there was something he had been thinking out for quite some time, and it was time to test a theory. While he ran, he began loosening his shirt. Gethsarade had been wondering to himself lately if what the stupid turtle had said was true: *There was some way squirrels could naturally fly, and if it was true, then how in the world did everyone know about it but him, a squirrel?*

He would have dismissed it easily were it not that he had made it off a plank not only alive but transported. It seemed the only explanation, despite the odds. So, if he were to test this theory by recreating the circumstances, surely it would work.

"Let's narrow the path boys," shouted Barrogan Black, emerging in front. The two lines of rats closed into one following them up onto the roof. More fell to the alleyways with each leap, struggling to catch the squirrels who, except for little short Tiburt, leaped across with ease. Nevertheless, he made it.

The squirrels spilled down, however, back on to the street after only a moment's gain, for a roof gave way. Still, they had a moment to think, "This way!" said Gethsarade, and he ran out.

"They'll catch up to us on foot at one point or another," objected Gy.

"I know, but I have an idea. They'll be easy to funnel now." He slowed, turned a corner, and held. They looked back at him. He motioned for them to get into a corner.

"There is but a second to do this, so only watch where I come down and stay in the shade."

They turned out of the view of the captain's corner, and Vincent waited until he could hear the rats just behind, and he took off again, sure they had seen him turn away.

Gy and Tiburt watched the captain run out to the edge of town while the crowd of pirat infiltrators piled after him.

"Heh, we got you!" they said. The captain ran on and on and right up to the edge of the cliff he jammed. Then he stopped and turned around.

"I know what he'll do, so come on, he needs us to catch him, hurry!"

They ran out to the bottom of the crevasse by another way, and Tiburt kept his eye on the general so he would not fall too soon.

"What's he doing?" Gy asked, huffing.

"He's believing!"

"Oh, good. In what?"

The captain looked on, down the crevasse as the rats hurled closer. Two rats slipped and fell to make a very flat impression on the rocks below.

"Oh, I hope I'm right. It has to be, or I wouldn't be alive." And he allowed himself to relax and drift backward down into the crevasse just as the pirat captain swung his rapier to lop off Gethsarade' head and just missed him by a chigger's chaps. He drifted out and away, buoyed safely on the waves of the wind.

"See how the skies do favor me, dare you pursue me any further! I am fated to evade you forever, Captain Black!"

Barrogan snarled and bellowed like a fat rat does, and just at that Gethsarade's two friends ran forth from the rocks they had made their way down from.

Tiburt and Gy gasped from far away but clapped their paws over their snouts. The adventure, as they had understood it, was over and nothing could ever be the same now.

"Wait," Tiburt said as their expressions changed from horror and loss to basking in a victorious miracle, for of all possible things in the wide world, the captain flew!

The whole town trampled up to the cliff's edge, barely able to stop one another, yelling, braying, bleating, piping, cawing, and roaring after the little squirrel who had jipped them all. Then, to dodge the crowd captivated by the distraction, Gy and Tiburt slipped over the side while everyone was paying attention to the squirrel in the air and they were forgotten.

Gethsarade jeered at the crowd, for where they were, so far from the city, they all knew they could never catch him if he didn't want them to. No animal could scale the whole crag all the way down and then back up again or go around the river and mountain and back before he could just hop and wing it over to the other side.

Naturally, they just made angry noises and yelled for him never to show his face in Otterdam again and then went on their way.

Gy and Tiburt were all safe at the river below, where Gethsarade flew down and met them. And after they shook paws in reunion, patted backs, and climbed back up again after losing much time, they sat down in a bottlebrush field, the reeds camouflaging them, swaying high above their heads.

7: King of the Sky

"You flew, old dog! You really are the hero of the magic book! The legendary captain! Uh, not that I doubted you before. Ha!" said Gy, clapping him on the back again.

"Of course, I flew. Squirrels can fly; you didn't know?" joked the captain.

"You didn't believe either, though, you told us. Who told you so? And how did they convince you?"

"A turtle. Named Bill."

"What, what? A turtle with a habilitation in squirrel studies?"

"I don't know. What education can a squirrel have about sharks? Sometimes more than a shark has about itself."

"What…?" The two of them looked at the captain, lost and afitside as to his meaning.

"Never mind. My point is, I don't know if all squirrels can fly, but I can, and I don't know if it's fate or not, but I need to find out why. And I have a feeling, again I don't know why, but I need to keep following this map to do it.

"We must go. I don't know if our theory is correct, but right now, unless we test it, we never will. I move we go to the place where the treasure in theory lies, and now move we, I motion, with reckless abandonment so we may have the time to decide for certain before our enemy arrives as swift as they can while being dragged down of course, by their common denominators. I only slowed them."

"Caution to the cliffs, aye," said Gy, who meant to caution the captain. His subtle warning was to no avail, as the swift progression of democracy encouraged the captain.

"I think…," Tiburt found no protest. The captain's reasoning was finally becoming worth its salt to him.

"I think it sounds very...sound" and so he fell silent.

"All right, let's go. The rat scums are afoot. Of that, there is no unhearing."

They hurried with all they had out of the ravine, following the river upstream to wherever they could climb up the cliff.

Then Gy had an objection, "I was wondering, as something just now occurred to me."

"What?"

"Well, the agreement was to go without knowing if where we're going was the right place, but I guess I had just assumed there was, well, some kind of understanding beyond what I had already reviewed, as to where the place was in the beginning...place, sah. So, out of pure curiosity, um, where exactly are we going to find out if the book is right or not?"

"Well. Um, I have a hunch."

"A hunch? About what? A person, place, or thing?"

"Just a hunch. A very hunchy hunch. If it were more particular, then it would be a hunchy-pothesis, but it's a regular hunch."

"Well, when our hunch gets any hunchier, please advise. For between your hunchy hunches and Tibbs' soundy sounds, I'm almost ready to try jumping in the river myself."

But the captain cut him off.

"Look," the captain's breath was getting a little sparse. "It's a hunch for a reason, but to be honest, I don't know what the reason is. If that makes sense to you. Like Tiburt said, if it seems like something is, then it probably is so, and you will never find out how or why unless you follow it."

"Follow WHAT?"

"My gut. I'm just following my feeling."

"Well, why didn't you say so?"

"Well, because if I had said so, you would never have followed me, would you?"

"No, because now we're all going to die."

"Good, so your hunch was correct. Now we'll learn whether this one is true."

"Before the river?"

"Before the river."

"Wait, what did you say then?"

"What about the river?"

"No, what was the precise thing you said?"

"I precisely said I was almost ready to try suicide by drowning if I had to listen to your wordplay any longer."

The captain thought a moment.

"In any case, we must keep going forward now, for I suspect those pirats shall pursue us to the ends of the earth."

"Someone will need to slow down the rats, and captain, you are the one they'll need up where we're going if the book's right, and it seems to be so. If no one carries this through this will all be for naught, so I'll be more than happy to slow them. We'll set traps, and we'll fight to the end. I swear," Gy finished, and Tiburt saluted for some reason.

"While I appreciate the sentiment, your plan has a fatal flaw," said the captain, "I need you to live. A captain just isn't a captain, after all, without a crew."

Gy said nothing more, but nodded and followed, with Tiburt panting behind.

They went along many hours without a hint of anyone behind them at all, and soon, all was silent as they clipped along and their surroundings drew them in. Very much soon thereafter, they had all but fallen asleep, their eyelids dragged down by the beauty and comfort of the forest so comely and gorgeous it was all but impossible to look away. The comfort of the distance between them and the pirats seemed too tempting after long. They agreed to keep one on lookout while they slept, a lot which fell to Tiburt, to avoid getting them killed and devoured.

Once the two others had gone to sleep, Tiburt sat down to relax, and thought, *I can doze lightly while standing up and still listen to the running of the river to keep me awake.* A little while later he thought, *I'm sure I can unproblematically go to kneel on one leg then another, for no one can go to sleep kneeling.* Then he thought, *If I can stay awake on one knee, then no doubt I can stay twice as awake if I am on twice as many knees.* Then he said to himself, *The fact is beyond debate, my back is killing me which is most distressing and distracting. So if I can sit back on my bum, with my ears straight up in the air, my comfort shall allow me to be much more alert than if I were standing even full upright.* Then he thought, *I remained awake all this time and am in complete control of my faculties, and sleepiness is but a matter of mind. I can put my shoulder here on this tree root with no issue and stay awake as well as anyone anywhere.* Then he thought, *My heart is stout and sure. In fact, I'll make proof. A stalwart thing like myself can stay awake all night like so. Even if I were to put my head down for just a small mo…* but he did not finish his thought, for his head sloshed into the leaves and he was hard asleep as asleep could be.

The next thing Tiburt knew, Gy stood over him shaking and waking him up rudely, yelling, "What have you done, you fool? You slept till morning!" This made Tiburt not a little upset, for as they say, when it rains, it snores.

Vincent looked about and said, "It's all right, I think. Our pursuers appear to have yet not caught up. Perhaps they enjoyed sleep as well. No harm, no foul, I say."

"Right," Gy muttered through his incisors.

"Well, since we're all equally rested, why don't we just go on, then?" posited the captain. They took a light pace for the beginning of their journey, and Gy at one point asked, "So how long do you expect we will go this way, Vincent?"

"Well, here's the thing, as I go along, I believe more and more my hunch must be right because I am made familiar with each and every step almost as if someone meant for me to gather the mystery along the way. As if I had been down this road before, under this here light, perhaps even by some strange machinations of fate, some power above any of us has lighted the way to only me. I would otherwise swear only to you that I saw all of this before."

"You sure, and you mean, like, 'hullo, I've seen that tree,' and not just you've seen a tree and now all trees look familiar to you?" said Gy.

"It just doesn't look, you know, right."

While they debated the nature of tree-ness, a sound like Vincent had never heard slowly grew and grew till it was piercing and yet lulling at the same time. Quite an unpleasant, droning sensation. And they looked up and up and up in a state of awe for the tree, and many others beyond, easily the tallest, reddest, beautifulest tree anyone ever looked on.

"What's that sound?"

"Hurdy-gurdy," said Tiburt. The captain eyed him. No more nonsense, just yet.

"What unearthly realm is this?"

"When you crossed Otterdam, you entered the realm of Acheron, Kingdom of the Owls," a voice spoke this behind them. When they turned, an owl stood with wings of white so big he could sweep them up inside of one, even just the anterior fold. He held his wings out, blocking the sight of everything to the right or the left. Only when the great white owl let his wings down again did they see such a fearsome troop of owls they shuddered. Little Tiburt came to whimpering. The great white fellow and his entire entourage had quietly sailed in and upon them without sound or suspect.

"I am this realm's king. Now surrender your weapons."

Tiburt shyly tapped Gethsarade on the shoulder and quietly acclaimed, "Hurdy-gurdy." The captain said, "What?"

Then shaking, he said, "Hooty burdy."

"Oh, well, we have no weapons."

But Gy and Tiburt had thrown theirs upon the ground.

"Oh. Um." The captain hadn't any idea he was the only one unarmed, what with Tiburt hiding a vest full of daggers and Gy's pants so loose and flowing one could not know if he had even more stored in them somewhere.

"Well, poo on you two. Why didn't you share that plan?"

"Sorry, didn't get the chance. We thought you would know all by yourself," said Gy.

The captain rolled his tail but said nothing.

"Don't bother; your weapons are useless before us. They are but pinprickers and nail trimmers." and the owls disarmed them completely.

"What are you doing in our part of the forest far from your place, which is to say, what are you doing in our forest? We caught wind of a foul odor, one of rodents none familiar, worthy, or welcome in our realm. Tell me, for I already know the answer, in my wisdom, are you these pests?"

The owls appeared to have come ready for a fight.

Tiburt spoke up first, which none were all too happy about. "Sir, I would like to share with you a poem, for the sake of goodwill."

But Gy and the captain stopped him, put a paw over his mouth, and held him back.

In all this, Gethsarade, being the master musician he was, he could not help his eyes drift to the strange instrument the Owl King played amongst his parliament to introduce himself. They just kept spinning its drum, which produced the most awful, monotonous sound. However, Gethsarade observed, attached to the oddity were all sorts of strings and knobs and pipes and such. By appearance, the instrument was not just meant to drone on and on, for it possessed, of all things, a headstock, from which strings strung, and over those strings were levers, which said to him this must be an instrument not too far off from his beloved and missed guitar.

"My dear king, I mean, your majesty, or whatever you would like me to say–"

"You shall say, 'Oh, great and powerful Hootley Toohoo, the Good True Guru' For that is my formal name. What is yours, trespasser?"

"My name is Ge- ah, Captain Vincent Poppaldi, you might have heard of me. I am Captain of the…"

"I know no such name."

"Well, no matter, heh-heh. These here are my traveling companions, Gy and Tiburtine. Though we are not worthy of your

114

presence, sir, I assure you we are not those beasts. We were their slaves, having just escaped, but only us three! And forgive me for changing the subject, Mister King Toohoo, sir. I was just wondering if you please, show me this thing here. What do you call it?"

"We are thinking of calling it a 'turny whizzy.'"

"Why? Never mind. May I see it?"

The owl gave the contraption over and Gethsarade tinkered with it. The thing was like a guitar with valves for frets, and a drum that rubbed against the strings as he turned the knob at the opposite end. The turning action made the box resonate with a whine like a violin, only the drone could be operated continuously. The captain was able to orient himself with some work to the turning motion, and soon he was playing his own music with ease.

"You play so well!"

"Yes, I have fingers." He went on playing. as it had been a long time since he had stretched his fingers over an instrument.

"Marvelous! All we can do is turn the drone over and over, which to us is still the most beautiful of noise, yet you took this treasure of mine and made the angels within sing manifold graces. Those, those things you were playing, making the noise go up and down, what were they?"

"Oh, notes? Yes, they make up a little thing some call music. This conflagr—I mean treasure, your highness, is, I believe an instrument of musical nature. It is meant to play not just one sound, but many, and rhythms."

"For this service of wisdom and skill, we will grant you one request."

"Well, we were hoping for a ride somewhere. Say, up to the top of the mountain, there."

"We are not some taxi service! I supposed you would ask for safe passage or something! Not bloody free frequent flyer miles! Gah, you think we great birds, we supreme rulers of the air, serve no purpose in anyone's life story than to show up whenever the time comes to shorten the plot?" Nevertheless, the Owl King was in a pickle to keep his word. So, he grudgingly agreed, gave them back their weapons, and they were off.

Riding on the wind on the back of the Owl King was as nothing Gethsarade had experienced in all his days. Even from the many squirrel stories above the sea, in the lookout's vantage box on the Tara Feen, nor even from his brief trip over the river's ravine outside of Otterdam had he seen over the tops of a tree, much less from what seemed like miles above the forest.

"Great King, sir," he said, for he took the back of Hootley. "I have seen only heights of small stature compared to this. To think you experience this every day. And from this view I can see things as I never saw them, things not so obvious to those of us stuck to the ground."

"Yes, I think I understand. A little perspective," said the King.

"Now, great King Toohoo. You may be surprised to learn many creatures believe the earth to be flat."

"Wh-Hah! Ha ho hoo," the king laughed. "Whoo whoo-ever convinced them?'

"For you, the curvature of the earth is plainly before you. But I, for instance, have only seen its true degrees just now in all my life, like many creatures who cannot fly. Consider a whole lifetime of only seeing the world one way."

"That must be the most crippling debilitation ever heard of."

"And yet the majority of the world lives with just such an ailment. May I share with you one more thing? I bet you would never guess I can also fly."

"Oh, yes, that's normal."

"How do you mean?"

"You're not from around here, are you? If not, perhaps I am wrong about them all. But all squirrels do in the land of Acheron, except those little peskers keeping their territory down on the beach. They have been quite a problem for years. The folks of Hesperia won't have anything to do with them."

"Hesperia. Acheron. I've heard of these places but only in books and stories told by drunken sailors."

"Books cannot tell of this beauty. This is the real Acheron."

Gethsarade said nothing, for he had not heard of any other books about the Acheron besides the one in his quarters back on the ship.

"So, if all squirrels here fly, then you have not seen a civilized squirrel that does not. I can give you something new to behold in your lifetime as you did for me. My friends over there, neither of them can fly, and they are not savages. They are new to this place, and this is probably the last time they shall ever see what you see every day."

"Oh, well, I have news for you as well then. For one of your friends is not a squirrel, much less a flightful one."

"What? Impossible, I have been with them every day!"

"The little one. He's a rat. You didn't figure that out?"

Gethsarade drew back, "What?" to which the king replied, "You can't tell? His tail is a fake. You cannot see the hair is an entirely different follicle in the sun than the rest of his body? Nor the odd piece of tape flapping about his bum? A little perspective Sir Captain. Or are you? Ha!" the king laughed, and Gethsarade became more than a little uneasy.

"You know, that explains a lot. I can see your powers of observance reach beyond the horizon, fair king. How can I persuade you to retain your obvious sense of discretion, if you understand?"

"You can't. Hoo! But I think, sir, I will say, you needn't worry about us owls. Our time in this story of yours is probably ended, for my kind and yours do not mix. The skies are a territorial place, and we do not wish for a fight with yours. Though it would be no match, we are not monsters and wish no undue harm on anything in our kingdom. Justice is for the unjust, and as long as the inhabitants there are just and honest, we would never interfere in their affairs. Only promise me, if an injustice so dire as to require the assistance of the Watchers of the Acheron arise, you will not hesitate to give a hoot-hoot. And then, you can show me a little more on our Hurdy Gurdy as your friend says."

"I shall, my liege."

"Look, there we are, your Nearly Mountain, and atop it, the squirrel realm of Hesperia. Down we go!"

"Wait, what?"

117

To their disappointment, the owls did not take them all the way. They were dropped only some ways beyond the base of the mountain, but close enough the city at the top was in view.

"Can't you just take us straight to the city?" asked the captain, and the Owl King said, "Absolutely not. We're not going that close, no way. They've got...nuts."

"Well, what was all that talk about our swords likened to pinprickers and nail trimmers to you? You're afraid of nuts."

"Not afraid. Terrified." He shuddered. "You don't understand. Big nuts." Shudders went all about. "You don't have to deal with our friend Boogle over here," he pointed to an odd owl whose head was very misshapen, apparently due to some unfortunate mishap with squirrels.

"Boogle, yes. He won't stop rambling these disconnected phrases. He got hit with one too many of those extra deadly nuts they keep on paw up there, for he often ventured too close unmindfully in search of voles. A shame for those things give one such cholesterol, but he never could control himself. He's been this way ever since. Watch," he motioned, and one owl turned to poor Boogle.

"Ok Boogle: uvula."

Boogle began slowly at first, but soon there came tumbling up from his glottals such an array of shilly-shallying gumflappery that the captain's head had a sensation as if his brain was being slowly sucked out of his eyes. They repeated the exercise with different words; carrot, rhombosis, funicular, javelot, shoehorn, and what on. They clapped a wing over the strange one's beak and arrested him, finally. Poor Boogle fell silent but still struggled.

"See? Never even saw it coming. He gets angry and can't stop himself," said the king, and the captain had nothing much to say. "Yes, the squirrels keep to their realm and we keep ours," concluded the king.

Gy leaned into the captain's ear. "We better hurry, sir, look." Gy had the sense to keep the spyglass, and put it in the captain's paw. "Barrogan Black."

Barrogan and his crew were a long way down the mountain but catching up fast. They were visible through an opening in the woods far below them at the river's closest point of approach, pulling some native-looking canoes up to the shore of their side of the river, and surveying the climb ahead of them.

"They will take some time to climb those rocks, but then they will arrive at the smooth slope, and speed will be our disadvantage. They'll probably catch up by land within the afternoon," said Gy.

"How did they do that?" Asked the captain.

"We thought we were ahead, but we had fallen behind, actually, Mr. Poppaldi," said Gy. "Probably had something to do with the nap someone took on watch."

"Sorry, again." Said Tiburt looking down blankly. He had been talking to a certain female owl.

"No matter now. We're desperately in need of treasure dear King Tooty-Hooty the Good True Guru. If I may, I believe we really could use a ride up to the top of the mountain…."

Silence came from the Owl King.

"The treasure awaiting us is truly massive, beyond all measure. I can promise you a significant share if you could just give us a quick ride, so to speak."

"Say it right."

"Say what?"

"My name. Say my name right."

"I didn't say it right?"

"No."

"Well, Highness Tootoo, Hoohoo?"

"No."

"Toohoo Vavoohoo?"

"Hooty Booboo?…Googly Booty? Hoosoo booboo tootoo? Boohoo Kookoo...the Hoodoo Voodoo."

"No, none of those."

"Look, dude, I forgot. This was going so well," the Owl King Hootley Toohoo gave a look, and the discussion was over.

"Can't help you. Bye."

"But I enriched your minds with new and spectacular dimensions of sound and fury!"

"Yeah, but you're kind of a showoff. Take care."

"You son of…" And they were gone. "Nothing is ever that simple is it, with birds," the captain sighed.

"Yeah, no. No, it's not. I mean, imagine what a significant income stream by offering rides to passersby. It would be a great way to make extra money and cut down on travel costs for the rest of us," said Tiburt.

"Yeah, but think of the negatives. I mean, about the true cost of logistics, you know, so much extra preening. Work-life balance, and everyone's so rude these days, and tips are a sham. Hardly seems worth the trouble," said Gy.

"We're getting off topic, here," said the captain.

"I'm just saying it could be a side hustle." said Tiburt.

"Yeah, well…while true…we've got to go. Big treasure and such," said Captain Vincent.

"Right, and we're off," said Tiburt.

"I say that. That's my thing. I'm the captain."

"Right."

"So, let's go."

"Let's go…."

The captain commander rolled his eyes. They hurried on, tiring with great tiredation of Tiburt's lightheadedness.

8: Hero's Welcome

As the owls descended and Barrogan Black's crew regrouped onshore, the light of morning broke over the edge of the slope like a herald of the advance of sky. Good thing for them, squirrels are generally faster than rats.

By now, it would seem the captain had all but fully accepted his identity as Vincent Poppaldi of the Tara Feen and savior of this new realm and so on, as one who ate his own medicine for so long he started to believe it worked to relieve his sorry condition. He ran as someone who believed they were on the way to some city covered in gold, Vincent the Master Commander envisioned for himself quite a setup, say maybe after he saves everyone, they'll just *give* him the gold. As they raced, he saw his life in moments of victory, clasping his paws in humble acceptance of utter adulations and smiles streaked across the faces of all his grateful subjects, tails swagging in song, notes of promise and letters of love raining down like the showers of an aristocratic matrimony. From this day on, only good things and riches forever.

If only they could figure out where it was. From their vantage in the sky, the Owl King showed them a city plainly in view, for it ascended to, and in, some places past the line of trees capping

121

the top of the mountain. But they had come near upon the top with no sign of so much as a gate or entrance.

"I don't understand," said the captain. "We should have arrived ages ago."

"Maybe it just looks bigger from far away," said Tiburt, once more doing his own special kind of trigonometry.

"I don't think so. We seek a place of incredible light. But as we climb this place is increasingly dark and covered with dirt everywhere; so dark that even the grass barely grows. When I saw it from the bottom of the mountain, the glow was so bright it was visible from anywhere. All I see is this canopy blocking out all hope. Oh, dog alive, I know how Barrogan knew about this place! He saw what I saw from the sea, where the trees don't block the view of the mountain from all places. Alas, look!"

And they did to where he pointed, for beyond the trees behind them, they could see they were so high up the mountain, they could look through an opening below the canopy and see the sea was plainly in view. And he remembered what he had seen at the Watcher's Stone.

"As one looketh to almost try," he whispered to himself. On the one side of the massive bay where they had crashed, there was the circle of stones, but on the other side there was yet another exactly like it. *It must also point to the same thing,* he thought. And the point he saw, where the light shone, was at the top of a mountain, but not one tall enough to pierce the sky. Were it and the mountain top not slanted off, then from his best estimation, the three points would converge to form a perfect equilateral triangle. 'Nearly a try,' he remembered the wording. 'Almost Tri. As one looketh to Nearly Tri.' Then it hit him, for he realized as he put together the geography of the region, he was wandering about on the one piece of earth shaped like the symbol above the doorway and imprinted on the book. "It's code for the not-quite mountain we stand upon. When I looked to it, I saw the blinding beam."

He knew then he had to find the un-miraculous, the unexpectedly obvious signs, which in the course of such findings, one can only un-deny they are on the perfect path. But it would be obvious only to exactly the one meant for it. That was the secret genius! They meant it not as a guide but a reassurance, a poem to instill confidence, not direction, and that was why he decided he would believe, even if he didn't.

"That's right, Captain. Come to think of it, one's not on the top till they're on the tip, and we've still got more a sight above us still. And if we can see it from the top, then the top is where we need to go to find it. Somewhere you can't climb up if you are bigger than a rodent, and you can't fly in even if you are a speeding bird. It's closed up! It's up, up, up still more! That's where they're going."

"Aren't there owls and birds up there."

"Not if there are nuts. The owl king said he won't go near the squirrel town for there is a loaded nut behind every tree branch. And I think we've made good with them."

"Oh, lord."

"Up we go, flying squirrels live where they can fly, I'll wager, and no lower."

"Well, best of luck, Captain, we'll fight the pirats off from here."

"Oh no, you're not stopping here. You're coming with me."

"We can't go up there, we can't fly."

"Nonsense, you're squirrels, aren't you?" Tiburt didn't object. The captain knew Tiburt was protesting for other reasons. "Just follow me."

Tiburt mouthed something mockingly but followed.

"I need help to find that treasure, for I know those pirats won't keep at bay forever, but we can get up this way as long as someone distracts whoever is in charge of dispatching battle-nuts."

"Aye, Captain." They followed.

Nearby was the first sign of squirrel life they had seen. It appeared to be what seemed to be a local nut farmer. He was bent over patting the ground with the most extreme care, as if he had just finished burying a priceless treasure, measuring depth and width of the lump in the ground with a demand for precision rivalling a world-class timesmith. Then, most peculiarly, he stuck his weathered claw in the dirt, and to everyone's disgust gave it a taste.

Then was about the time the captain gave out a cough to catch his attention for he was fully engrossed as a gopher from the

123

Sloughs of Ungleaw, as we might say. "Quick, my friend, you must tell us where the city is!" said the captain, fully grossed. The farmer's face was remarkably plain, and it was clear in a word, so were his sentimentalities.

"Whut?" said the chap. They were both confused, the captain that the other looked discomfited at hello, and the other that the captain was speaking in outright contradictions. They didn't even know each other. The captain looked about for help, but his friend Gy went off somewhere fast, and Tiburt was not the kind to sort intricate, high-stakes social contexts.

Tiburt popped up anyway. "Now, I know as well as you two. Anytime we get to this point, it usually means the way is right around the corner." They looked for a corner, but nothing; pretty much just trees and dirt.

"Yes, yes, my friends, look around," the farmer kind of chuckled to himself. "What, what do you know? Don't you understand we must get in the city and stop the pirats! They're on us!" The farmer just chuckled again and said, "No, I think we will probably be just fine."

"Don't be coy with us, let us in on the secret about the city on the mountain! Now! Or I will rattle you about like a pup's dandle with my great sorcery—" Tiburt there fell directly down, for he in his rage had forgotten to maintain his balance, one would suppose, accidentally as he threatened his magic, so that being so the captain stepped over top of him and went on missing n'er a beat.

"Where is the city's key?" shouted Gethsarade, "I demand you tell me."

The farm squirrel stood there. "How do I know you're not with them?" the farmer pointed, his tail, and his hat, swaying in annoyance.

The captain turned menacingly "Because I am a squirrel and they are rats. I am good and they are bad."

Then Tiburt, getting up and having a thought, turned to the captain's ear, saying with the back of his head towards the farmer, "Captain Poppaldi, sir, don't look now, but I think he's one of those that thinks he's smart, but only because he's not!"

"Yes, Tiburt. I know."

"Fair enough," said the farmer. "They shall allow but only the hero fated to return to the city free access without question by order of the House of Tadwick, even in a time of woe and tribyuh-lation. Otherwise verily you will be met with the guards at every tree and they shalt thoroughly pummel yew with many pummelments and *gree*-nuts with their big muscles. It says so, and you'll thoroughly not pass in shape or form as they are over there, standing guard at every third tree, but there is a secret way unavailable to you who doth not be the savior. It is exceedingly undecorous of squirrels who fly to enter by crawling. So, the way you'll not be going, and thus gettin' past all the guards and quickly all the way to the top and inside, is just over there at the tree where the trail approaches and yet stands unguarded. This tree we ever allow no one to tell of, which is why no one has told you of yet, nor ever will."

"Well, thank you for not telling me. Suppose I won't be off now to not go over to that tree."

"No problem, Bob-lem." The farmer gave a howdy-doo wave, and the captain motioned to the others, Gy who was highly indisposed with a certain young squirrel-acorn maiden who wandered up in wonderment of the three stout figures at the gate of their roast, and made eyes at the stoutest of them, that being Gy, who made eyes right back.

"Later, my friends, later. Let's go, with work to be done, fools to squander, and much treasure for the having."

"I'll say, Captain. *Captain*. These squirrels are *different*."

"Yes, Gy. I *know*."

Tiburt said, "Captain, do you really think he was trying to do one of those winky things, when someone is trying to say something but not say it and then just end up saying it anyway, or was he just stupid?"

"Don't know, don't care."

"Ho there!" yelled a guard, eyeballing the captain who eyeballed him right back as they approached the right tree. The guard had some impressive armor, a cuirass of polished silver with a fine mail skirt and on the breast was a relief of a crossed sword, a golden nut, and two squirrels chasing one another.

"Now you listen just a minute, that is no way to speak to the great Commander Vincent—"

"Shut your foreign adversarial muff. There is no time for this. There's a rabble about! Show me your admissions."

"Admissions…eh…," said Gy and Tiburt.

"Never mind my compatriots. They're slow. We have none, the very ratfinks up there took them trying to get in your city and I intend on stopping them."

"Well and good, and my condolences about the finks. Those things are awful this time of year, 'specially on children. But under the laws of our city, you may only gain unsolicited access to the city if you are, one, in possession of the city's key, or two, being of the magistrature of our vigilations. The meaning is, no one may enter."

Vincent looked at him for a moment and said, "Except for the hero...?"

"Right, well, yes, but it's just kind of a rhetorical statement. It's-it's as if I said, you must either be a citizen or a person of undeniable and absolutely mythically impossible greatness. No such thing."

"Well, problem solved. I'm the hero. Let me in now."

"Uh, huh. So, you're going there with it. Oh, well okay, then. Let's see it."

"See what."

"Sangareth?"

"Gesundheit."

"Very good. But no."

"What, no?"

"He shall possess the key."

"What's this key, Cap'n?"

"Cap'n?" asked the guard.

"Yes, *Captain*. Don't you know, this guy's famous all over the world, as he the great Vincent Poppaldi, the leader of the Free World Army, and right now there's an impending invasion of pirats, a veritable apocalypse, and you'd best get out of his way if you'd know what was good for your rank," said Gy.

"Well said; most grievous apologies, Commander. And you're the Free World Army, you two?"

"Yes?"

"Well. Nice. But I cannot let you pass."

"What? I have travelled the world and now come back to claim my place as your leader. I don't know what this key thing is, but if anyone's your savior and it's not me, there's a problem! You've got an inferior prophecy on your hands, not to have the world's greatest commander in to save your town. So, let me in! All right! They're getting away up there! What is wrong with all of you?" Vincent said as he threw out his arms.

The guard stood a moment, stared at the three. Then he shrugged and stepped aside. "Okay, works for me."

"Wait, what 'works for me'?"

"Well, you're a flying squirrel, aren't you? Go ahead on in! It doesn't matter if you're the hero or not; your wings give you automatic citizenship by virtue of excellence granted you by the Great Nut with those patagiums. You are our kind, so get in. Why didn't you just say you were a citizen?"

"Pata-what? Okay, you know what, works for me, too," said the captain and in they went to the stair leading to the heart of the town. Then the squirrel locked the door behind them and took off and up to join the battle.

It occurred much too late to them that at some point there might be a confrontation to the captain. And as he raced to his likely and impending doom, he wondered what on earth he was doing, and along the way, he devised the best course of action would be to hurry before they get there at all, and then run before they arrived.

They scurried up the branch un-arrested, and a few of the guards noticed the captain and his crew of two in the fray, but the captain flittered around as they went up. The guard assumed they were all flying squirrels, thus honorary citizens and no threat. Meanwhile, the pirats continued to fall one by one, but Barrogan Black held his position, frantically swinging his sword about, but eventually even the pirat captain himself went down with his crew, rolling down to the floor with a crash.

"So, question, Cap'n," said Gy

"Here it goes," said Vincent.

"What do we do?"

"What do you mean?"

"I mean once we're inside."

"Easy, we get the treasure. I am the only one who knows where it is." He had no idea.

"But what if they just follow us, or someone in there finds us out?" asked Gy.

"Don't worry, I have a plan." He did not, other than to run, which to him sounded fine.

"Pardon, you don't mind my asking, but what's the plan, in the most precise of terms? Sah?" said Gy.

"Well, we run."

"Sounds fine."

"Yes," the captain's breath was getting huffy.

The only problem with fine-sounding plans is they is no way to plan at all. In fact, it should be noted here, Tiburt the fool of the three, thought to himself quite some time ago about this problem, *I better come up with some very fine magic for this plan, or we will probably die,* which he was not even a little fine with. So, he some time back had worked up a plan of his own, a little magic of a different kind, as one will soon understand.

Now, imagine one should suddenly, and though with even a little warning, encounter such a sight as they never dreamed possible to see. Imagine the moment a doltish secret fantasy you once held as a child, such as perhaps one could someday learn to turn into a fish and swim to the depths of the darkest and most fantastical waters, then to turn right back into a squirrel at will and go on about your day.

Imagine one day you came up on a vision of others like you but different, doing something you wouldn't yet dare, as if this was the normal thing of life, perhaps cleaning the dishes with magic, or walking through walls. Well, dear reader, it was such a moment as this when the captain walked through the door at the top of the flight they ran, panting with all their might.

The vision caused his breath to forget itself and nearly felled him faint. All about him were squirrels, all looked very much like he and Gy and every other squirrel he had ever known, but all doing the one thing warned to all rambunctious children is they ought not leap off of trees in fancy and try their paws on no one, for in theory no squirrel could fly. But here they very much were, all about the three, flitting about, some carrying packs on their back, others hurrying it seemed to work, saying hullo to one another settling down to walk the rest of the way and ruffling their collars and clasps to get themselves back in good decorum. They all bore the expression on their faces as if they weren't doing the most fantastic thing anyone had ever done ever. Flying!

They all looked about, taken, but the captain had to gather himself, whistling a sharp whirt to the others, and the two bent their chins so they didn't look new to town. Yet someone had noticed, as this was so typical of a reaction of first-timers to the city. Likely, it was because those two were back to open-mouthed staring in a moment. It was some time they spent wandering around trying not to catch an eye, but also trying to find the treasure stupidly as if it would just be lying around.

And Tib and Gy were asking, "Captain, where's all the gold?" For all the wonders they beheld, there was not a hint of gold anywhere, muchwise a city made of it. Everything there was made of its perfectly normal sorts. The shock! The captain had to shush their eager hearts more than once as they tried to stick together, but the same someone found them again shouting, "Sangareth!"

He turned, avoiding eye contact, and tried to duck into one of the side alleys around the ends of the humongous elevated court. But it was to no avail, for soon the everyone in the yard was stretching their necks and hopping up on top of one another to see who was yelling, and the nook only served as a stage, inescapable.

The captain felt an old familiar feeling, the one of a show he knew was about to go badly. Then someone shouted, "Sangareth!" again, which the captain thought to himself they were sneezing, so he said, "Bless you," and they bowed low and said, "O thank you, sah, thank, oh, thank you!" and bowed out of sight, and the captain thought aloud, "Boy, these squirrels really are *different*."

The one shouting again spoke, "I'd know that face anywhere. I know your smirk, that mischievous grin. You are the ill-fated Sangareth!"

"Is there a cold going around?" the captain asked. The stranger had old eyes, but looked at the captain as if an old friend had just stopped in for a surprise visit.

Everyone had stopped and were staring at him and his two companions, who did not get this was not something in the plan, until the captain shushed Tiburt rather emphatically as he was smiling and waving at the attention.

"I most assuredly assure you. I am not ill-fated. And get some wipeys, please," the captain chuffed.

Just when all of this could not have gone in any worse a direction, then Barrogan Black appeared again through the other side of the back alley they had just come through, brandishing his sword, and held it right to the captain's throat.

"H-ha!"

"Whoa!"

"What? How did you get up here through the guards?" A few said guards of the city appeared, gasping, for Barrogan had thwarted them, following the three up of late by the darkening, even though the secret path was inside the trunk of the Great Hollow. Now the rats who survived the journey with their captain, about 30 of all sizes big and small, held up the whole town square, captivated by the shock of their presence and the pointiness of their blades.

"Think like a rat, if you must know," Black replied. "For if you see one on the outside, you better know there are a hundred more already in your walls! Ha! We were just waitin' for the right door to show itself, and I served as the bait to get you thinkin' you would beat me, and lead me straight to the door. Just like you predictable, over-competitive squirrel types, you think the only thing that matters is bein' first. I say there's one thing better, that's being right behind, with a sword! Ha-ha!"

"*Mi coppa,* you are very tenacious," reflected Vincent.

"Swat you, Guardians, you are worthless! How have we defended our beloved city all these generations with you at our aimless helm?" said one in the crowd, and they all nodded.

"Don't be angry with them, as you are all obviously easily distractible. I waited for them to finish celebrating their victory and stop watching entirely, and then I stole inside with a light thrashing of your incapacitant guards! Ho Ho!" Everyone gasped. "Ha! Yeah, but then when that didn't work either, I just asked one of the local idiots, and they showed me an unguarded gate. Not sure why he did so, but…."

"Dagnabbit, Farmer Daggerouth!"

"He's such a bloody blabbermouth!"

"Yeah, he tells you in detail what he will not tell you, as if then saying 'but I will not tell you the thing,' somehow makes up for having just told it! Gosh!" one proclaimed, and the crowd noted their agreement with lots of forehead smacking.

"Yep. Yeah, that's what he does. Moving on. Now, quit your lamenting and tremble in despair before me! Surrender all yer gold!" Barrogan Black exclaimed.

They looked around, quizzically, "I'm sorry, dear sir," said one, "But if you've heard of this place as one of riches, it was only a metaphor. We treasure only the clothes on our backs, all of us, and in the realm of Hesperia, our treasure is knowledge, the only thing of any true value. Please understand."

"Yeah, well, bull," laughed the pirat captain after a moment, "That might work for this idiot here," and he batted Vincent on the head with the flat of his blade, "But not on me."

This deeply annoyed the captain who knew Barrogan Black was exactly right. At the moment, they all began hurriedly taking off their jewelry and baubles and throwing them at the feet of the pirats, on a heap that grew and grew.

A few of the ladies sobbed and whimpered, which thrilled the pirat captain to spur on, "I'll take it all, thank you. Any objections I am happy to address here! Ha!" He motioned with his rapier and pointed to a spot on the deck boards over which his hilt hovered, making a sick, twisting motion. This worked well, causing the squirrel ladies to hurry even more at devailing themselves of their goods.

At all the whimpering and sobs the great Vincent could take it no more and shouted impulsively, "Fear not, my friends! I am here. Your savior!"

Everyone stopped, including Gy and Tiburt and looked at him.

131

"What?" said everyone, including Barrogan.

"I am here, your beloved and long lost...."

"Sangareth!" Everyone shouted, to which the captain replied, "Bless you." They swooned at this grace. However, one objected at his side, whispering, "Though, didn't you just say, you weren't Sangareth?"

"Vin-CENT the hero, Vincent Poppaldi. Should I have come with a hanky? I don't understand what is happening. Why is everyone sneezing?"

"Sangareth, cousin to the house of Beethorn!" said one, a-gasp.

"Come to return us to our glory! I, *Vincent*, am your redeemer and liberator, as I have done for the many nations of the world, you must have heard."

"I...uh," Barrogan said, confused as all, but for entirely different reasons.

"You don't know Sangareth, do you?"

And the captain could not pretend he did.

"It was the book, sah. I do think," said Gy.

"Oh, I thought it was like a saaaa-aaah, like a cry for help, or something, you know?" said Vincent.

"Well, no one does that, and you're really in the pot now."

"Shush. Keep playing." The show must go on."

"So, are you going to do some saving or something?" said one of the fair citizens.

"Yes! Just ah, right here around, this...ah," The captain knew not what to do, "All right, charge!" He pointed. No one moved.

"It's hard to command an assault without a rapier," Gy pointed out. He drew one and put it in the Captain's paw.

This made Barrogan suddenly very confused. "Wait, but you said...."

"You honestly think I, or anyone else would listen to a word you say, after you show up here and threaten the great hero?!" cried the captain before Barrogan could say it.

But he said something anyway. "Very well, I'll bite. And in that case, I challenge you, commander, hero, whatever your title is, to a duel!"

132

"Oh?" said Captain Vincent, who was now very sorry for having said anything.

"I propose the parameters. You must stand upon that porch up over there and hop to that tree."

"That is all?" said Vincent.

"That is all. If you accept and succeed, then I'll grant the first swipe at my head, and thus the decided advantage against us pirats in the battle for your lives, whereupon you shall win, and we will leave you alone forever. If you decline, then I shall ravage this city for all the life and gold within its walls and raze it to the ground. What say ye?"

"And what if I reject your proposal entirely?"

"Then you shall be a coward rather than a hero for all of recorded history here from this day forward, for you shall fight an unwinnable fight and you shall die and everyone with you."

"I accept," Everyone gasped.

"Then on with showing us what a true hero you are. For I believe your antics upon the cliff were a hoax. A fluke. So prove it."

Vincent got up on the porch in front of everyone and did a little mental prep. *All right, self. You flew over an ocean. You covered a deadly and dangerous cliff, so this ought to come as nat'ral as butter. No problem. Easy. So easy, I should just jump right. There's nothin' to even stress. So right. I'm off. Then.*

After a good half minute more of him standing there stock still, someone shouted, "Ey, go mate! Mutha, you're slow."

"Right, just thought maybe there was a go signal, or what."

"Go!" shouted literally everyone.

He jumped. He kept his eyes forward on the tree, but it shot up in front of him and he slammed into the ground before he had time to realize he fell like a rock.

"Ow. Oh. Oh, ow. That was a warmup."

"Yeah, try it again," said Barrogan, in his usual mode of insidious grace, to which Vincent got up and retried, falling on his face, and got up again trying to laugh off the incredible pain and extreme confusion he was in. "Heh, sorry, I tripped."

"Prepare to die, non-hero," said Barrogan matter of factly raising his sword, somewhat bored.

Two squeaky voices that sounded a lot like Tiburt and Gy piped up. "I feel like I saw a bit of flight there."

"Oh, yes I did, too, look such a little tiny space, you know you can't get a good bit of momentum set up!"

"Yeah, give 'im a chance!"

"Whew, go Vincent, go…," the voices trailed off.

"Nonsense, I say we fight!"

They turned to Vincent.

"How do we know he's the hero, mum?" from another voice.

"Shush kid, it's *going down*," said his mother.

"I don't know, it's pretty basic. I mean we've all done it in school."

"Well, he is from out of town, or maybe he's out of practice."

"Maybe we should give him the benefit of the doubt. Not all squirrels have access to such a good education. Doesn't mean he can't be a hero, right?" said the squeaky voices.

"Right…?"

Gy hid his mouth with his collar so no one saw, put a paw over his snout, and disguised his voice. "I think so! I really do! I want to fight for him and saaave the tooown!"

"Me, too, let's fight! Yay! Weeew heeew."

"Right, thanks. Now. Everybody, fight! Aah!" Tiburt gave a yell, grabbed a pot and smashed a pirat right over the head, then quickly realized he was the only one to do so. At this, the lot of the heinous crew drew their rusty swords and lowered them in unison at the squirrels all standing around them, shaking.

And just as Tiburt realized the full extent of his mistake, backing off with his paws in the air, another pirat went down, a large clump of sandstone of the type from the beach having come down on his head from the sky.

Up in the sky, and to every single one's total surprise, there were the silhouettes of owls out in the middle of the day, and down from their claws was the rain of stones deadly to rodents. But it would appear they were aiming for the rats!

"Everyone grab a rat!" yelled Vincent in full relief. Suddenly confronted with the prospect of winning the battle with ease, everyone did so. With only a little struggle, they proved an easy batch to outnumber with but a few cuts and scrapes. Each pirat dropped one by one, and soon Barrogan Black was alone, still with his rapier at the Captain's neck, but yet now it seemed a posture of vain defense rather than domination.

"Ha. You never could see my stall game coming. Could you? Of course not. Now. Be gone from this place forever, you and your crew," said Vincent.

"It's true—the savior has returned!" said one in the crowd.

"That's right, fair city. I am your hero, returned to take my rightful place amongst you once more. Yes, got it now?"

Then before Barrogan Black could utter another word, the captain said, "But at this moment, this vile bringer of hatred and darkness must be vanquished. Who is with me?" They rushed the dottied pirats and were successful at beating them back, not by much help by Gethsarade who pretended only to fight, and soon the pirats were gone, one and all.

Now, the captain was equally surprised about this development with the owls. And as everyone looked to him, lifting him up in celebration and glee, he himself searched for a clue to why his fortune should so suddenly and unexpectedly turn out so well.

Gy and Tiburt stood next to each other clapping for their leader, and Gy just caught Tiburt blowing a kiss somewhere above, and he spied in the sky the troop of owls flying off, and one of them gave a wink and blew a kiss back down. The one now newly identified to all that would know him as Captain Vincent turned to the townsfolk, to find they thought it was him. To this he knew not what to do of this but accept.

Gy turned to Tiburt and said, "You're okay with this?"

Tiburt thought about objecting, and then not. "Of course. I see the power of belief at work here, and no magic can interfere with that!"

Gy said, "What did you do?"

"Not talk about it, yeah. Ever," said Tiburt waving Vincent off and looking around wide mouthed while being hoisted up. He shouted over and Tiburt shot him a thumbs up and clapped with Gy.

Captain Vincent's illusion was complete. Now it would seem, the great Captain Vincent had found his way indeed.

9: The Revealing

Captain Vincent and crew were received as heroes, hoisted up and handed pretty prizes and things while laughing, and his new friends shouted his fake name and cheered, "Go, Vincent! Go! Hoorah and yay!" and so forth and so on.

"Wait, is he this Sangareth or...?" Tiburt began. "Just go with it, the sooner they give him the key to the city the sooner we get the gold, and the sooner we leave," said Gy.

"You're Vincent Poppaldi! Really? I thought you were the great Sangareth, but no matter, it's just as well, right?" someone in the crowd asked him incredulously.

"You want to know who I am?" he shouted, and they all screamed "Yes!" at him so hard, he rolled onto his haunches, at which point he brandished a guitar that just somehow happened to be there and hit it with a copious rasqueado, straining to get all the shakes out as he felt the good riff jive course through his knick-knacks.

Just as the crowd was sufficiently wowed, he started in on his ripping tale, and everyone was receiving him so well, it seemed, he never wanted to leave the moment.

"Now let me tell you all just exactly who I am! Behold the tale of the Five and a Half Hour War!" Another strum pattern and they reeled and began to dance up and down to the rhythm. This was what it was supposed to be like!

"What in the holy hell is going on here?" said someone from way in the back of the crowd, so loudly that all stopped, with folks dropping a few things.

Even Captain Poppaldi, right in the middle of the party, stood in silence, somewhat shaken in his confidence, and saw his challenger. He was so old he had the shakes, and the hair all around his face and ears was stark white. Yet he had a hard set jaw, the kind only possessed by squirrels of high resolve, who needed no introduction or solicitation, the kind that don't even admit when they've absentmindedly sawn off a finger because they shouldn't be allowed to handle sharp things at their age, but they do it anyway out of spite. And who never, ever slept past two in the morning.

"Who are you?" The old dog was clearly and highly suspicious. But then, sitting right there in his rolling chair, he squinted and suddenly and for no apparent reason became wildly startled, "Oh! What? You are a ghost, a ghost! Why did you come back to haunt me? Ack!" He bent over in his chair trembling and choking.

"Enough!" spoke up the lady squirrel who wheeled the old dog in his chair. Up until this point, she had said nothing, too busy tending her elders, but at this she had had enough, and when she spoke, the crowd stopped and listened.

"My grandfather is ill and has not the energy for this. And I'll soon take his place anyway, so I demand you tell me now, what is going on?"

The old dog even stopped, looking back at the one speaking.

"Hello, my lady."

"Shut up and spill it."

"Okay. I or we, my friends and I...." Gethsarade motioned to the other two, "We...." Then he remembered he was a hero and gathered himself up to start again, "I came here from long way away aboard the ship Ta—never mind."

"Tanevah Mind? Never heard of that galleon," she laughed.

"Well, you my heard of me if you'd been around much. I am the great...."

"Sangareth!" one shouted from the crowd. He's the hero who's come back to help us escape the apocalypse! O where have

138

you been all these years…. Didn't you see my lady, he just did it! We're saved!"

"Oh, is that right? I missed the apocalypse, then," she said.

"Yes! It's true, you did! All thanks to him who until recently was Sangareth!"

The captain was more than impressed with himself now. "Well, thank you, you should have. There is no one anywhere hasn't heard the name of my ship. It has sailed far and wide to lands I can't even tell you about for your own safety!"

They gasped. He had them lock and key. He had always hoped for an audience such as this, a dream come true. "Let me tell you a true tale, truer than any you've ever heard."

As he spoke, in the middle of his speech, she slapped him. Hard. She had been turned away from him while he spoke, helping the one very senior to her to his feet, though he fussed and refused the help with his cane and of an elbow to walk and lean upon that he very much needed.

He was very cumbersome of pace, and the former conversation had taken place up until she had finished walking him all the way up from the back of the crowd. She stepped forward and straightened up to the speaker. Gethsarde felt as if a watchfire beacon were shining into his eyes even as he twaddled the crowd. And that was when she slugged him a goober right in the face, fingers spread and everything.

He was blind for a second and his ears rang, and hopefully didn't appear to lose balance briefly. While he regained, his tale came out little more than sputters and half-witted drawls, adding still to the unimpressed look on the strange kit's face.

It was the word 'war' that seemed to pique her interest, for she did not turn her attention from tending to her aging companion until he had uttered it and, through the flush and fever, he tried to continue recounting his tale. She instead held him, and as it were she seemed quite unimpressed.

"And what war shall you bring to this land, warmonger and stranger?"

"Stranger? He's no stranger! He's famous!"

"Oh my, a *famous* warmonger. Pardon, I didn't realize."

"Clearly," said the captain, "I will allow it."

She sneered at him.

"I bring you no war. In fact, it is as you said, I just saved you all from it. Celebrate!" said Vincent.

They began to shout again but she quieted them with a paw.

"Just because there is a fight the moment you show up and you win it doesn't mean anything but that violence seems to keep a tag on you."

"But I'm a savior and, having done some saving, I'd say it's more than a coincidence."

"Balder and dash! Poop on a stick!" yelled the old coot in the back. Poppaldi took a step back.

"You heard him." she said.

"Well, facts' facts, my lady. And in any case, you are saved, of that there is no ill question!" said Poppaldi. He had won the audience. "Hail! Hurrah! Hail!"

"STOP!" She hushed them again, "What is your name if you're this savior?"

At that it occurred to him they were saying a name, not some cut down or conniption. If only he could recall what it was, "Come on, sah, it's the name in the book," said Gy. If only, the captain thought, he had read the rest of the book!

The captain just went with his original plan, since he was on the spot. "Well, my name, if you must now allow me to tell you, is none other than the Great Vincent Poppaldi!"

The crowd was somewhat confused. "But it's Sangareth that's supposed to come save us. Sangareth." *Ah, there's the name,* the captain thought.

"Well, I'm very sorry to be the one to bring you the news, but it was all a misinterpretation."

"Poppycock!" Great Father spoke up, and this time he hobbled up to Vincent and took him by the shoulder for a moment, walking away from the crowd and talking in a hushed tone. But then as he spoke his expression changed. "No, you're...you can't. You are gone, you are my...age. You are not here. But I'm old. You're the same, the very same as you left. Nice hat, though. Is it really you? Your face is far, far...But what, what, what, what do you, you, no, you've come, come here to, too... do what? Why back now? Is it time already? No, no, can't, can't. Can't be. You can't be!"

The captain's head tilted at the unintelligible phrases being uttered at him while the old squirrel surveyed him, whispering, muttering, grabbing him here and there. The old mutt had the most offended and confused look one might ever see, and yet for some odd reason, there seemed, once that is the captain stopped and stared hard into his eyes a good while, inside, down, and far, far back, in his head came the faintest compulsory show of joy, perhaps relief. But then the look was gone and one might never know had it not been completely unmistakable.

Then the old one stopped his gibbering, and his eyes flitted. He stood up prompt to speak out loud. "Alright, you must be wondering who we are, stranger." So, all was settled that needed settling. "I am Great Father Tadwick, and this is Amalie, my very great daughter. I run this town, and I see there can be no denying you saved us and you are owed gratitude and remuneration. I grant you whatever you wish. Old boy," he said, leaning in, "what is it you want?"

The captain straightened up, "Mr. Tadwick, sir. I'd like...a date with her." The crowd gasped and murmured. Everyone but the late arrivals bore a look of objection.

Some in the crowd were saying, "But he's not even a millionaire. I mean, is he?"

Captain Vincent simply said, "Mark my words, old friend, all revolutions are begun by not being paid. I think you will find there be no one better in all the land to suit one way or the other."

Great Father Tadwick blinked a bit, then simply said, "Okay." tapped his cane matter of factly on the deck twice, then turned without another word back to get into his rolling-chair and motioned for Amalie to tend him away. She, however, was still stuttering in protest. "Ah, he, what, just, hey, I."

"What's the matter, my dear?" said Great Father Tadwick.

"I...." Apparently, she had been quite confident Captain Vincent would be denied this fashion.

Instead, he was carried off with cheers and dragged down to the celebration. Once he and his friends were inside and being handed all sorts of drinks, Gy and Tiburt approached him and whispered, "Did you see it, Captain? Did you see it?" And he asked, "See what?"

"The sign. Go look."

He stole outside to get a look before he was nabbed back into the tavern for more favors, just quick enough to read above his head in mostly washed off gold paint, "Persimmonia's."

10: A Moderately Important Date

Later in the evening, he walked up the laborious walk from the low side of town. From the inn near the same street as the tavern which he and his friends were lodging, his poor feet perseverated through an atrociously massive gate, across the laboriously long processional to the exhaustingly huge house of Tadwick and rang the bell at the door.

He did a quick breath check and adjusted his clothes once and then again. His collar was too wide, and his sash dirty. He straightened his hat, but it was worn and white from the sun and stinky like the salty sea. He took it off, considering ditching it in the bush for a moment. He smelled the brim. It did not help. Disgusted, however, he put it back on, having seen himself in the dark glass of the lace-curtained window in the porch light, realizing his hair was worse.

He fancied to himself all the fun ways the date would go, her laughing at all his jokes and such, et cetera, when just in the middle of his thoughts the door opened. The house was breathtaking precolonial, and he hardly noticed Amalie's mother, and sisters or perhaps cousinlings, who along with everyone inside an absolutely a practiced prim and proper little poppet.

She came out. Until now, her astonishing beauty and her throat full of fire was all he knew of her. Though he maintained his bearing, he could hardly breathe, figuring correctly it would only be a point of leverage against him, if he let on that there was not any single thing about her he did not find incredible.

"Good evening, my lady."

She said nothing.

"Shall we?" he said. She complied, but as soon as they had strolled out of the view of the house, she slumped her shoulders and sighed the relief of one who knew better not to when anyone of value was around to see it.

"On our date," he said, "I thought we might start out with a walk about the Hundred Trees."

"Okay, this date thing...whatever. But here's what will not be a thing: me caught dead walking next to a practical urchin. *Especially, especially in some kind of bizzaro trophy parade before my neighbors.* You will get some new clothes if you're going around with me." Gethsarade gulped and followed her to the tailor.

There her commands to the tailor, the captain, and the help were curt and of the type of business of having none of it. Soon, they buttoned, eye-holed, stitched, velloured, cumberbunded, snipped, and cropped him all over.

The new squirrel in the mirror appeared about as comfortable in this gig as a general of the line with ruffles and flourishes meant in the daytime. These types spend their time giving featherhatted orders over tea and numpets, and little figurines of war, rather than the kind who winds up burnt out, with one leg and scars, as he once appeared, gave a salvé back at him.

He pet his ascot and traced the feather with his fingertip, so fine and soft he hardly felt it. Triple-stitched chaps replaced baggy, urchin pants. The oversized vest, lent to him by Gy after losing his own tattered shirt when he took the leap off of the cliff, had been turned into a gentlesquirrel's tuxedo with tails. His own tail swished from a triple stitched, custom opening in the back. The poet's shirt fluffed out, it felt, at all the openings but still he could tell his body filled it better than the last garments. It could have been that his muscles had become wooden, proud even, from the long days helping his crew with the lines at sea. But then maybe it was the light playing on the mirror, for the face looking back at him even was the same, yet somehow different, handsomer: confident.

He could have sworn the reflection winked at him. A second look, and all was normal-ish once more.

"That's better. I mean, you still look like a hog-toothed gopher, but at least you appear to be trying," she said, and they left with his new clothes shielding his disturbed respect. They went walking down the lane in the middle of the town, and the captain tried hard to think of something neutral to say.

"This is truly a grand place, is it not, to think someone could grow up here," he started in hopefully, but did not finish his thought.

"You mean there is no place like this back home, o great master of greatness? I had supposed you're merely passing through to some other grand arena," she went on. "You know I thought for all the bravado you showed this afternoon, you'd be more...wordy in front of a lady."

"Uh, sorry," he said. "It's just, I'll be honest, I have never been on a date before."

"Never? Ha!" her laughs echoed. "I expected as much, and your confidence wanes so quickly in front of true confrontation."

"Well, maybe I've been a little busy with my life, you know, adventuring and swashing and buckling and all, as you see."

"More nonsense! I see perhaps you are right, for it is one thing to pretend to fight a battle, and it is another to handle the flames of romance, were there any! Ha-ha!"

"I'm sorry, wait, you could tell. I'd hoped.... No, you're too perceptive. You could tell, I can't pretend in front of you. About anything. Can I?"

"I'm a lady and ladies know the first rule of all males: they lie to get what they want."

"That in itself is a lie. It must be, all absolutes are, necessarily."

"Is it true for you?" said the Captain.

"Well...."

"Then you have no idea if it is a lie or not, so again, you are only lying once more in the safety of another lie," said Amalie.

"You are...really something," he said.

"And you're a bore," she said.

"Thanks. I saved your town, you know," he said.

"Did you?" she said.

"Okay, this is getting off on the wrong foot."

"Well, how should it be going? Should I be howling your praises in front of the masses? Should I be delivering myself to your bosom willingly in swoon and submission? You extorted your supposed victories of circumstance, I say at least from what I could tell and probably many more, so you could have forced me here."

"I *forced* you?! You forced MY paw! How was I supposed to act? Just let you embarrass me in front of everyone!" said Gethsarade.

"The truth comes out," said Amalie.

"No, you have no idea who I am."

"Oh, not yet then?"

"I didn't mean...Argh! You are impossible! There has to be a way to win with you."

"Unless there doesn't."

"Look, you want me to be honest? Fine. I'll tell you exactly who I am. I was a stowaway on Barrogan's ship. That's how I became an 'adventurer.' When I boarded, it was to avoid creditors, for I was a thwarted musician avoiding rent. Because life outside of privilege is hard. Then Barrogan took the ship over and I have been running from him ever since," he said. But she had stopped, and her look had changed.

"You do seem familiar, and maybe that's what Great Father meant when he spoke about you."

"You're so strong willed. What unearthly force convinced you to actually come out here and meet me anyway? We both know it wasn't the orders of your Great Father, whatever that means."

"Bite your forked tongue, twice. And he said there was something about you, and he wanted me to find out what it was. To find you out."

"You're just going to tell me that?"

"We're both being honest now, and besides you want this 'date' to keep going? Then don't make a scene will you 'dear?'" She smiled, her demeanor did not match her words out in the square, but their conversation remained congenial from a public distance.

"Well, there's the truth from both of us, so there. And from that point on, everything has been a complete accident. I'm just playing along trying to survive. There. Happy? The savior's ship of gold isn't even mine any more than it was Barrogan Black's. I just took it from him. He took it from someone else. Maybe they took it from your real hero. And I am only trying to find my way and taking care of me, understand?"

"Of course, I understand. I understand the male and his utterly present concerns. There is little not to understand about it. Everyone understands that."

"Then," he asked, "why did they still fight?"

And she said, "Because you look so much like him."

He said, "Like who?"

"Like Sangareth."

"Bless you."

And she said, "You don't know? But I thought you were the savior," she laughed jokingly.

"Well, I never really admitted to that. Not that way," he said.

"Oh, yes, you did!" she said, laughing out loud.

"Okay, you've got me. I know nothing; I was just playing along, you know, to inspire them."

She said, "I know, you did well, and for it I thank you."

"So, are you going to let my secret out?" he said, smirking sheepishly.

"No," she said, "I won't tell anyone Vincent Poppaldi is not the true son of Sangareth. One, no need to, they will find out for themselves. Two, I don't believe the stories anyway."

"What stories?"

"Right. I mean the stories written in the lost book of our history, the book of the Eloran Era, covering the 2047th Wintersfall. It is still the greatest controversy on anyone's lips to this day."

"Yes?" he said.

"You see, we keep a meticulous account of our history and traditions here, and every great thing that happens gets written down. But a general named Sangareth tore out the pages written about him after a debacle he caused. He stole off to some land no one knows of, and no one has seen or heard of him since, except for one lost survivor, who washed up on the beach most emaciated, and he claimed in a state of insanity that the general had been borne a son who shall return to restore his name and…."

Vincent cut her off there, and he said, "Whoa, whoa, this is all a bit much, where is this book you are talking about?"

She said, "I will show you." And she took him to the library of the Great Commons Hollow. He stood mouth open and tail flat, for the inside of the library spiraled down and down and down inside the tree until he couldn't see it anymore. "All books, and especially the section on history, were kept in meticulous order."

He said, "Why, you must all know who your ancestors are for hundreds of generations."

And she said, "Longer, thousands upon thousands."

"Must be a wonderful feeling," he said. "Let alone being able to fly."

"You can't fly?" She said.

He said, "No."

"There's a surprise, considering your sizeable wings."

"What?"

"What? How do you mean, what? Did you not know of your own wings?"

"I-I…I mean, I don't have wings. I mean birds are magic. What?"

"Yes, you do, silly. Look!" She reached and unbuttoned his shirt, "Whoa, slow your roll shipmate, we're all professionals here!" he cried, and got a real laugh out of her.

"Don't be an idiot, look." She opened his new shirt, lifted his arm, grabbed him by his side, which tickled considerably, and pulled, which tickled even more. But to Vincent's surprise, his skin came with her. "Why do you think the guard let you in? Why do you think you passed yourself off? You raised your arms in the tailor's shop and *I* knew. Something you were saying had to be true. Even," she laughs, "even if there is no son of Sangareth, there can still be a hero. This is better."

"Wow, I just thought I was flabby there. Those are wings? I thought wings were just, you know, the kind on birds."

She kept on, "There is no one way of being anything in nature. I don't think hero-ship has to do with declarations and prophecies. It is blood."

"Blood?" he bit.

"Yes, and maybe you are a hero, but Sangareth was not, despite what many believe, so I'm glad you're here. Forgive me for my skepticism, Vincent, as you can see, my family's beliefs are definitely the popular sect, which stands to reason why it's the most convincing. But it is the one true account, and this it rules powerfully. So, while there is cause for a healthy skepticism of certain institutions, you will find, sir captain., I am only here because I only do not question the integrity and wisdom of my Great Father. His blood is perfect."

She seemed firm, and Vincent could think of no more to say. It was all so overwhelming: wings, blood, history. He thought, of everything he had been through up to this, and then it came to him, "Hey! Want to see my ship?"

"Ship?" she said.

"I've got something that might sound kind of crazy to you, in fact, about all this."

"What is it?"

"Now that you tell me all of this, I think I might actually be the Hero."

"I mean, of course you do," she said, sarcastically.

He rolled his eyes. "I'm not being facetious *anymore*. Follow me, I've got something to show you."

He produced the telescope he acquired from the ship like any good captain after taking her to the edge of town where all could be seen. "If Hesperia can be seen from the ship, then...Ah, ha! The ship can be seen from Hesperia!" There from the tallest, highest part of town, he let her look through the glass, and she gasped.

"What do you think? Hard to see from here, but there it is."

"Oh?"

"It's the *Tara Feen*!"

"Oh! It's beautiful!"

"Do you want to see it up close?"

They climbed up to the end of the highest branch at the top of the tallest tree and stood up. "Do you see it?"

"Yes. But I'm nervous. I only flew once before. It was a miracle I didn't die, how bad I was, and I could have sworn it was some angelic power bestowed on me."

"What like you were some kind of sorcerer or something?"

He laughed. "Yeah, it seems silly now."

"But you can make it from here, right?"

"*You can?*"

"Of course, it's down all the way, so it should be one shot, five minutes tops. Although it will be a little longer back up. They're not actual wings, you know, they just help us buoy ourselves in the air, but we can do a lot of things not even birds can with these."

She jumped up in the air, somersaulted, and then changed directions in midair, spun and did so again, coming down right where she was before in a gymnast's landing pose.

"Wow, I'd like to learn that."

"Well let's go, then."

"This is going to be so embarrassing."

"Don't worry, I will guide, and you just do what I do. Trust me, as an adult, you'll pick it up in no time. It's in your blood!"

"Okay, I'll try." And with a one-two-three, they were off.

It had taken three days on foot at the foot-pace of a squirrel and the help of the Owl King's Parliament to get to the base of the city. He struggled at first, but she helped him with a few hints, and then she said, "Hey, you're catching on," and then she started to pull back, or so he thought.

"Easy, she said, don't get ahead of yourself, easy, hey. Hey, wait!" But he was unsure how to slow down. Suddenly he was rocketing down the mountain with ease. And the five minutes she said it would take were shortened down to two, with her struggling to catch her breath, landing a full three minutes behind him." He was dusting himself off, checking for all his teeth, and desperately looking unhurt, for apparently his landing had not been orthodox.

"Okay, show off, you can too fly," she said half angrily.

"I swear I did not know that was going to happen, I didn't know how to slow down. And I don't think I want to do it again anyway, it was painful," he gigged himself up.

"Yeah, whatever. Typical oversensitive, yet arrogant, showoff male."

Vincent just sighed. "You've got me all wrong. Anyway, here, I brought you here to show you this." He took her to see the book of *Wintersfall*. She fell silent and felt the triangular emblem scrimshawed on its cover. "This book is actually a replacement of the pages taken out if the original is what I think. We cannot be sure of its contents. Sangareth took them, we suppose, not wanting the days of his life to be written by those who opposed him so righteously. His own followers left with him or were banished."

"Wouldn't you just replace it and not worry?"

"These books are sacred, and they are revered in all the land for their accuracy, objectivity, and thoroughly excellent style–our history told in first person by those who lived it. You can't get truer. Our history runs so deep, as you can see, and must never be compromised. It must be kept at all costs. The fact that this book has been written outside of this canon is evidence enough to throw it all into question. Do you see?"

"I'm sure it will still mean much more to yours and your kin than it does to me."

"It was stolen once, so this portion was written back down by the honest paw of my Great Father himself. Instead, it's filled with propagandist lies, as expected."

She went over it.

"This is incredible. It's nothing like the story I've known since birth."

"But there's no way I could do this."

"I think you could."

"You were nothing but contemptuous of me out there."

"Well, now I know you a little better. You're not who I thought you were."

"Maybe you've more to learn yet," said Vincent.

Little could they know, there were shadows about that day off behind the folds of the cliffs and shades of the trees, there were more than a few watchers. But they held, silent, and under the cognizance of Barrogan Black, no one made a move against them. They watched from the darkness as the two stared deeply into each other's eyes, aware of nothing else.

"Shall we, Captain?" asked the first mate.

"No. We wait."

"He's right there, sir! What do we need to wait for—agh!" those were the first mate's last words, for Barrogan ran him through and left him where he fell. All the others fell in line, trembling.

"Come here, Bock." He motioned to another crew-rat. "You're the new first mate. Now, supposin' yew isn't as dumb as the last one, tell me what you see up there."

"I'd say I sees him up there havin' found hisself a lovey dove, suh," said Bock.

"And how would yew describe her to yer mates?"

"I'd say she was a mite pretty bitty."

"And?"

"And…" Bock looked closer. "Oy, suh, she looks a right bit loaded, suh. Must be old money."

"And yew know how?" Black squinted at Bock.

"I'd say it's by the dress, suh. You see, townies wear them simple dresses, and when they want to get all gussied up, they sews in a load of ribbons in their old church clothes."

"Very good. Now…?"

"This one here, though, she's got a silk dress on, no frills, as it were. At's a Victorian rococo style, spring range, reminiscent of Feiberguialuxchzeg (pronounced "Frebe"), late period, top designer. You look at the shoulder and can see the pick stitching, suh, brand new, five hunnred fiftey thread silk. Cut and put on her piece by piece. You don't get an accentuation of the shoulder unless you pat it down by paw, then lead the cloth into the fold, highlighting, but not overemphasizing the balance of shoulder to hip. I'd say, you don't come across talent like that any old d--" Barrogan Black ran poor Bock through. Everyone around him let out a breath, then sucked it back in again.

"Everyone shut it. Now, here it is. She's up there with him, and she's likely well connected, for I knows the look of stuck-up old bew-gee-oy-see anywhere. We attack now and get our revenge, but we'll alert the whole force of the city on our heads without a chance of escape. We need the element of surprise. So, we wait."

No one had any more problems, and they seethed and waited together, watching with eyes of pure hatred the two aboard the *Tara Feen.*

Meanwhile, on the ship, the two continued to get to know each other. "Don't be so dramatic. The fact is I was wrong, and I couldn't help but notice you are quite an inspiring character," said Amalie.

"So maybe we could replace the book now since we have the real thing?"

"I don't think so," Amalie said.

"Don't think so?"

"Maybe you don't know our folk here. Try to tell them their 'canon' is flawed? They could never face it; better to work with one willing ear at a time. They make it their whole business to stay within their comfort zones. Our library is a publicly funded Bias Control Center (some interaction with the librarians offers some evidence of that fact). Our church, the Universal Church of the Nut, you couldn't tell the difference between it or a community-sponsored Comfort Zone Reinforcement Space. What do they do for the world?"

"I don't know."

"Exactly, but you *know* they're in there."

He chuckled.

"So, you see what I mean," she said. "They do nothing. They believe it's their theological mandate to not do anything. Action is the harbinger of change, and change is heresy, which means the Great Nut is wrong. Not us, but the Great Nut, for our rationality is unquestionable. Therefore, better to be irrelevant yet comfortable than risk the unholy sacrilege of altering one's step."

"I get it, yeah. So, is your rationality perfect about my alleged father, still?" he walked as they both walked the deck of the wondrous *Tara Feen,* strolling casually.

"Sorry, I get carried away. So, you see what I mean. When you got them to move, and even to fight, that meant something. Winning a battle takes far less strategy than getting someone out of their safe space, their comfort zone—same thing after all. It meant you have a gift, and if only it were true, perhaps you are the hero and maybe we are wrong."

"Well, it's easy to get others out of their comfort zone when you've never had one of your own. It sounds nice, in a way. Just having something like that. Why would I want to take that away?"

"True. But my point is that you must be different to inspire. And you are. You do. And if I do say so, Vincent, it seems an awful lot like you are the hero."

"No, it doesn't. This is all stuff from a long time ago and it's just coincidence. I mean, what are the odds?"

"The odds are pretty high if it's the truth."

"Yeah, well...but...I mean— no, you're not getting me there. I'm gonna get you," he said.

"Nope. I win."

"No way!"

"Way times an infinitely large infinity," she said.

"Okay, there's usually steps to the game."

She peered into his eyes and muttered. "I don't play games."

Then he kissed her since he had the chance.

"Oh! You! Little! Twerp!" she screamed. "I didn't give you permission to do that. And if you ever try it again, I'll...."

The commander huffed on his nails and polished them on his jacket. Feeling cocky, he looked at her with one eyebrow raised, "So ya like my ship?"

"Oh, you do not get to be like that with me right now."

"So, you're saying there's a time in that it *is* appropriate. Ha-ha, yes!"

"You want to think about what you just said?"

"I did. You do like me!"

"No. I...NO!" Then she and he collapsed into a final fit of unregulated and remarkable honesty and laughter.

Then he kissed her again. And she let him.

"I still hate you." Kiss. kiss.

"No, you don't, you like my ship."

"You are such a f—" she didn't get the word out, whatever it was, for he kissed her some more, which didn't bother her at all.

"Now I've got something to show you! Let's get back to town," she said.

Perhaps this, he wondered, would be the final piece, the way to the treasure, whatever it was.

"But before we go, there's something I need to know."

Then, suddenly, Vincent heard the thung of a twine string snap, and low whistling sound, turning him around just in time for an arrow to zip right in between his ears; the miss wouldn't have been if they hadn't ducked smartly. It *thwammed* into the thick rail of the ladder behind them.

"Did I mention natives?" he said.

"You didn't think to tell me before?"

"No, you didn't know about them either?"

"I've never been outside the city walls. What's your excuse?"

"I don't know. I guess I just got carried away by the moment."

"You idiot!"

A spear went flying past their heads and banged into the back of the room.

"Gah! Let's go!" she screamed.

"Oh, doggit, I really should have thought about this!"

They ran and jumped just as the ship became quickly overrun with the savages, who seemed to feel the ship had now become a part of their property.

"Come on!" He put his paws out like she did as she easily hopped from the fo'c'sle of the ship to the nearest banyan tree, but it seemed he hadn't quite mastered the technique. Dodging this spear and that arrow, and five trees ahead of him, she clapped at him with, "What happened to your big skills? You can't do a quarter-hop?"

"I don't know. What am I doing wrong?" Then, suddenly, he found himself trapped in a cut of the woods where it was not thick enough yet and quickly was surrounded, looking about frantically as the ground squirrels climbed.

She gave a sigh and jumped back into the fray, resorting to pushing him in front so he could make it from branch to branch.

After quite a while of this, finally the squirrels on the ground began to disperse. "So, they can't take the hills, eh? Guess they are getting tired."

"Never mind it. When they realize we're headed up the mountain, they will leave us, for no one wants to tangle with the guardians."

Vincent trusted her, and she turned out to be right. By then it was relatively easy to dodge the invaders, seeing as they could not fly. After they dodged enough spears and escaped back to the safety of the walls of Hesperia taking slightly over an hour, they spent the next few minutes catching their breath.

"So, the guardians must be pretty famous, huh?" he said.

"More of a historical reputation, but still one intact, thank goodness. Who knows how many more generations that will last."

"What was that all about?" Then before he could say he was sorry for getting her in so much trouble, she got up from her brooding position and slapped him again,

"Ow!" he jumped.

"That's for nearly getting me killed." she snapped.

"I'm sorry. I just wasn't thinking."

"No, you weren't," she said, back in her cool, boss-lady tone, and then she sat quietly for a long moment. "...but it was so much fun. Hey!"

"What?" he said, anticipating another slap.

"A real adventure. I've never had one of those."

"Yeah, well, I guess it's good to know I'm not getting my ship back anytime soon."

"Yes, that's terrible. No true matter, though. I will let Great Father know to dispatch a troop to repair and recover the ship. No sense something so beautiful going to waste. Like I said, the natives won't mess with guardians nutted to the teeth."

Gethsarade, finally feeling himself a little, chuckled and bowed to the lady. "I and my crew thank you for such generosity." but he had to stop himself from reflecting out loud how easy money could make one's problems. It would be improper, and Vincent knew better. "A true lady," he said.

They both sighed, despite the excited fluttering they both felt in their hearts, unsure whether the feeling was the adrenaline rush of narrowly escaping death, or perhaps something else.

"Well, before everything back there happened, what was it you needed to know? You were saying something about a last thing."

"Well, if I'm truly to know if I am the savior or not, I need to find the key, and as I'm aware, it is in the place called Almondale, or Almond Avenue, or something." He would not say anything, but he had changed his mind and decided she was definitely trust material, what with saving his life.

"Hmm, can't help you there." She furrowed her brow. Something she, the lady of Hesperia, didn't know about *at all?* "But I know this…."

She took him down to the dive in town. It was roughshod and obscured, but when he could make out the sign it read, "Persimmonia's."

"Oh my *gosh*," he exclaimed exasperatedly. "It's a pub?" as if he had never been there before.

"No surprise there. In history, the pub has been the logistical center of all revolutions well conducted, as it's visited most by those who don't get paid well, as you say so accurately. Loud music and hushed talking in many dark corners, with lips disguised by the rim of a drink. It's a time-honored tradition of criminals, and for the unindustrious, all the birds in their hearts with one stone at the bottom of a glass. Shady, cash-only business and all.

"But, of course, you the professional know this," she elbowed him. "All I *personally* know is this name and location is associated in some way to the Sons of Sangareth, and wherever and whatever they do. Maybe it's some meeting place for them to conduct their evil conspiracies. But no one tells me much. They all know who I am."

"Hey!" shouted Tib just then from the far end of the joint. He and Gy raised their glasses with their shining, cheesy, grins in a 'go-get-em-tiger' gesture.

"Yeah, thanks guys," He waved them down and rubbed his forehead.

"Ha-ha, relax, I think they're cute. There's no way they, as outsiders, could be involved with the likes of the Sons of Sangareth."

"I don't think the Sons of Sangareth are evil either, though. Sangareth wanted the hero to find these guys."

"Well, whatever the truth may be, I hope you find it."

"Me, too."

And that was the end of the conversation. They picked up their glasses, raised them to one another, and cheered.

"To adventure!" Gy looked at Vincent, who assured him with a look.

They laughed and talked about many things in their seat at Persimmonia's Pub until late in the night, and watched Tiburt and many others make total fools of themselves by dancing and slobbering all over the place.

The end of the evening was a dream. Gethsarade and Amalie talked until it was time for her to go home.

"I had a wonderful time. You were only kind of an idiot," she said, as they walked up through the archways and trellises lining the path up to the House of Tadwick.

"Hey, I put your life in danger only once."

"Well, thank you for not getting me completely killed and showing me my first real adventure."

They arrived at the door. He smiled. She smiled. He leaned in. She avoided his kiss and ran in, shooting him a quick smile as she shut the door.

What a quirky girl, he thought, chuckling to himself and trying not to take it too personally. *She is playing hard to get even now?* He walked to his room out into town weary, but in a trance.

Meanwhile, inside the House of Tadwick....

She closed the door and dropped her breath.

"Finally," said Great Father, having waited up for her, and she sucked her breath back in. "What did you find out? How much does he know? Does he trust you? Did he lead you to them?"

"No, he did not. He has no idea where they are or who. But he is the one, and he trusts me, to be sure. In enough time he will infiltrate and we will wait when they show themselves. He has revealed everything, and he trusts me completely."

"How do you know?"

"Because here is the book. And his ship, the real *Tara Feen*, needs repair and I expect you'll handle it. Is there anything you want to tell me?"

Great Father waved her inquest off, but his head was exploding on the inside. "Excellent work, my lamb! But how does he not know where to find them? The map inside should lead them to it, he is the savior, so he has to know its interpretation."

"Well, he may be the savior, but he's also an idiot and kind of illiterate. But not to worry, they will find him soon enough. They'll flush themselves out. We'll just watch."

It was only after having loyally handed the book over without thinking, she might experience some doubts. She went to her balcony, alone with the night, and considered whether to betray Vincent. He wasn't who she thought he would be. He wasn't who anyone thought. So different.

What she had seen just seemed so much more real than the legends. It just didn't seem right, the whole thing. Then she realized what she had done that night wasn't excellent at all. She had just made things very difficult for herself.

She wandered into the moonlight, staring out into the water, if perhaps she had gone undercover by order, deep into the heart of the enemy she had heard of all her life, just so she could rediscover the hope she had banished from her chest ages ago of one day leaving this place. She felt a flutter of olden revival in her heart that she should, through hopeless submission to the old tote, find a means of escape.

Perhaps she could even think again of sailing off to some far shore and having adventures just like the ones Vincent so richly described, just like those star-crossed lovers, Alya and Milowe Sangareth, the most tragic of all loves in their library. She had so joyfully read about them in the legends, which she no more took realistically than the old nursery stories of the Old Guard. She properly reviled them, yet secretly she longed for a love story for herself like all the young kits. *But what if*, her heart called out to her mind. *What if?*

Nothing is for certain, but perhaps at least I can protect him.

11: Son of Sangareth

As it goes with dreams, one wakes to find things not so after the frosty night. The day is a little less bright, ah, the sad disadvantage of being a dreamer, yet are nightmares not better reserved for the midnight hour? But as our hero woke, he found the world had become a strange new kind of nightmare. The next morning, he stretched himself up, bright as the simmering sun shining on the dew, and found out the engagement was already news all over town. Apparently kissing anyone was a big deal in Hesperia.

In the night, wedding plans hatched, in the absence of objection, as excited prospective parents-in-law are wont to do, words spread and signs, yes signs, posted, which was the medium of communication about this matter to Vincent himself. Parties attended by second and third-paw friends seeking favors and engagements from those one hasn't seen in years until there's someone getting latched up start popping.

Still groggy, Vincent walked into the Persimmonia's Pub, and ordered a stiffy, to which the bartender only objected on account of it being eight-thirty in the morning. Vincent replied, "Try to imagine a situation in which you would want a stiff drink at eight o'clock in the morning, now what would that be like?"

The bartender thought for a moment, then said, "Well, I'd like to think I'd just been told I am bound for eternal slavery or something awful. Why do you ask? What did you do?"

"You're not far off. Pour."

Then his loyal friends showed up, who had undoubtedly heard the news, and came to confirm it, also in the same manner of celebration. "You work fast. What did you do?"

"I don't know," replied Vincent, laboring his ale.

"Anyways, let's celebrate!" said Gy.

"Wait, you sound happy. Why?" said Vincent.

"We found it, Captain!"

So, the captain said, "Well, where's this Almondale place?"

After a few short turns, Gy brought him over to their table, which now seemed to be held in subsidy and showed him the scrawl above the lantern in the ceiling where they sat: Try Lady Persimmonia's Special Brew, ALMOND ALE, Today! Gy clapped him on the back, laughing, saying, "I dare say, my friend, some things, just maybe is what they is."

"But what does it mean, though? Is the hero supposed to own this bar? That sounds ridiculous. Maybe it's just a product gimmick, you think?"

"No, of course not. I'd wager a guess, your dear old dad was saying you should not forget to have a good time. You're on the right track and so on. Take a load off for a while."

Vincent shook his head, "Look, I had no plans to marry when I went to bed last night. Someone is rushing this along and there's no way this is the Shining Way."

"I'd say," they said, sarcastically, not realizing still.

"Oh, shoosh. But why? Now, that I don't know."

"So, what of the old plan to get the gold and get out?"

They leaned in, "Tell us, Captain, how does this help us get the gold out?"

"Well," he leaned in as well, and they ducked their heads low, "I've realized wherever this treasure is, Amalie is somehow tied to it. I was thinking we get Amalie to go with us, now I...."

Then they suddenly all were talking at once. "Know what they say about females on ships and all but...."

"Absolutely out of the quest...."

"I think that's a wonderf...."

A pile jammed in, interrupting them, of squirrels headed by Great Father Tadwick, smiling, something clearly very hard for him.

Vincent was growing suspicious of everything he did. "For he's a jolly good squirrel, for he's a jolly good squirrel, for he's a jolly good squirrel, which remains yet to be seen, hey!"

"What? I don't think those are the words, are they?" Vincent said to his companions, but Great Father seemingly intentionally thwarted their plan-making, along with his ultimate plan to skedaddle from town by escorting in two fair maidens for the two next most eligible bachelors ever, Gy and Tiburt. And they were totally and completely smitten.

The friends quickly disappeared with their new *concomitantes*, and the party swept out into the street on its own momentum.

Vincent just snuck out the back and left.

The following, dear reader, is not the thing to happen to those who go pooping out on parties, although note one should not rule it out. The captain felt if it was his party, and so he could poop if he wanted to. Whereupon after his departure, he was immediately blindfolded, punched in the face a lot of times, knocked out, and revived somewhere dark, messy, and unpartylike.

When the covering was removed, he was greeted by masked squirrels holding him, and there was someone mouth-breathing behind him, and just when Vincent realized he was there, the dumb brute whacked his head on the table.

"Ow, what?" Whack. "Now just stop!"

Whack. Whack. Whack.

Vincent, now thoroughly disarranged, could only combobulate unintelligible threatening and growling and yelling for a long time, coming through the very muffling ski mask jangling about in front of him. When he came back to, Vincent said, "Okay, I don't mean to offend you, and maybe it was just stress, but I honestly didn't get any of that."

Then the assailant punched him in the face again, pulled up his ski mask to uncover his mouth, and started yelling, and alas it was the exact same.

"Still nothing," Vincent burbled.

The assailant reared back and then paused, "Wait, are you not, like, frightened?"

162

Vincent replied, "D-baa-hugh, words. I need....my head for the word. I can't make words without my head, please."

The assailant said, "What?" which sounded like "Uuub," to Vincent, and he was punched again for good measure.

"Stop hitting me. God...." He put his words together, then said, "Have you ever met a mentally unstable shark? You remind me very much...."

"Yeah...no."

"Well, I know one. Good friend of mine. You two should meet," said Vincent, smiling deliriously.

"Oh, wow, really. Friends with sharks. What's that like?"

"What it's like is, it's like, I'm not scared of you."

"No? Wait, are you threatening me?"

"No. So you can stop." But he punched him in the face again.

"Ow, ow. Why are you doing this? Are you just bats? It is not effective. Could you just talk to me with mouth words?"

"Um...I don't know if I'm supposed to."

"Well, I'm still not scared of you, so I think we're at an impasse. So, go get someone else, please."

He snarfed and left into the next room, and Vincent heard muffled talking, making out only, "He's good. Lots of mind tricks. Watch yourself."

A new squirrel came in with a cup of hot tea and sat it down. He untied one of Vincent's paws, smiled as he took a sip, and said, "Now, you'll get the other paw back if you tell me how you learned about the location of our hideout and our secret word."

"Who are you? Where am I? Why?"

"I'm not telling; you just answer the question."

"Well, how am I supposed to tell you how I learned the secret word if I don't know the word to which you are referring?"

"I am asking the questions, and you are answering them."

Then Captain Vincent just sighed and took it upon himself to take a look around and noticed among the piles of junk, refuse, and old dirty clothes, a pair of older squirrels sitting in almost worship like fashion around a game of Squabble, who glanced his way and checked their masks, tight, and went back to their silly game.

The scene was next to a substantial pile of cheap takeout, and another pile of disassembled board game paraphernalia. Vincent surmised: first, these grown squirrels lived like adolescents, second, it was pretty cool, and third, there was a scrap of newspaper, (apparently only used for waste) and on it, there was a scrap of text.

A-l-m-o-n-d D-a-l-e.

Almond ale. Almond Dale. It was two things. "Almondale. Is that right, is that how it's said, is it actually a place? Someone said it was like a drink. Is this Almond Dale?" Then Gethsarade gasped excitedly, and bounced in his chair, "I need to be here, this is where I'm supposed to find…. The key is here! The key, where is it? This is Almondale, or Almond Dale or whatever, right? Come on, out with it, I haven't got all day."

The squirrel stared at him momentarily, then went out and there was more muffled talking. "Carl, are you trying to learn how to spell again? Stop it!" Whack.

He came back and sat down nicely again.

"This is ridiculous." said the captain.

"I agree," The nameless squirrel punched him in the face once more.

"What was that for?"

"You didn't answer the question. That's what this is."

"Okay, look, I know how this story goes. I say I'll never talk, but most likely I will, since the person who knows nothing always talks first. You don't believe him, and you just kill or cripple him. Either way, the innocent from whom you get nothing gets the short end of the stick, whereas the ones you're after invariably escape and leave you, conversely, crippled, because the ones actually at play in the story always have backup. Right? So, how about this: you just tell me who the heck you are, and I will see what I can do to help you. Win, win."

They looked at one another and then knocked him out.

He came to however long after, and he was at a nice dining table. There before him were the now not-so-rag-tag-looking bunch he recognized from before, wearing perfectly polished armor beneath beautifully embroidered black robes. One of them spoke up, saying,

"We are the Sons of Sangareth. We apologize for knocking you silly. This is Almond Dale."

"S'aright. Can you by any chance untie me?"

"No. But we need you to hear us." To which Vincent replied, "You just don't know how to persuade, do you? Where are my friends?"

"Friends?"

"...He's got friends."

"Guys. He's got friends." Vague whispering.

"Yeah, 'friends.' I bet," the punchy one lolled, then fell silent.

"What's it like? Are they cool, I mean like, you know, viewed with social favor?"

"Guys. Shut up."

"Right, boss."

"Yes, apparently they don't come in thick supply with your type, well, actually I suppose I just got smashed up with them anyway. I take it they're alright since you don't even know about them," said Gethsarade.

"Well, who are they?" They got up to grab the masks and knockout knob.

"No, look you're not punching ANYONE ELSE IN THE FACE today, not until you tell me why I'm here, and probably not afterward either. Better, tell me why you're here, and why I'm supposed to find you."

"You're supposed to find us?"

"Yes. The hero shall find the key in Almond Dale."

"What do you know about the hero?"

"*I'm the hero*," he said, getting bouncy again. "It's me!"

"How do we know?"

Gethsarade replied:

> "Where a terminal moonlit pillar
> A geyser's upward broken stream
> Is Elora's angled message sender
> Averse a blinding, blinding beam."

The others stood suddenly as he spoke and ceremoniously recited the rest of the poem with him, half of which they seemed in some entranced state, then they said, "And of the half written down which only is spoken between us, from the survivor of the demise of the *Tara Feen,* Good Knight Bramble Beely, never written down but committed to the memory of the Sons of Sangareth alone. What of it?" Gethsarade recited the rest.

The one appearing to be the leader went out of the room. There was a very audible whoop, then he came back in. "So, we're sorry."

"Good. So, where's the key?"

"We thought you had it."

"Well, I thought you all had it. I thought that was why I was supposed to come here, to get it from you, right? The key to the treasure?"

"Treasure? What treasure? We've been waiting for you to bring us a key to a weapon."

"Wait, does the poem actually say anything about either one of those?"

"Of course it does. Wait, hold on. Oh, let me think, no actually, I don't think it explicitly does, either one. Oh my goodness, how did I not notice before, it says absolutely nothing about any of my preconceived notions," said he who was apparently the leader.

"Well, does that make all this a useless farce?"

"I don't know.... Maybe there is a meaning there yet to be discovered."

"Yes, the simplest answer given all the facts we don't know is definitely the truth."

"Hm."

"Hm."

"Well."

The captain clicked his gums. "So, I've got some questions now. Why are you all here?"

"Didn't we cover this?"

"No, I mean why are you *here*, here. Like, shut up in a hole instead of being praised by the world for your apparent heroism. What happened since Sangareth left?"

166

"We are hiding because for the longest time the Sons of Sangareth have been vilified. The Great Father Tadwick would tell you one story, but we know another."

"Oh, I think I know about the version you're about to tell me," said Vincent.

"How?" said one whom the captain remembered as Carl.

"What do you mean how? Of course he knows, he's the hero." said the leader.

"Well, I don't know. That was more of a play for convenience. But actually, I read about it in a book I found, you see."

"WHERE IS THE BOOK?" They all shouted, falling over each other. "Yes, where? You must tell us; inside that book is the key to our victory."

"I don't think it works like that." He didn't want to say he had just given it to their rival.

"No, no, he wrote a message to the Sons of Sangareth, you know, and said, just believe, so anyone who believes can receive the blessing of the savior. The *key*," they said.

"No, I think he means the actual, biological son of Sangareth, son singular, and I don't think I need to bring you the book, first because I've decided I don't think you know enough shut up in your hole here to be trustworthy if you even wanted to be. You guys have been in isolation too long. Second, I know the message. I tried to decipher it so long it could not be hacked from my memory with a rusty hanger."

"Well, please understand, we're not exactly the popular ones in the story, seeing as our leader was excommunicated, killed, and banished, not in said order. Um. But we are the real Guardians." They showed him the breastplate of Elorus. "The others are just terrible fighters because they're not guardians at all. They're a pretending faction, using tactics they're not built for and don't know them. They just think the techniques are super-hard to master because they are, for them."

"Well if you, the Sons of Sangareth, are the real Guardians of Elorus, are you guarding now?"

"Why, yes."

"What from?"

"Exactly."

"Well, we pretty much guard ourselves these days; it's tough work, being on the outside, on the inside. But we dealt with *you*, didn't we?"

"Fair enough. Tell me something, if the Guardians are so mighty, why do they seem to lose all the time?"

"Against whom? We guard. It's hard to deal with conspiracy when one is doing one's job. You can't guard a society from the inside, too. We don't boast those kinds of numbers."

"Yeah, area of cognizance type stuff. Jobby, knowledgey stuff." The leader took another cheeseball, "Yeah, gotta know that stuff. It matters."

"Yeah, yup," they all agreed.

He said, "Look, I've got to get back before someone comes looking for me. And I'm the most eligible bachelor in Hesperia, promised to the most eligible maiden I might add, the daughter of Great Father Tadwick."

Gasps went about the room.

"But you're not even a millionaire."

"Right, I did good, so, respect. Yeah?"

"He really is the hero."

"I mean you've got to be something special with how ugly you are, landing a slice of hot chinga-chinga like that. Chinga-chinga winga-winga!" They fist-bumped one another.

"Okay, whoa. First of all, barf. Second, it's not like—."

"I mean, what's with the sash, how do you even come back from that socially, much less land a girl, much less THE girl?" said the leader.

"Right...," the Sons conferred.

"Yeah, good on you, because you're not doing well in the looks department, and no money? Totes horriff, man, totes horriff."

"Well, maybe I'd be a lot more attractive if someone hadn't recently beaten my face into strawberry jam! Anyway, that being said, you don't want my kidnapping sitting on top of your already bad reputation."

"Sounds reasonable," they said.

168

"Moving forward. So, I take it your interpretation of the text says, you're the winners of this situation in the end, right?"

"Right. Of course."

"Of course. And I'm the hero. Meaning I am to lead you to alleged victory."

"Yes. Splendid."

"Which means you are to do what the leader, me, says."

"But there's no weapon."

"Maybe he meant us to find each other. Maybe we're the weapon all together," said Vincent.

"Hm. The poem was the key, and we're the weapon."

"Hm."

"Well, that means we're supposed to get everything back with just you?"

"Yep."

"Well that sucks."

"Yep."

"So, what do we do?"

"Well, I think we should first stop wasting our time playing Squabble. Then we should figure something out, like a plan."

They sat a long time on this.

"You can call me Stag," said the leader after much thought.

"And I'm—." They shook paws, and his tail froze for a moment, for he had come too close to letting his true name slip. Then he thought, *they of all in this world would know me.*

"Although I thought the Son of Sangareth had a different name, Gaga, Saga, something. Not sure, as it's been a while since I read it."

"Yeah, we don't exactly carry library cards, not being welcome to the world and everything."

"But we know you, Vincent Poppaldi, leader of the Rising and Son of Sangareth, Hero of Elorus and Savior of Hesperia. Remember, we trust no one."

"You mean trust no one else. Heh-heh. Right, got to go. I'll let you guys know the plan when I get a little more information. Meet me back at the pub in three days. Right, got to go." said

Vincent. He wiped the blood from his face with his kerchief and left it with the crew.

"Of course. Sorry, starstruck. Hee-hee! No problem, sir!" and the puppish squirrel closed the door with a thoomp.

It was with that Gethsarade walked out alone and sweating. Acquiring a few more titles seemed to be the trend everywhere he went. He needed to get the book back. If it truly had his name written in it, in the version known only among them, it meant he would be exposed soon by his own name to the enemy if he wasn't yet. It also meant he truly was the hero of fate. *Mi madre, how awful, all of this,* he thought. *I really should read the rest of the book!*

Three days. Three days ought to be enough time to keep them out of the way, he thought and headed out, not knowing if he meant to use the time to find the book or the treasure.

12: The Dream Within

When he came out onto the street, he realized he was not far from where he had been taken, just a hop down the alleyway behind the pub. Then it dawned on him: he was 'tween Persimmonia and Almondale. The treasure had to be somewhere around there. But for the time being he had to get back, for meanwhile the party still went on out in the street in front of the pub, as he could tell from the noise.

After avoiding being seen and crossing a few streets, he found some familiar area. Soon, with some asking, he located the sign to the Pub. There, wandering around, apparently looking for something or other and avoiding the crowd as he was, was his lovely bride-to-be who seemed to be looking for something herself, and in seeing her gorgeousness he couldn't help but for a furious scowl to overcome his face. Upon sight they approached each other swiftly asking at the same time, "What did you do?"

They both replied, "I didn't do anything!"

"Then who announced we were engaged?"

Vincent grabbed a paper off a nearby board, which was the announcement of the wedding between the Hero Vincent Poppaldi and the Lady Tadwick. "It says here it's in three days. Three days! How does anyone…never mind, it's not important. This is insane."

"I agree." She didn't.

"How could we possibly know whether we would want to spend our entire lives together after one day? Ludicrous!"

"Um, yeah." said Amalie, suddenly slightly flushed.

"What's the matter?" he asked. Just then, they both had to move out of the way of a much more serious crowd suddenly making its way in the direction Vincent had come, but he paid it little mind. It passed by without interruption.

"Nothing…nothing is the matter," she said. "Come on. I need to show you something. You'll need your wings. But before we start up, here's a pro tip. To stop in midair from a high speed with your type of patagium, you first loosen up, then kick out so your body goes vertical."

"Wait, you don't want to talk about this?"

"Not now, as right this moment I need you to trust me. Do you? I need to show you something very important. Back to your wings, you will need to force the air out yourself, so reach down with your arm outstretched, grab the flap, and rotate your wrist to draw it flat manually, then draw your wings in close to your body as needed to slow even more, like a brake for emergencies. Doing that won't work without doing the other first, though, and you'll just go faster. Then do the kick. Understand? Okay, let's go."

"Do I get a minute to practice?"

"No. You'll be fine. Do you trust me?"

They started up the nearest tree and soon they were flying at breakneck speed. This time she made sure and held on tight, and yelled up the commands, "Left now! Right now!" until they got where they needed.

"Okay, we're here."

They were on a platform, but one so huge it failed the eyes to see the ends of it. A giant, grand, single tower stood in the middle, which seemed to serve as the main control of operations, and all the time there were squirrels all gliding around it, up and down, going in and out. Most of them all wore the same thing: flowing white robes with the same gold embroidery all over them, hood to toe. The style very much reminded him of the robes worn by the Sons of Sangareth, but the armor was missing. Instead, they wore their rank on patchworks, and their uniforms were solid colored and plain. The tower stood up out of a cropping of several expensive-looking schoolhouses and extending from them in all directions were all sorts of gardens, landing strips, and exercise grounds for combat and et cetera, Vincent guessed.

"Have you ever seen anything so grand?"

"Wow...oh, um, yes, it all seems quite fine."

The place was absolutely splendid, with painted stone and wooden reliefs everywhere depicting what Vincent could only guess to be the ancient heroes of the Eloran Order built into every building. Statues of squirrels in mid-flight stood in the courtyard. Fountains sprang from place to place amidst of gardens all about the main deck. It all reminded him of the artistry infused into the construction of the *Tara Feen*. However, much of it did not seem right.

"What is this place?" Vincent shouted close to the top of his lungs in such shock at what he saw.

"This is the secret training ground of the Guardians of Elorus. It was built upon an ancient, sacred place we call Elderwood. Said to be the birthplace of Elorus the Hesperian."

"Wait, you mean, what? Secret?" he shouted again, but she motioned him to calm himself. "Secret means I shouldn't be here, doesn't it?"

"Stop!" shouted a squirrel wearing exceptional garb, sporting the uniform of the day. He bounded up to them. "Lady Tadwick, I honor your presence, but who is this?"

"This is my guest, and your superior in fame for the time being, and shortly in rank as well. Any more questions?" This was a phrase used often in militaries everywhere to mean, you, underling, will not ask any further questions.

"By your leave, madame," the officer saluted. This was a gesture that could be roughly translated as *please allow me to go as far from you as possible.*

"Very well."

She enjoyed her inherited position very much sometimes. She had the guard, all the while grumbling, led them to Elderwood tower and she dismissed him there.

"Right this way. Hero."

She smiled, and he caught it and smiled back. He didn't understand what it meant, however, and decided to keep himself on guard.

"Down this way."

She led him through an unlabeled door on the side of them and descended a spiral of stairs that seemed to get darker and darker as they went down.

"As one approaches the base of the tree," she explained without him asking, "the holes that are drilled for light and air get deeper, so it will only get darker from here till we get to the room."

"Room? What room? Where are we going?"

"You'll see. Trust me."

Then suddenly they were at the end of the tunnel and at an unmarked door.

"What you are about to see is the beating heart of this city."

His own heart skipped.

She went on, "Only certain members of the ruling class are allowed inside here." She opened the door with a special key she pulled from her robes. The door swung open and lodged against a wedge stone that propped it open. Vincent squinted.

"There it is."

What stood before Vincent inside of what seemed like a basic cellar on top of an apparently highly overused pedestal about his chest height was a glorious, gleaming walnut many times the size of a normal one. It radiated what told him instantly could only be the magical shine of pure gold.

"Wow." This was the only word that escaped Vincent's lips for a long time as he beheld it, examining its every feature. "I don't believe it."

"We all believe *in* it. I brought you here because I'd like to tell you the story of how the Great Nut protected me so you can understand what all of this means. There was a family, the Sangareth family, long ago before I was born who tried to create an uprising.

"Well, my grandfather was friends with this family until they had a falling out, a difference of opinion, because her father wanted to hold to principle in the face of threat, and Sangareth wanted to take the Great Nut and hide it from even the Guardians, as a reactionary response to the threat of invasion and infiltration from within.

"There were some who agreed and sided with Sangareth, so there was a conflict from within, and a beloved family member of the Tadwicks died (Great Father's would-have-been first wife, Nada Beethorn, the sister of Sangareth's second in command, Staghorn Beethorn senior).

"As a result of this quarrel, one dark night Sangareth decided he was fed up and tried to steal the Great Nut for himself and fled Hesperia as his only intentions were to use its worth to make himself rich. But the death of Nada Beethorn devastated Great Father, leaving him in grief. He vilified Sangareth, and banished him and his family from town. They left on ship and were never seen again. Since then, there has been absolute peace.

"I was told the story by my relatives, and they described how Sangareth was a vicious, terrible rodent of purely evil devices and everything he did was because of his hot, terribly foul blood. My father always said so. He knew Sangareth personally, even before all that happened."

"How personally?"

"They led the army of Elorus together before Sangareth tried to wrest the favor of Hesperia away from him with his quest for power. He may have had terrible blood, but in truth I believe in his words. They ring so true to me. He was right that no one faction should control the truth. You want to know something?"

Vincent asked, "What?"

She said, "Goodness and badness are just in the blood and that's just how it is. But the blood of that nasty dog is not in you, though you believe in his cause. The perfect combination. Someone different."

"But…with the same faith."

"Against everything, I realized you're not a part of all this," she said and then continued to tell him the story and the feelings she had begun to develop for him won out over her suspicions as they had the night before, and she kissed him on the cheek and said, "Thank you, for showing me different was possible. Now, we've got to teach you how to use those wings!"

"Really? You'd do that?"

She smiled. "But first watch this." She took a lever by the door and flipped it with some effort. Vincent heard gearwork, it sounded like, start to turn through the wood, and after a moment the pedestal on which the Great Nut sat began to rise. He beheld it lift up into an opening in the ceiling, and it rose and rose.

"Where's it going?" he asked.

"It's going toward the sky. Up at the top, there is an arrangement of mirrors and torchlights. They create a beacon that shines the golden light of the Great Nut over all the mountain skies." she said, and he marveled.

"So, this serves not just as a mere symbol...," he reflected.

"But also as a real light to all who are lost, and it wards off evil ones who would come here and do harm, for it shows the world the shining truth of our strength, that our spirit is ever strong."

She led him up to the door where she called some guards, "These Knights will teach you everything you wish to know about flight and airborne defense. Kneel." He knelt, and she drew a sword from a Knight's sheath, tapping his shoulders. "I dub thee Sir Vincent of the Knights of Elorus. You now know the deep secrets of our city, as all our true members of the order know. This makes you one of us now."

"Wow! I mean, you know, that's cool. Thanks." He was sure he wasn't grasping the full import of what she was doing, so he made to appear as appreciative as he could but not totally overwhelmed.

They're just giving me access to every ounce of power and fortune I ever imagined possible, he thought. *This is awful! Now what am I going to do?*

The day was spent flying and falling until he was weary to the bone of it and had forgotten all about his trouble. He went home elated about all the new skills he had learned. So elated, in fact, he forgot entirely to go find out why the Great Nut was not 'tween Persimmonia and Almondale, that is, why the opposing force possessed the treasure of Hesperia. Since he forgot to do that, he couldn't figure out how to steal it unless he snuck out again.

But something bugged him about Amalie. She had shown him how to use his wings and fight. He went to the inn to wonder about this story. She had explained all the meanings of the many squirrels and times pertained to in the book and the ship, but it was such a sudden change of heart from such a stalwart individual.

That night Vincent, knight, captain, commander, fiance, hero, and all types of other such names, sat alone in his room and wondered, *this is all so incredibly complicated, what do I do? How am I supposed to find my destiny, let alone act on it when I find it? Why is it always so dog-awful hard to know what to do? I don't want to fight anyone. I'm not a fighter. I just want to be loved. I don't want to kill. I gotta get out of here.*

Or wait. Maybe I won't have to. It doesn't say I explicitly must kill or fight anyone. They say it, not me. There's plenty of misinterpretation going around. Maybe I just need to stick around and see for myself. For three, no, two more days. And then I'm screwed. Oh, nuts.

Let me think. I love her, I'm pretty sure, but I'm going to be found out if I stick around much longer. But if I leave, at least before I get my paws on that treasure, I'm ruined and stranded. But if I go any further, someone's bound to figure this out. There'll be no explaining why the hero lies about who he is. I'll be ruined.

So, he wandered home. But as he walked, he tried his wings out every now and then, taking his time with the new skills. Then, his thoughts drifted to a better light, and before he knew it, he was imagining life in the sunshine with Amalie, skipping fences, coasting from forest to forest, or whatever it is flying squirrels do just for fun.

By the time he got home, his heart was as light as a feather. And by the time he opened the door, he had forgotten entirely, as seemed to be happening more and more, that he was trying to steal a priceless treasure and betray literally everyone. He locked and latched the door, and he turned to find Tiburt standing in the corner of the room, waiting for him.

"How was the thing?" Tiburt asked.

Vincent decided not to let him in on anything just yet, for Tiburt seemed to be in a funny mood, even for Tiburt.

"Ha-ha!" he exclaimed. "I found my destiny and is it not grand indeed?" Vincent asked Tiburt, who seemed for some reason suspicious.

"Or is it the fate of another?" said Tiburt, and walked away.

Vincent's mind was brought back to earth. Despite his best efforts to convince himself, he could not think Tiburt would say such a thing unless he knew, but he could not imagine how Tiburt could know. He thought back to the time he picked out an impostor when no one else had even suspected a thing right out in daylight back in Otterdam (Oh, how far this journey had taken him since even then!). Nevertheless, he knew all along there would be sacrifices.

However, Tiburt's words had jerked him back. Whatever he meant, he kept wondering to himself in the night as he tried to sleep. *What the heck am I going to do anyway? And what am I supposed to save any of them from, exactly? And more importantly, why, again, am I supposed to be the one doing it? Oh, only for Amalie, if only for her, I suppose I should stay.* He thought long about the words Tiburt had said, and he remembered the last time he had said something like that was on the ship when they were talking something about fortunes. He got thinking finally about his now knowing about the Great Nut. Then it hit him—a way out of it all.

Soon, he was at Tiburt and Gy's room, "Gy, get Tiburt. I have a plan. I'll explain everything on the way, but I know where the treasure is. And thanks for the lessons, by the way." He flashed the key he snagged from the folds of Amalie's dress.

Tiburt got up. "Well, sorry, it's just me tonight. Gy's out on a date. So where are we going?" Vincent looked somewhat startled yet impressed, but said nothing, only motioning to follow. Tiburt got up right then and was ready instantly, for he wore his day clothes to bed, and off he went.

But there was someone else with a plan that night. Barrogan Black, having been chased out of the town, had hatched a new plot, and of the time between the moment he was flushed out of Hesperia with the small band of his remaining crew he wasted none of that time. He set immediately back to the ship's port and found the band of slaves had formed a new colony.

"But what if there are more of them than you think?" said his new first mate.

Black replied, "I met the natives, and they are not fond of the band led by the one known as Vincent. They are starving and diseased. Though they are many they lack proper leadership."

So, as it happened the night the bond began cracking between Vincent and his crew, Barrogan was busy forging a new one all his own. He popped up out of nowhere among them as they were busy preparing the night's communal feast of roasted bark and dirt cakes, and he raised his arms high to get their attention.

"Natives, brothers, true possessors of the land of the Acheron. Hear me!"

At the sound of the word Acheron, their ears perked up and they listened despite not understanding anything else he was saying.

Then one of his two surviving crew said, "Captain, I think they might not understand anything you're saying," He sighed exasperatedly, and he bent down, scribbling real quick. He held up a drawing of Captain Poppaldi with his wings. They instantly yelled in bloody rage. He stabbed the picture. They yelled louder, and he motioned for them to follow him, and they did, picking up their spears and foaming at the mouth.

"Do you think they will be enough, Captain?" said his new, new first mate, whose name won't be bothered with.

"Not remotely. One stop left to go. Lemme see, they can't be far from the ship…." And sure enough, after climbing the rope to see from a tall pillar, he spotted an encampment across the bay near where the ship *Tara Feen* was settled on the rocks, pushed upon them by the tide. There were small fires and smoke. He had been right in surmising the Happenlings survived the wreckage, and likely used their labor skills to gather and create supplies, thus allowing them to trade with the crazy natives. From his vantage point, he saw the *Tara Feen* had been placed on stilts, and the Happenlings were attempting to repair the ship, probably in hopes of leaving. *Now,* he thought, *they will learn why they should stay.*

"Friends!"

They stopped their hacking and chopping and sawing to see who on earth was calling them friends. They spied out on the water a boat of rats, having tied their tails together to form a flotation device, a little thing rats sometimes do.

It has been speculated in legend that rats occasionally tended to tie up their tails into big knots and go rolling around. It should be heretofore known to those outside of the rodent kingdom that,

179

although some very unfortunate times, these bundles are found irreparably caught, the majority of the time rats do this deliberately. Those who cannot untangle themselves are left to their own as a favor to the rest, it is believed.

There has been wild speculation upon the causes of this phenomenon. Some believe it to be the cause of rats in hibernation sleeping in their own droppings and getting stuck together. This is obviously flawed, as rats are actually quite fastidious, and would never allow such a thing. Just ask a rat, he or she will tell you.

Others believed sometimes rats play too hard, and they get confused and end up all twisted up like so. This is also clearly problematic as no rat would never admit to doing such a horrid act as playing.

When the pirats floated up in their rat-boat, claiming a show of benevolence and favor, with the lone Barrogan Black standing inside with his arms open in welcome, the squirrel Happenlings immediately speculated it had to be some sort of king. They took up spears, clubs, and whatever they could find, for we all know what happens when rulers and subjects confer; this is why they were called Happenlings.

However, Barrogan had a plan. As soon as his boat bumped ashore, he stepped off and spoke loudly as they started to rush to him. "My fellows. You may not know me, but I am a powerful ally to have on your side in this war."

"War?"

"Yes. War."

"What war?" they stopped, confused. Mostly because no one ever said anything about a war.

"I'll tell you. But first, you must be wondering if I am friend or foe. Also, you must be starving and tired, for what slave isn't. Today, I free you. Today, I give you relief from the pain of toil and hunger, it is no more."

"How are you going to do that?"

"Do you know the difference between a slave and a master?"

"A lot, but I have a feeling there's a convenient enough definition coming." This was spoken by a squirrel, gray in coat, who knew much more than the rest about the world.

"My name's Scurrid. And I am leader here," he turned back and eyed the crowd, "not master but leader." With a grun he pulled a club of considerable size from the pile of gatherings they had amassed, "And I have been teaching my mates here how to fend for themselves, since they're out of chains. I think we've been doing pretty well so far, so what can you offer us we can't get for ourselves?"

"What I give is just as I said. Right now, you are not slaves, but you are not masters either. This is a shrewd world we live in as you must know, and the only ones who live apart from the pain of daily struggle to survive are those who know the difference between slaves and masters. The difference is...belief."

"What do you mean?" said Scurrid.

"You were once slaves aboard a ship, waiting to be sold, were you not?"

"No, the Great Vincent was going to free us, well, till we crash landed here and I led us off to fend for our own."

"And why did you do that, rather than follow the Great Commander to fortune and fame?"

"Because we are simple folk; we don't care about that. We just want to live in peace and make a life for ourselves with the sweat off our backs. It was freedom now, or freedom later; we chose now."

"Or did you? Let me ask you. Are you free? Is this the existence you want for your children, and your children's children? While others right up the mountain dwell in security and riches, in carefree wealth and solitude, you honestly are telling me you wish to live like scum in comparison to them? They are the masters of this world and they hold wealth untellable. It is a place where squirrels rule, and no one dares hunt them. While you all, perfectly capable, smart, squirrels scratch out a living for no other reason than you believe you don't deserve that life and they do."

"So?" Scurrid knew his philosophy was starting to shake in the minds of the others. It was clear their life was hard, and it was not getting better quickly.

"Look at yourselves. How long will you fare this way? And why should you struggle, and they live in prosperity? The truth is, your beloved *master,* Vincent Poppaldi, was not going to free you from anything. He was going to sell you off to the rats up there. Why do you think he never removed you from your chains?"

"Now that I think of it, I do think I might have overheard that. Great Commander, perhaps, but he was sure an opportunist."

"He spit on me." said one. "And he never apologized!"

"Don't be fooled anymore by the legends you've heard on the seas of this vile person. In fact, I know him personally. I was abandoned by him. Threw me overboard like a piece of trash and you know why?" said Black.

"Why?" they asked.

"Because I was one of his crew, and I demanded a fair share of the fortune he was after. And now he's up there livin' it up no doubt, with the rest of his followers eatin' scraps, or worse, in the brig for thinkin' they could join him at the table. Does that sound like the real Vincent to you?"

"You know what? Maybe I just wanted to believe something because I wanted hope. But you've made some good points here, Mr. …?" said Scurrid.

"Barrogan. Barrogan Black. And I'm not done. I told you the difference between slaves and masters is belief. When the whole world believes you're the slave, it's true. But that also means when the whole agrees you're the master, well…you are."

Barrogan went back over to his crew. "There are only slaves and masters and those on their way to being one or the other in this world and you better believe it. I told you I would make you free this night, and I further vow to make you the masters of your world tomorrow."

He went over to his crew, and as they were still tussling to get their tails all free, Barrogan took a stick and drove it into the middle of the knot. The seven of them struggled and pulled but could only make the knot tighter, as Barrogan twisted it so they were all stuck back to back, helpless. They eyed him, too shocked to speak as the used the stick as a handle to maneuver them up the beach and into the thick of the crowd as he pleased, and he released the stick into the crowd.

"Slaves or masters. Your choice. This is my gift to you; my former crew. They are good workers, but it is a sacrifice I am willing to make. This world, as you can tell, is giving no one a break any time soon. Be realistic. Take my offer. You won't get another one."

They paused a long time and no one spoke. Scurrid bent down slowly after a long while and picked up the stick, keeping the shaking rat crew in bondage, saying to them, "Well, let me say what I know we're all thinking, friends, we all want to be free, but life is business. And I'll tell you, I'm tired of being on the unhappy end of it. Nothing personal."

Then, still holding the stick in his paw, he raised his arm, much to the unhappiness of the rats attached to it, for it caused them to bend low, forced into a bowing gesture that to a rat would be most embarrassing.

"Barrogan's right: masters tonight, tomorrow kings!"

The former Happenlings all cheered. But just under his breath, Scurrid asked, "Now, Mr. Black, how are we, numbering only a couple hundred, going to overtake a kingdom?"

Just as they were at the height of their happy yelling, Barrogan whistled, and out into the clearing on all sides stepped the Nicky-nacky tribe by the hundreds—a number none could count.

"I believe you've all likely met," said Barrogan. "Now you have soldiers!"

"How did you get them to follow you?" asked Scurrid.

"Magic. He-he. Now. Anyone of you can stay here. However, follow me, and this time tomorrow you will no longer eat wood chips and straw. But if you betray me, I'll kill you all. Nothing personal."

"You're a shrewd one."

"What can I say, I'm a rat. Now, let's get that windbag Vincent and what's rightfully mine—I mean ours! Ha-ha!" He guffawed. Then the rest of them guffawed. They went on guffawing for a good long while. The tribe squirrels watched, barely understanding what was transpiring, and they asked their chief what was going on. The chief, being perceptive, explained to them all in their native language, "Fathead Redtooth just sold out his own crew to Silverhair Dirtyface to get them to help him go kill the

183

Crazywings. He go big crazy. Better do what Fathead says. Many eat-ums for the gods, big, big harvest forever, no doubt. Oh, and we're all gonna get to take turns stabbing that Vincent guy."

This caused much cheering and elation.

Then the chief said, "Yeah, then we'll kill all these other idiots too, and once we're done with them, let's party!" and they all did, celebrating their impending victory until the wee hours, and then they set out hard and fast for Nearly Mountain.

It was then they met with unexpected company not long into their drive inland. The Happenlings, the Nicky-Nacky Tribe, and the Pirats heard the rush of some airborne legion approaching.

Captain Black held them back with a paw in the air, and they listened. Then, through the trees and out of the cover of night, the Guardians emerged. Unbeknownst to them and the politics of Hesperia, Great Father kept his promise to his dear granddaughter. It was all so unexpected neither party could think much on words. They set upon each other with brave blows. But all the training and might of the Guardians could not overcome the sheer number of the invaders, and they were taken. Barrogan Black knew, however, their cover was blown.

Once the Guardians were beaten and dispatched, Black set them off full speed for the mountain top, for he learned from the first journey and from the tribe squirrels to travel up the river on the North face, rather than around the south bend and through Otterdam.

"Time's up for Hesperia, boys!" he cried, and word of the rise was heard even in Otterdam, where residents shut their doors and cowered, letting the numberless legion pass underneath unchallenged. Some even had the courage to pray under their breath, far from the ears of hateful Telmarus, for the doomed Hesperia, and some cheered. For it was clear to all by the next morning, the Golden City would be ashes.

13: Reckoning

Way back up on the mountain, Vincent sat in a jail cell, staring across at Tiburt. Their attempt to steal the Great Nut did not end well. They were instantly caught the moment they entered the base and were taken blindfolded to an undisclosed location.

"So, um," said Vincent.

"Yeah, we shouldn't have tried to do this without Gy. He's the only one of us with any sense."

"Okay, okay yes, agreed. But what do we do now?"

"Are you asking me, Captain?" Tiburt said, genuinely overjoyed to be finally honored with the solicitation of an opinion. "Why?"

"Never mind. I don't know," said Vincent.

"Oh, wait, I know! We could get Gy to come bail us out!"

"Good idea. Except how do we tell him we're being held in a secret prison in a secret location we're unaware of because it's secret?"

"Ah. Well, we could...I don't know."

"I know," Vincent sighed, then he patted his feather and sash down. He sighed some more. There's not much to do in jail.

Tiburt occasionally raised his paw when he had a new idea, but he never voiced it, and then he just put his paw down again as quickly. Vincent figured he hadn't worked past the problem of no one knowing where they were, including them, and they had no contact with the outside.

"We were so close," muttered Tiburt.

"Yes, supposing only you hadn't kicked that mop bucket over. Or those other eight mop buckets. Or knocked over that rack of armor and that rack of bells. Or, when they stopped us for questioning, you hadn't shouted, 'Oh, don't mind us, we're not stealing the Great Nut.' I think it all this could have helped our situation not to happen. Don't you think?"

Tiburt said nothing.

"Tiburt, don't you think?"

"Yes, okay? I get what you are saying. It's not my fault, I just struggle sometimes controlling my, you know."

"Entire self?"

"Okay."

"Do you think you could magically conjure up some basic sense of discretion?"

"Okay fine. Just leave me alone."

Vincent sighed. "I should have just gotten married."

"Yeah, probably."

"I feel like this is a common occurrence for us."

"Uh, huh."

"Perhaps it wouldn't be if you hadn't started singing in the middle of the court and chasing fireflies absentmindedly while I was trying to hide from the guards."

"Guards! Guards! I demand due process! Amicus curiae! I demand you hear my argument a priori. I demand you give me my right to a good loud yelling, and I demand a divorce, a quo, a fortiori, animus posteriori ergo erratum et cetera and everything else. Please!"

The guards then barged into the cell, thrashed him with a shillelagh, and left before he could say anything else.

Tiburt sat up rubbing his erratum posteriori.

"That's what happens when no one understands what you are saying?" Vincent dug in.

"And what of when no one knows who you are?"

"What does that mean?" Vincent stared at him impatiently.

"I mean—oof!" Tiburt's backside still hurt. "Darn those old squirrels. No one ever lets me say my peace. I mean this. I spoke to you about a palindrome."

186

"Yes, well? Isn't a palindrome just a word that ends the way it begins?"

"Yes and no. You see a word is just a symbol. A palindrome is just a word written in a circle. A symbol, a bit of magic."

"Why is it always magic with you."

"A palindrome isn't always just a word. Anything can be, if it ends the way it begins, and here's the real secret. Everything ends the way it begins because everything is a circle. You will realize the truth and meaning of your life when the pattern comes into view."

"When the pattern comes into view. When will that be?"

"I can't say."

"Of course, you can't."

"It's not for me to say, only to tell you, once it happens, everything will become clearer."

"My life began in a boat. So, it will end in a boat? Well, you're wrong there because I got off of it." But he shuddered under his coat.

Tiburt threw his paws up and drew silent.

"Some prophet you are."

"To prophesy and to speak the true truth is but one and the same, Gethsarade."

Gethsarade, too shocked just at hearing his own name, looked at him but said nothing.

Tiburt went on. "This kind of magic is not to be fooled with. Dark magic and light magic are the same—just depends on what you do with them. But you don't mix them. You don't get what you want when you do. No one does. You will make everyone the enemy of yourself."

"Maybe you're the enemy."

"I will be if I have to be against the evil you are doing. You must tell her. I mean this not as a prophet but as your friend."

"Oh, shut up. You have only looked out for yourself since you got here."

"We all three have, but you are looking at danger."

"Says the prophet of nothing."

"You know me so well, apparently. Do I know you? Maybe I'm just along for the ride. Maybe there's more magic in the world than you think."

"I won't even act like I understood that. Know what? You think you are this inexorable sorcerer, but you might find out when you least expect someone's been sorcering you."

They sat in silence, then after what seemed like an hour, the sound of a key clanking in a lock startled them. Suddenly, there were several guards in the room, standing outside the jail cell.

"Take him, guards! It was all his idea, so spare me!" they both shouted, then eyed each other. The guards stood silent, and they all stared at one another, some a little confused, but yet all disapprovingly.

Slowly through the still open door hobbled Great Father. "Shut up." He eyed them and tapped his cane.

As the guards unlocked their cells, to the amazement and confused joy of Tiburt and Vincent, Great Father hobbled back out the door, out the jail, and into the boughway. Everyone followed, including the warden.

"Sir, I strongly advise against this. These miscreants need to be brought to trial and shown who they are and what they've done here to the entire world," said the warden.

"Shut up. The first shut up was pre-emptive."

Being unlocked and unchained, Vincent took the opportunity to stride up to the old dog,

"Sir, I must object to such characterizations, as we were just out for a stroll and shooting the breeze. It was pure chance we came upon this place. I promise this will never happen again."

"Oh, stop being so dramatic. Trespassing is a misdemeanor. You were only trespassing. You probably would have gotten away with it if you hadn't brought your idiot friend. You're one of us. Right?" he turned to the warden. "My good citizen, you must understand this is all a grave misunderstanding."

"Sir, they are like the snake Sangareth—"

"No, he is not like Sangareth at all. You must understand. This Vincent is of such noble mind. His intentions are of totally different context than that scoundrel."

"But he is blood to that one."

"No, the interpretation is wrong."

"No, it's not, it's a prophecy! It says—."

"You fool, I wrote it! Is it not said, 'blood is thicker than water, but loyalty is thicker than blood'? I am loyal to him. He is my future son-in-law, and that is who he is, never mind anything else. I am elder Knight here and he has earned my trust, which means he has earned yours."

So, the guards said nothing more to their high commander and went back to their posts.

"Thank you," said Vincent, but Great Father Tadwick whirled around, stuck a finger practically up Vincent's nose and said, "You opportunistic little twerp! You better not cross me again. I did this because you are betrothed to my granddaughter and I've got plans for you, too. If I find out I am wrong, and you are like the foolish Sangareth, and you hurt my lovely little girl, I will find you wherever you go and I will chase you to the pillars of the earth, just like I did to him. The ignorant ones speak of a hero. Well, they got it wrong. I saved this town, and I will do it again. Now, get out of here before I order you shorn and spoliated, and try not to screw anything else up!"

"Of concern for your kin, this all was...I appreciate your help in all this, but tell me, was the same welfare in mind when you announced our wedding plans? Or, excuse me, I mean your wedding plans? Am I right in assuming this arrangement was all about you?"

"You have no idea what it is like to run a realm. You couldn't. There is no such thing as private concerns; you do what's best for your city in all ways. And wait long enough, just wait. You are not being granted anything. This life is a curse you will soon come to know as well as we do. Of course, you could always just go back to your big important adventures out in the wide world, I'm sure. But your only option here is to do as I say now or else I will tell them all what tonight was about. You want to run this game like your fath..." he cut off and turned away.

"What does that mean? What do you know about all this? Tell me! And why do you believe so well he's my father? Tell me what you know!" But the shouting went unanswered. Great Father simply disappeared into the night.

Gethsarade and Tiburt said nothing more and went back to the town, both going their own way.

Gy was at the door to meet him. "Well, sorry about Tiburt, as he just gets so passionate when he comes up with some new crazy conspiracy idea. I honestly don't know where he got this name you speak of. I'm sure he'll be fine once he blows off some steam. So, what's the plan now, Captain?" he asked after Vincent filled him in.

The Captain forgot for a moment that was one of his titles. "Oh, I don't know. It was a one-shot deal. Now I'll marry off, I suppose, before I can work out another crack at that nut."

"Not such a bad thing. Not such a bad thing at all. Just another kind of treasure. Tell me," he paused.

The Captain stopped smirking sheepishly at the floor. "Do you think she's worth it? Do you think she's…the one?"

"Well, I hadn't thought about it, but I suppose I do hold feelings for her." Then he caught his breath, "She's wonderful, actually. She's strong, far stronger in mind than I ever knew one could be. Being with her makes me so happy." He reflected for a moment, Gy nodding at him with an enthusiastic half-grin on his face, but he was still waiting for Vincent to answer his question.

Vincent fell silent for a moment and then said, "Well, tell you what, I'll get up and meet you back here in the morning before dawn, and let's try to talk and see if we can't take one last shot at that treasure and be off this log. Does this sound sound?"

He patted Gy's shoulder and turned to leave, but his friend was crestfallen. Vincent, for whatever reason, had not picked up on the signal.

"Well, something I've been meaning to tell you, Captain, is I sort of, kind of, found someone myself." He was the one now being sheepish, scratching the back of his head and raising his eyebrows in hopes Vincent might give his blessing.

"What? Are you leaving me then? What'll I do with only Tiburt as my crew? You are coming with us right, still? Right?"

Gy's face fell even further.

"I mean, you aren't going to let this sudden relationship prevent you from achieving our goal, are you?"

"I'm sorry, I didn't realize that you were the only one with rights to change the plan by finding love, Captain."

"What, who said love? I didn't say I love her. I mean, we have only known each other a couple of days."

"But I can see it in your eyes, Captain, so be honest. I been thinking a lot tonight since we got up to do this. I mean, look at everything we've both found here. How much is that compared to a hunk of gold? I thought if you were getting married and settling down, then we were kind of maybe gonna stay here. It's better than anything either of us ever been, Tiburt too, ain't it? Well, ain't it?"

Vincent stood, realizing so much.

"I mean I know what we came here to do, but I just thought…."

"Never mind what you thought." Vincent popped. "All of this I was doing was just a play to get the treasure. You would know if you had only asked me."

"I didn't know I needed to ask you."

"Well, you should've known. Now you need to decide."

There was a long pause, during which the Great Vincent barely withstood the time he held his gaze into the hurt eyes of Gy, whom he could tell was searching hard for a crack in his resolve, the kind of resolve he now knew a squirrel should bear as a leader and was all too eager for practice.

But that was not what Gy searched for. He was not trying to convince the squirrel he had come to know as his best friend, even above the better-meaning Tiburtine, to change his mind. No, a good squirrel knows when a good squirrel's mind is made.

Gy searched for a long time, and this great leader he had come to so admire was suddenly being so incredibly, unbelievably, and undeniably selfish. And he was trying to get over the shock of being so let down by someone he so admired.

Gy said finally, "I'm heading back to bed, Captain." To bed he went, and that was all there was to that.

14: That Awful Name

He dragged himself out of bed and into the pub after a highly unsleepful hour.

"Good morning," said the bartender.

"How do you know what kind of a morning I'm having?" said Vincent.

The bartender, who seemed a good-natured chap, just smiled and poured.

Vincent drank, trying to figure out what to do with his day, the last day of his freedom. *Don't they usually throw some kind of party for this?* He thought about perhaps spending some time practicing. His wings were still very awkward. But now knowing how to use his wings and not being afraid to fly anymore might help him get along better in town after the — *no, idiot, you're trying not to think about that.*

He thought perhaps he could convince Amalie to go with him. With this new confirmation of Sangareth looking more and more like his father, he now had new questions, like, what are the odds? And he discovered within himself a new motivation to be the hero he was told by the teachings his father could have been.

He thought of going to talk to Amalie. *Oh, but each one I talk to makes me completely change my mind! I cannot make it up this way! What does the poem say?*

But then he had the compound problem. If he did fulfill this, someone would object to his false identity and he would be forced to explain everything else, along with his real intentions. Or just run away penniless. Bah. Rather take another cliff wall to the face.

He considered the idea that the poem meant for him to continue his journey since the situation about maintaining his identity was becoming increasingly less ideal. *Oh, fiddles, and I never thought my name would ever mean more to anyone than Vincent. I never knew my name was written down anywhere anyone would see! Maybe I should just tell everyone the truth, for that would certainly end it all. And then if I live at all, it would be back to Faro, if I could even live with the shame of memory. Oh, what to do!*

Then he heard a familiar voice, "You've got to tell her," said Tiburt, who stood in the back, having plucked up and brought himself over to confront Vincent. He instinctively noted a scant populace in the bar, just the regulars.

Tiburt said it again, as he closed the door to the pub, preparing for full-on confrontation. Everyone there watched, but no one said anything. He tapped his glass. But as Vincent glanced about, the bartender caught his eye and gave a wink, and he realized the bartender was not the same one he knew before, and suddenly didn't seem so good-natured anymore.

Tiburt distracted him back, "You've got to tell her. The hero has a name, and Vincent is not it." He leaned into Gethsarade's ear, "I can read, you know I saw your doiley before landfall."

Then he said it a little louder, "I saw it."

Again. "I saw it. You knew all along and yet you still lied?"

"That is what you think?"

"I saw the name, that ridiculous name. I saw it and, at first, I laughed and thought it was a puzzle. But I learned better. We found the book, and I knew right then."

"You knew what?"

Tiburt backed up so everyone could hear.

"I knew you were nothing but a self-interested coward. You knew exactly what you were doing this whole time, planned it from the beginning, and got us wrapped up in it. You could have chosen anytime to be who you were born to be, but I will show them. Now, you are implicated. Found out! I thought I would give you a chance because Gy asked me to, but he doesn't know everything."

"And you do?"

"About magic, yes."

"Oh, magic again?"

"Yes, magic. And you know exactly what I mean. It's not about making sparks fly from sticks or leaping into the air from brooms. It's about making them *think* it is. Magic, dark magic, is about power. Not having it, as you know, but if one can make someone think you do, by all means, you do. Or it could also basically mean just kind of generally being a liar. But I am too smart for that and for you."

"I can't do this metaphor anymore. You are a deluded lunatic, Tiburt. I don't know what else to tell you. You've assumed everything from nothing."

"Nothing? How is this for nothing?" He reached into his jacket, but when he did, several of the others present, who had been hiding and watching in the shadows, reached into theirs.

After a tense moment, Tiburt slowly held up the rag Gethsarade normally kept in his boot. Gethsarade snatched it back, for it was from his beloved old mama, but not before everyone saw. There was only one conclusion. All onlookers knew something else, too: the last of the Sons of Sangareth was just made.

Tiburt, who had not read the room, continued. "This foul creature here possesses the name of the hero your books prophesied about. He holds the name and was born with it, but I tell you, my friends, he is no hero."

Several of them stood, and one asked, "What do you mean? Is he or is he not the son of Sangareth?"

Gethsarade sat thinking while Tiburt went on stating his case. "Oh, he is by line, but not by principle. This son is corrupted, not unlike some believe the one of old to be. I have heard all these conversations. I have heard all your legends over these few days of how this town is divided all over who he was."

"Well, I tell you now who is right and who is wrong. And no matter, for I present to you someone with no intention of fulfilling the birthright and destiny you claim him to have. For he has come here under the guise of someone else. You all believed it until now."

194

"There, in his own paw is his true name and the proof of his lies and deception. He has told me himself of how, like Sangareth, he would sooner take over this town and seize all power for himself for the sake of money than embrace his true destiny."

"He planned to steal the Great Nut, as some we now know rightly did. We thought he was here to save us, but we were wrong, all wrong, and they were right. Sangareth was evil, and as so is he."

Half of those in the bar were standing, and the other half sat motionless, as if holding their breaths.

"Let me see," said Great Father Tadwick, coming out of nowhere. He had been waiting in the back, staking out the Sons of Sangareth as they had staked him out right back.

Vincent and crew were still unaware of the full politics of Hesperia. They had found Persimmonia and walked into the middle of a silent standoff, running for as long as anyone could remember. The Sons did their business there and kept cover, always careful not to reveal themselves to the wrong squirrel. But now everyone took a step back, for the game was up.

Great Father snatched the cloth out of Gethsarade's paw, turned it over and over and read it to himself, then read it out loud. Then he finally said, "How do we know this is real?"

"What?"

"You say this is damning evidence. How do we know you didn't just make this to give yourself an out, young compatriot, if your little plan didn't work out? This, by itself, proves nothing."

Tiburt stumbled over his words for a moment. All this while Gethsarade had been thinking, and he had come to a conclusion: *Something's got to give, a right and proper sacrifice,* he reassured himself. *This must be the time. So be it.*

"Let me ask you, Tiburt. What would a villain do in this situation? Would I deny, deny, deny? Or would I confirm it all, reveal my evil plan, and find the first chance to run?" He paused for effect. Performance art was his thing, after all. "I think, Great Father, we know the truth is not so simple, is it?"

"No! The truth is the simplest thing there is! Why, you two are in cahoots! That's why you're against me, why just a while ago, you...," said Tiburt.

195

"We what?" said the Captain.

Tiburt was stymied.

"Curious to know what your so-called dirt on me is, I really am…. Great Father is also curious, I'm sure. But perhaps you just don't understand the truth. Even while it is the simplest thing there is." He stood at the bar next to Great Father Tadwick, the leader of the Army of Elorus, and reclined on his elbow.

He now realized he could not keep the illusion up forever and sighed in resignation.

"But still, I don't want to do this, Tib."

"I must admit, You're the third-greatest sorcerer I've ever known," said Tiburt, but Vincent knew it was not a compliment. "Second only to me, and I only to Mouse-tradamus!"

"Funny you mention mice as you are one!" He went over and with an easy jerk removed the furry covering Tiburt had been wearing over his tail all the time. This time it was Tiburt who stood without speaking.

"It pains me to do this, but now everyone must know it is actually you, Tiburt, who has lied to this good town, and you have been made. Without another syllable of your sorcery and propaganda-isms, I, by my martial authority granted as a member of the Army of Elorus, condemn you to the deepest most silent reaches of the prison in Promises' End!"

Five squirrels took off their outer coats to reveal themselves as Eloran Guards and took him by the arms.

"Ack! Why, why are you doing this to me?" Tiburt shouted, and then broke out into laborious sobs. "Why, why, why. I'm so sorry. Why!" he sobbed openly and without abashment, but the Captain held firm, in spite of a quivering lip, as he knew he must make a right and proper sacrifice to get his prize and make off with the Great Nut.

"That rat was poisoning all our minds, Poppaldi, and you are our hero again," Tiburt heard over the feinting and pathetic whimpers of his once friend as he was carried off to suffer and make his spells in futility.

Tiburt was taken down to the jail, all the way to the depths of Promise's End, weeping and begging for the forgiveness of one who could no longer hear his cries.

"Aye, mate. What yew in fowah?" said some surly sod after the jail door shut.

"Leave me alone."

"Doesn't seem like he wants to talk, Bubby."

Tiburt broke down into tears once again.

"What's ya name, bo? Oi, I'm Algern, and he's Erl. There's Carl. We have really cool code names, but I don't think there's any point in them now. Did you ever hear of the Sons of Sangareth?"

They all bowed gracefully, as did Tiburt. When he looked up there was not a pawful, but a legion in front of him. They were still emerging from the dark; some had been in prison so long they were emaciated and decrepit.

"Soh. What yew in for?"

"I was betrayed by the untouchable Captain Vincent Poppaldi, leader of the...."

"You don't say."

"No, I do, I just said it."

"Yeah, he screwed us over, too," said another who rose in the back and came forward.

"You don't say," said Tiburt.

"Call me Stag."

Back at the tavern, Vincent walked out with Great Father, amidst the aghast looks of those he now recognized as the ones who had taken him captive, at least some of them.

"Up, boys, and let's go. I think we know what we're all dealing with here," said the captain of the Guard, turning to face the others.

"You are all under arrest."

"On what charge?" challenged one of the Sons.

"On the charge of revolt by attacking the Guardians while working under orders to secure our borders and their murder."

They were all too shocked to speak for, of course, they were innocent. As the door closed behind Gethsarade and Father Tadwick, the rest of the patrons all put up their paws and resigned themselves to prison in their silent horror, undone, The last blow of defeat was dealt to the Sons of Sangareth in their own hideout at the paw of the one they trusted to bring them honor and victory.

"I cannot thank you enough, again Great Father."

"Good work...Captain Poppaldi." He spied about and gave him a look. Captain Vincent understood, nodded, and they parted.

Vincent went home amidst the rising cheers of others for the deed of exposing a liar and a witch; indeed, the whole poisonous crew of the Sons, as they were paraded about in public all the way down.

But as he started to make his way to the inn, retiring victorious from the day and relieved at finally making up his mind, he was stopped by Gy.

"So, this is how it is, then? Abandon with all abandon, your friends, your home?" Gy stood steadfast between him and the way. "You know he ain't done nothin' to you."

"It's a sacrifice I had to make, Gy. I promise you'll understand when this is all over. He was going to get in the way of the plan. All of it will work out."

"I think you're just enjoying this. We should have been gone long ago."

Then before Vincent could reply, Great Father appeared, having been watching from the back, realizing something had better be done about Gy as well.

He said with a voice thunderous, "You need to let this happen. Or else you may stand implicated, young Gy. This is our law, stand with the accused or stand against, there is no other way to stand."

The commander looked on a bit surprised, but glad for this more fortunate turn, only he had begun to grow increasingly suspicious as to why Father Tadwick was helping him at all, much less in every possible way.

Gy was silent for a moment. Then he spoke, "You know as well as I, Cap. He ain't done nothing wrong and, as a matter of fact, he ain't done nothing to nobody. Nobody!" He waved his paw at all the crowd, and they gasped at his boisterousness.

The commander put up his palms to calm him, which proved most ineffective and their tails all twitched quite tensely.

Vincent spoke in low tones, "Gy, look, I know, he was my friend, too, but I am in position here to uphold now, and one has to do things one does not like when they are in a position as mine. Now, I wouldn't have done this if there was anything else I could do. I tell you the truth. But I promise I will take care of everything."

"How about a fair trial?"

"But here are the facts!" The old one held up a facsimile tail, a rather roughshod, wraggly thing to make off to everyone as a disguise. Now everyone took a real look at it. The murmurers confirmed to themselves that this was open and shut.

"Blood is blood, and a rat is a rat and there is nothing else to discuss. No one else here is on trial," said Vincent.

"Maybe that's the problem," said Gy.

"What are you trying to say?"

"I'm saying you ain't who I thought you was if you can do somethin' like this."

"You have no clue who I am."

"Truest thing I heard all day." He walked off, and they all went home shaking their heads at Gy's poor, poor, overburdened system of reality.

The Great Vincent went off alone. He spat on the bough, raging in himself, They just don't understand, they don't understand the burden of destiny, of greatness. I am the Great Vincent... He hung his head down, for he had finally remembered he was not something he was not.

Then there was the rag he kept in his boot. He pulled it out and unfurled it and examined it in the moonlight. "Gethsarade, my last of hopes, my hero," it read, for the Lady Ridroga had stitched over the scrawled the letters with her own paw to preserve them long, long ago.

Oh my, mama, he thought. *What do you want me to do? You told me to find my destiny. I didn't listen, did I? Am I on the precipice now? In this moment of lucidity, mama, am I stepping into the door of madness when one actually believes one's own deceptions? I only went this way because it was made of me when there was no other way. Now it seems there is no other way but...* and with that he turned and went the other way, taking off into the air, albeit awkwardly, as fast as he could.

A few minutes passed, and he stood at the door of the house of Tadwick, knocking and panting. And a few moments later, Amalie stood before him.

"Good morning. What are you doing here? We can't," she said.

"I'm just trying to sort things. It's all coming apart. Would you come away with me? I just want to talk."

"Sorry, other plans," she said as she didn't want to say she was helping with the wedding decorations. "Anyhow, we're not supposed to see each other before the, you-know-what."

"I'm certain you and I are well acquainted by now, so when have either of us been accused of concern for social propriety?"

"I am and always will be concerned with my duties. Thank you," Amalie said.

"I didn't refer to your duties, for duty and propriety are seriously different ideas," he said, "Let's just get out of here."

She looked about and said, "I can get away for probably 10 good minutes."

She popped back in and then out again, making sure no one saw her grab her coat, and they scurried off somewhere quiet. All the while as they walked and sometimes flew, straying from sight, Vincent, talked distractedly of the surroundings and on and on about the pressures and pains upon him.

When they arrived behind a grove on the back of the property, she sat down with him and said with a smile, "I understand, very much. I do. But that's Hesperia for you."

"How do you manage it? You've been here your whole life, whereas I've been in this place only several days and I am clawing at my brains to get out of here."

Again, she laughed and he didn't.

Then she just sighed and said, "I could never leave this place. There is too much history here. Plus, my family. I am confident things will work out for the better. They always do."

200

All of this was just playing the part, of course, for after a lifetime of watching the opera of her elite life this was merely a lady's way of asking to be persuaded.

"You don't understand." He put his paws to his face for a moment, and Amalie instinctively caressed his shoulder to comfort him.

"Tiburt, my friend since the inception of this adventure, my friend...I just came from sending him to jail," he put his head back in his paws. He liked being comforted by her. "Would you believe Tiburtine is a rat?"

"He's always been honest to me."

"No, I mean, he's physically a rat. His tail was a fake, a coverup. The shock of it all. I am betrayed, and on top of all of it, I suspected his intentions all along were to gather others against me. He tried to take the Great Nut of Hesperia for himself. But to usurp my skills and prowess as a commander to infiltrate this place and then upend it all? He spoke such awful, vicious lies, and I dare not repeat them."

"What did he say?"

"Well, first..."

"Never mind, if you are revolted by even uttering it, I won't bereave you by belaboring it. You are soon to be my husband, after all, and we are to trust each other completely."

"Yes."

"I shall reassure you," she interrupted him again, "If any part of what you said was true, then you are absolutely in the right and your actions constituted a worthy sacrifice for the good and safety of Hesperia; you did the right thing. If you are to dwell, dwell on that."

"Those words. Why does they feel so wrong?"

"Because you are good, and because of that you care not just about the right thing but about your once friend. That is not bad. But you're a protector now, and you have a solemn vow to uphold, and you upheld it."

"But he was my friend all the same. I don't know what am I protecting if I am alone. Only myself?" he said.

"All the time I am seeking only the fate of another. I know now what he meant, for this is definitely not what I want, and yet I can't stop myself even now. This is not who I am or how could this not be for I have done it? Oh, I'm so lost."

He looked up with what she could not decide was either a pang of regret, whatever it could mean, or perhaps the spark of affection. But she remembered herself before he finally quit his blubbering and looked at her again. "Do you ever want to just…get out of here?"

"We are already far from the house."

"You misunderstand me. I mean don't you ever just want to leave all this behind and go off to live free of all this?"

"I had never dreamed of it," she said, but what she meant was doing such a thing was the life-sustaining hope of her constrained existence.

"Do you not want this? I mean, what's wrong with life here in Hesperia?" she asked, testing him.

"Nothing." He lied. She waited for consolation. His resolve could not fade so soon before the big day.

"I do want this," he said, which, of course, meant: *no, this is absolutely not what I want. I want to run away screaming.* "I will be fine."

"I think I hear the approach of Great Father and his entourage, for he comes about this way over by the south. I come here so I can see him coming without being seen. But I must go. I am so, so sorry to leave you this way. I will see you in the morning?"

"Yes, my dear. I mean, yes, I will see you in the morning."

She made sure she was clear to leave but turned back and said, "You are not alone." This obviously meant, *I love you, and I shall forever, if you would but take my paw tomorrow.* She decided to take his last words as a means of comforting her, and with a final expression of piercing sincerity, she took off.

"Of course, and thank you." and at the end of his saying this, he had to stop himself from uttering those fateful words when lovers are unduly parted: *goodbye, my love.* But, of course, to say what one means is quite never appropriate. But for a brief moment, and against all the odds, he realized he actually meant he would be there in the morning.

Amalie was just in time to meet Great Father Tadwick at the door, "Afternoon, Great Father," she took his elbow.

"You are not to go out tonight. Stay home and prepare for tomorrow, your big day."

He continued, "Something is amiss, for the division I sent to repair the *Tara Feen* has neither returned nor reported to me. No worry, I am sure all is very well. It could be anything. It did give me a pretext to exact a victory on another front.

"It was all thanks to you. You really pulled one over on that Poppaldi pinhead. Granted, he did a lot of the work himself. Why, he even turned out his own friend."

"I thought I was going to be hiding in corners picking out the spies of that ruddy bunch for years to come. But he, the dunce! He walked in and blew them all out of the water in one turn. I tell you, you were wise to induct him, bring him into the fold, while still an outsider, for he has proven one thing: a fool simply wanders lost. But give a fool just enough wisdom to make him dangerous, and he will destroy everything in his path. Brilliant! Anyhow, are you excited?"

"About Tiburt?" she hadn't been paying attention to him.

"No, about marrying Vincent. Was this not the arrangement? Are you well, dear?"

"No, I mean, was it Tiburt he sent to prison?"

"Why, yes, and how did you know?"

"Well, he only has two friends. It wasn't a hard guess."

"True, true. Yes, it seems little Tiburt was not just a little small and fat for a squirrel. He is a rat, masquerading as a squirrel so as to work his way into our society and destroy it from the inside, I'll wager."

"Tiburt would do something like that?" she feigned her shock at having heard this news for the second time.

"My dear, you can't put anything past someone who is already past everything you've got. Anyhow, enough. We're home. And I've missed so many preparations, I should like to see what's been done."

This conversation was had in front of all those present in the household. For the next one, Amalie politely excused herself and requested a moment with Great Father.

As soon as they were out of shot of eyes and ears, she bonked him on the head. "What were you thinking by arranging this! I'm not to be farmed out by you."

"Do you love him?"

"Yes, but that's not the point. I'm saying, it's supposed to be my choice."

"Then marry and trust me. All will come in due time. I mean you no harm, but please trust me. I order you."

"I need to go to him. There is business to which we must attend."

"Darling, you know you can't see him now, as there are too many decisions you must make here, are there not? Is this not something you want?"

"I told you he was a suitable suitor, which is not to say I wanted to sidle up with him for all of time. I didn't know you intended to make me find out about my own wedding by way of the morning news cycle."

"Don't you want to sidle, as you say? I do say, it seems I know my little girl better than she knows herself."

"That's none of your business! And you are entirely too direct for my level of comfort about this."

"Charming, but we've still have the preparations for tomorrow, my girl. You should go on now."

She broke down, "Yes, Great Father."

She walked timidly back into the foyer, and then Great Father burst in after her, "I just remembered, I needed to tell you something, dear. Please, sit."

She did not.

"I thought I had to get to my business, choppity-chip," she said.

"It can wait a moment," he said. She did not move.

"Anyhow, something has come to my attention about this character, Vincent. He is a person of interest in many parts of the world. I don't want him gallivanting off to some ordeal, leaving you a widow in your youth."

"It is my sincere hope he stays here, but here his very name is tainted now with the accusations of Tiburtine the turn-tail Tabbit. I don't want such a stain to follow him either. No, I wish the both of you the best, but now he will carry the rumors and ramifications of his past and all his monikers into your life and become a matter of constant worry for you."

"And you?" she finished. "How can you call him a fool in one breath and then in the next seek his loyalty?"

"I meant he was a fool in the general sense like all young squirrels, but doesn't mean they're not useful," he winked. She rolled her eyes. "But Tiburt has cut his name deep this day with accusations and rumors I fear will follow his name, and thus you, until your dying days. Something must be done."

She moved about a bit, agitated and eyeing him ironically, and then stopped in the middle of the room and stamped her foot, prompting the onlookers to immediately leave, for in the realm of Hesperia, it is improper to stand about with an angry lady in the room.

Her tail seethed and twitched at Great Father.

"This is outrageous. How could lovely Tiburtine make such wild accusations after all Commander Poppaldi has done for this town? I can't believe Tiburt, bless his troubled heart, would try to go and taint his name. Pot calling the kettle crazy, too, with everything he's hidden in plain sight. A rat, true."

The old Great Father nodded but said nothing for a moment, and Amalie did not realize in her furor that he was taking the time to choose his words wisely.

"Speaking of names and such, I know you adore your future husband, and he is indeed a good boy if even a bit troubled."

"He's great."

"Well, I had something I wanted to say. I don't think you should take his name."

"What?" Now, it should be noted, after all her acts, she decided during the night and after her last meeting with Vincent that she indeed truly loved him. So now she intended to convince him after describing her dream of being away from this place forever, of sailing the world with him and having all sorts of adventures. She now understood he was not the savior of the realm of Hesperia, but the savior of her.

"Now, I didn't mean it to say you should not marry him. I mean to say, I don't think you should take his name, but I wouldn't stop you from marrying him, love. There is a difference, and there is a reason."

He turned for a moment and then turned back, "Actually, I think I must demand this thing. As your Grand and Great Father both, I command that you may never marry Vincent unless he takes the name of the Tadwick family, so he may find acceptance in this place, not as an outsider coming in, but indeed one of us."

"So, what if he's an outsider? He's a superb outsider, a pure-hearted outsider as I discovered, and you intend to keep him here forever as your puppet and make him like you."

"Do you think truly so? I mean for all the squirrels to show up at the door of this city in all the world it should be Vincent Poppaldi the intrepid, and albeit with no army? To do what again? Get married and settle down, make puppies and smack on biscuits? Forgive me if it sounds a little strange."

He only said this to throw Amalie off the scent of his true intentions. In Hesperia, it was actually not common to expect incredible adventurers and heroes to settle down there, as they believed and reminded themselves everyday they all lived in Hesperia. Such a thing is not uncommon anywhere neighbors don't get out of town much.

"You're jealous. Someone better than you comes along, and you can't handle it, given such an ego you always had," said she.

"You don't understand the politics of this place yet, dear, as you are young. But I assure you, you will."

"Don't give me that naive youth crap!" she waggled her tail in a battle pose, "You only think about yourself! You just want to keep your line going because all you ever had was daughters."

He waved his paws in front of him, acting more amused than perturbed, because he was actually the opposite. "You've got this all wrong, dear, please."

"No! I refuse to live my life under your shadow! I refuse. Furthermore, and out of curiosity, I don't suppose you would want me to confront my love immediately, would you? I thought not. He should, and ought, to fly off screaming this instance."

"Now, I know, It's not the kind of card you want to deal first. You could wait, say, until you were ready to sign your names, and once the parson asked in the official manner, you could say something like, 'oh, it's all right.' That's something he wouldn't want to say anything against, you know, and it is soft, but firm. Please, understand, dear, it's all for the best, and you will thank me in the years to come. Don't worry, I'll be there with you all the way through and make sure you aren't alone."

"Read me well: I will have my wedding day on my terms," she threw her cider into the fire and started out.

Thereby, he lost his patience and thrust his chest forward in indignation, "You shall keep my name or you shall NEVER MARRY! My word is FINAL!"

He stormed out without another word, because in their world, they both knew it was indeed true. Everyone heard and the help staff all peeked in, expressing their compassion silently as they knew as well as Amalie that to defy him would be to defy the face of the Earth itself as concerned Hesperia. To be a Tadwick was to be chained forever to the legacy and burden in this one place, a prison. For to be a master in Hesperia to her was to be no less a slave than any bilge-creature. She sank down to the floor in tears.

At the inn, Gethsarade never went to sleep that night. He had not been alone since he could remember. His friends had been his constant companions for months at sea. In the three days they were in Hesperia, they had either been by his side or Amalie's. But now it was the day before the wedding, a thing which three days ago would have been inconceivable to him. Four days ago, he had entirely different plans, plans to be retired on some beach by now, partying it out. But now, five days since they had unwittingly landed in this realm, they had been all but torn apart.

That night, the night before the wedding, he concocted a plan, *I know, I shall simply take Amalie with me and go off forever. If*

I stay here, I will just end up wrapped up in all this like everyone else. His thoughts turned to Amalie: *Maybe she really loves me, but I don't know, and I don't know what I don't know. Everyone lies to everyone here. This is all such a charade. Geth-charade. Maybe I'll have another go.*

He laughed to himself on the way, now realizing how silly his name could sound to a stranger, not having heard it himself in his own head for so long. *Oh well, maybe I won't need to worry about this anymore. There has to be some way out of all this lying, and if I can take the chance, I better take it now.*

He picked some flowers to go and surprise Amalie by climbing up to her window and, all the way he practiced what he would say. "My Amalie," he whispered as he flew, "I know this is so inappropriate, but my dear, won't you please go with me? I'm so tired of all these politics. Can we not simply go and make a name for ourselves somewhere far away and grander than this place? Elope with me, please. Let us go now before our wedding night, let us steal away forever where no one would track us. Let's just go. Marry me, right now. I love you."

He climbed up to the trellis with pansies in his paw and was about to knock but heard something, so he stopped for a moment and listened at the window.

"Oh! What a horrid animal! I can't believe it!"

"What is the matter, Amalie?!" shouted the servants, struggling to prepare her for bed as she rambled about. Their consolations seemed muffled glurbs in comparison to Amalie's and Gethsarade could barely hear what they said.

"That's it!" he heard her cry, "It's that terrible, ugly name again, so stop saying it! I can't get away from his name. No, I'm not just talking about that, I'm talking about him! Now look what I've gotten myself into. Marriage! For sham and for shame! He's finally sunk his filthy claw into me and I'll be hearing it for the rest of my life now. How do you deal with that? No, I NEVER had a choice! Great Father arranged all of this, it was all his idea, don't you see? He's going to be right there everywhere I go and I will stand for everything that name stands for, and I'll never get away. I'll never get away from that horrible, awful, doggish, brutish, slavering, conniving, corrupt and indolent shell of a squirrel. I have to, though. I know now, I must. This is my solemn duty, and as long as I live, I will never leave this place. I will die burdened with this curse." She sobbed quietly and they comforted her with coos and whimpers.

He stepped away from the door in shock, not seeing her silent sobs from behind the curtains, but only hearing her. *The name isn't that ugly is it? Perish should she discover my real name. Am I so disgusting, no one should desire me unless it was forced upon them? My goodness, after all, she never actually said she loved me, did she? It was all a lie!*

He thought for a moment about bursting in to defend the last bit of his dignity, but after a moment thought better of it. If she hated him so much and so secretly, being creepy and ugly right out in the open would only solidify it. So, he left the flowers on the step, stepped off scowling, and did not look back.

After the end of a few more sobbing rants, she threw open the windows to get some fresh air. Should she be so surprised? It was his way after all—everything for Hesperia and what is good for the golden goose is the same for the gander.

But she never realized that just a moment ago her hero was there to make his whispered dreams to her alone come true, once and all, had she just kept her fool mouth shut. She looked out onto the sea, miles off down the mountain, and cursed into the lonely night air wishing for somewhere to breathe.

It was then she saw a paw-full of flowers, wrecked upon the balcony deck, trembling in the cold breeze, and she wondered what they meant.

At the same time, far below her, there was a stirring in the dark—a shadow unseen. A farmer whose simple-minded ideals had him out in tending the soil at that completely insensible hour and watching for critters who might come digging around for a midnight meal. He had a reputation to uphold, after all. Couldn't be turning up a low crop now.

Then his vigilance was for once rewarded, for there was a creature over past the row-posts but hard to see. In a moment more, they were upon him.

15: A Heart of Cold

Early in the morning at the bridal shower, Amalie went on and on at her vanity, saying she was so excited to get away from the Tadwick name and its politics forever and go off into the world for once in a lifetime and have all kinds of romantic adventures.

"Are you feeling any better today, Amalie?" said one of the maidens.

"Much better, for I am getting married!"

"You are and it's so exciting!" they squealed and giggled the giggles of dray-kits whose lives finally crossed paths with one living out their own fairy-tale dreams.

"Isn't Vincent too dangerous?" they asked, but she giggled.

"Sometimes, a true hero must be prepared to appear as an enemy. And besides, the danger is to not be one's self. I had a thought about it, and I'm not so mad now, for I know my Vincent will go anywhere with me, so it doesn't matter what we call ourselves while we're here." It seemed to the maidens she had made peace with herself.

Through the door of the bedroom and downstairs, there was a commotion heard. It sounded as though Great Father's presence was being requested for something as usual during days of family importance. She sighed, but then her eyes lit up with the realization that if Great Father were not there, he could not force his will upon the nuptials.

But just as the full plan came to her mind, Amalie and the bridesmaids heard a faint chiming. The bell! And just at that, someone broke into the room shouting, "The Great Nut is missing! And there's a fire!" And she ran out with half her makeup on, foolish girl. Then she thought for a moment, and ran back to her dresser, throwing it open and feeling for the key in her dress she wore to see him yesterday—gone.

Then, running to a balcony window, Amalie peered out of her room and took off for where the maids and household help house knew not, but she knew she was heading for the coast.

16: To Elderwood

Earlier, before sunrise....

After his moment on the balcony, he had stolen off finally with a single purpose in mind. Before he left for the base under the cover of darkness to get the Great Nut, however, he had stopped by the inn to summon Gy.

"Come, I am leaving, and I need my first mate."

"Can't."

"I'm asking you to come share in eternal and endless wealth with me. I will have the Great Nut in my grasp tonight. Come on!"

"I'm sorry."

"What do you mean you're sorry? You'll be sorry. It's time we're off, so let's go. I'm leaving as there's nothing else for me here, no more business to be had, only treasure."

"Mate, there's more than one kind of treasure, but some kinds you can't carry off with you. But the fortune I found needs tending right now. I can't."

"I thought you wanted this?"

"I did then, not no more now, mate. No more."

Gethsarade became a little frustrated. "I am going away to go back to the Algarve and live as a king supposedly, seeing no other way out as I'm too mixed up here. So, I need my first mate to get on board. We got what we wanted. So, let's stop all this ridiculous drama all set upon us by this place, put it all behind us and go."

"So, you would sacrifice all of this just to go get yourself a little more money? A few bigger nuts in the vault, as it were? What's happening to you?"

"What's happened to *you*? Are you ready to sail?" Captain Vincent asked impatiently, not getting through Gy's head.

Gy did not move.

"I'm travelling back home to Algarve. When they see what I have become, they will appreciate me and finally treat me like someone."

"You think so? My friend, what is enough for you? You got out of that ruddy sod-town you came from. Just that is more than most. You travelled the seas, all the way across the whole bloody planet. You became a captain, a commander, you've bloody well done a lot of things no one has ever done, let alone all of them together. Now you are shacked up with the brightest star in the sky having fallen right over in love with you and you are so blind by your own anguish from lying to everyone to see you already have it all. Stole it right out from under them and the folks love you anyway. What more could you want? You have everything to be had!"

"It was all by accident that I stumbled into them. I wasn't trying to do any of those things. I didn't ask for any of it, and I didn't want it. I wanted...I don't know."

"You're right. But it wasn't some cruel twist of fate that it happened, as if the gods were just trying to keep you down, or from your audience, or whatever. It was because that's just life. Life's not about getting what you want or not. Following your heart isn't about it either."

"The life you found was the life meant for you. You know it because you followed your heart and found something bigger than you could ever imagine or do alone. Hey, followin' your heart, that's fantastic, but that's just what gets you in the door. Know what I mean?

"If yer doin' it right, what happens after that's gonna be bigger than you. After the followin' yer heart stuff ends is when the real test begins. It's about finding out whether or not you've got the humility to accept where your heart has taken you and keep following it, or the take pride in throwing it away. Havin' the courage to keep on even when it plays out all wrong is real exploration and real courage."

"That's a bunch of hokey-cokey is what it is. In any case, I don't care anymore and I'm going home."

As he turned to go, he thought he might get out what had been on his mind since he met the old rat, "And you know what? If you sincerely believe all your cockamamie crap about chasing your heart and accepting your fate and all, why don't you do it yourself 'stead of...." He stopped there.

Gy's face went up slowly, his throat trembling, and said in his cracking voice, "Oy have been, mate. Have been. Always have...I don't know if it's proper, I don't know much of anything, but despite everything, or maybe because of it again, I don't know, but I know I love you. I love you like a brother, a bloody piece of me, but if you do this... there's no going back for anyone."

"I...," Gethsarade looked him over as if having seen him for the first time. "I can't. I'm sorry, friend. One more to disappoint, like I do best. Parting glass and all."

Gy fought back a tear and said with a huff, "Don't I know it?" he said, choking in his sobs.

Gethsarade shrugged, "I'm going home. Goodbye," he said, and hung his head all the way down as he left the shack with a tear.

Gy wouldn't be let down so easily, though. "That's what you don't understand, mate. You are home! I'm sorry, but I just can't let you leave like this," Gy said, following Gethsarade out.

"No, home is somewhere where others are like me and like me, too," said Gethsarade.

"How do you figure?"

"A shark told me so once. Besides. I overheard something...." It surprised Gethsarade that mentioning this was as hard as it was.

"Amalie doesn't love me. She thinks I'm silly, and she's only marrying me because Great Father is making her. He has a strange way of showing it, but apparently he's enamored with me, actually, and, if I had to guess, he threatened her with her inheritance if she didn't marry me so I could be locked up with his sick excuse of a family like the rest of them, and he could have one more thing to put up on his wall."

"I don't know for sure, but one thing is true: she thinks dirt of me. She's being made to be with me, and I don't want that. I can't live with that. I once dreamed I could endure all the hardship in the world if I but had someone to kiss my cheek when I came home. I now know there are worse things than being alone. So, I'm going to be alone."

"What are you talking about? And what is it with you and sharks? I don't know what you think you heard, but once you leave, mate, you're going to get back there, and you're going to realize neither one of these places will be the same. The world moves on."

"I'm counting on it."

"Look, I just want you to find the happiness you're looking for. But promise me when you find everything you wanted, just ask yourself if what was in your heart was a desired circumstance, or a pile of stuff, or squirrels with ideas, or poetry, or love, or any of the stuff you think is so worthless now. I did find them right here."

"I don't think much of anything anymore. And all I know is I want what I want."

"So, you're just going to leave us, then? You're just gonna leave us?" Gy could not help the lump in his throat swelling up and he couldn't sound authoritative anymore.

"I guess so."

Gy's words were at once finally failing him, and Gethsarade felt he hadn't seen anything so pitiful in all his days, but he held up his head.

"Well, maybe you'll keep searchin' forever for what's not in your heart cause you ain't got one," Gy said to Gethsarade's shock.

"Maybe you're just kiddin' yourself, if you can leave us like this."

Gethsarade said nothing, for at that there was nothing more to say, and he turned out.

After a long time down the bough, he turned back and Gy was following him.

"I thought you weren't coming?" he asked.

"I promised you I'd be your first mate, and that meant I'd help you until I couldn't anymore, and I intend to keep my promises, unlike some. That's all."

After helping Gethsarade angrily, yet silently, to the edge of the tanglewall, their interaction was simple.

"Ever the teacher, my friend," said Gethsarade.

"Goodbye." And they parted.

Once making his way under cover of night to Elderwood, he stole the Great Nut easily, relieved of Tiburt's heavy distractibility, as well as Gy's overweight beliefs, and his speed quickened the fact he had been granted full status as an Eloran Guard Commander without any question. Though, it was fairly certain such an action was a ploy, Great Father had provided the ease, and for the second time around, no one dared stop him, even as one of the guards saw him streaking along in the dark towards the tower. The guard who saw him simply saluted, begrudgingly, and continued on, probably didn't get paid enough to deal with the Tadwicks again.

Once inside, it was doggish labor getting the statue down from the pedestal. Once outside, however, he simply rolled it off the nearest edge with a few kicks and hip thrusts. It fell to the bare forest floor with a thud on to the dirt. He checked if anyone saw. He saluted a nearby guard who didn't pay attention, and then was gone off the side.

Once down, he put the Nut and a few extra boards in an abandoned farmer's cart he found riding down the mountain, which the Great Nut had no problem providing him with the appropriate inertia. He coasted by Otterdam, waving hello to the gate guards from the safety of the far cliff. There didn't seem to be anyone to see him, but it was fun anywhat. At that point, the roll was low and he travelled at a breezy clip, and he was able to brake with his wings and steer with his tail. Its immense weight made the trip hard enough, but it was a statue of the most cumbersome of kinds.

The curve of the hill took him back the other way up the river's path, and he stopped when he saw the spot where Barrogan Black's forgotten canoes still sat, as he had planned.

Gethsarade dumped the Nut at the cliff's edge, abandoned the cart, threw the boards down, and repeated the kicking, thrusting, and falling process, whereby the Nut fell lazily to the sandy bottom, and he floated down after.

He looked around with a farewell sigh, and with angry tears that came on unexpectedly. He placed the boards in between two boats, placed the Nut on top of the boards, lashed it all together with what vines and rope from the beachhead camp he could find, got in a third boat and used the other two as a tow. From there, he used his tail as a paddle and a rudder, coasting and crying and laughing all the way towards the morning sun and the end of the land.

There he found something magical. His ship had been repaired. "Magic! Fate! You see? Fate rests not in blood, but opportunity. Vincent is dead and I'm gone."

Back in town, Amalie went straight for the ship, stopping breathless only at the edge of town where she found Gy staring off into the horizon.

"Where's Vincent?" she said over the still-ringing bells.

He bowed his head in his paws, and heaved laborious sobs. "He's gone my lady. He's gone. I tried to stop him. I don't know if he'll come back. We've got to get you back home, as it's dangerous out there."

She stared at him in disbelief. Her throat locked up for a moment. "But," she stammered, "how can this be? We are engaged to be married this day. How can he leave me? *Leave us?*"

Gy tried to comfort her, but she tore away and flew with all her might down to the shore. She called out for Vincent over the water, but Gethsarade simply rolled his eyes at the hearing of that name and pretended not to hear it off in the distance. He bowed his head.

What a sham it all is, he thought, as he drifted out into the sea with her calling after him. He stared off at the horizon, away from the sound. Her screams and sobs faded into echoes, and then slowly, ever softly, they became indistinguishable from the wailing of the wind through the turnbuckles. *What a shame. It will be roughly a month,* he thought to himself. *Dreadfully long time.* Still, he hoisted the sail set the boom, and waited. *Only forward, forever,*

217

he thought, have to keep movin' on with the world, right? But his thoughts did not answer him. *Maybe my heart is to just keep movin' forward forever on just like the world when we say goodbye,* he thought and shoved on.

Not long after he had passed over the horizon, he passed out from lack of sleep.

17: For the Fate of Another

Days later....

The trouble with stealing off in a ship was one might forget to bring enough food or water and after the rush, it's all over.

The day strung drunken fairies cross the bulkhead, cast by the half-hurried patch job done by the repairers: a laughing, lolling sinusoid where still the night should have been, inviolate line dances, curtseying in united regress and progress about the cabin, and Gethsarade's brain stamped about in his skull like a half-lit suitor. Then the light would go away, and the next moment mock his eyes again. Now, he felt the feeling of a sailor at the end of his wits, trapped in the midst of the turning, yearning sea.

Gethsarade's eyes opened slowly, as the sleep fell off, and hunger struck a hammer blow and held him down. All those nights might soon end. He wiped out the dawn spirits and reached for his guitar, but alas, it was without any more strings. He groaned under the savage reminder that he was truly alone on a ship at sea with no promise he should ever return a voice to his sweet Lucinda, to scurry their hesper dreams and banish the literature, he would have no more of it at all. He had gone out so far and so long, who knew but the stars and the days? He had lost count of the days. All he could remember were the light of the sun to guide him.

Knowing that spell of glory was over, he drifted in the sea dance, and thought it a fainter happiness, and it should be a happiness with a grain of peace in his pocket, which was more than he could have had with all those riches he once thought so proud and fair, all he gave up the night before to endure a life of torture.

Alas, he deserved it, fair to only see her face again. It all seemed so directionless. It all seemed so new. This new kind of loss. No one would understand why he should go and then return, much less he should come back only to a sure sentence of innumerable tortures. And to think he would do so with a singsong heart.

He pondered if he should have gladly given back the golden idol he thought of as his salvation, which now sat glaring at him with its addling fissures. Give it back to those who truly deserved such things. Just think…scoff at the fate of another one dancing directionless…still lost at sea.

But something happens out there. Not many who have ventured beyond the borders of this fine place know this kind of thing about the briny deep. There are no landmarks, mostly because there ain't no land, but the point is, it's really easy to lose the way.

Even the best sailor can forget what time of day it is in mid-afternoon, get turned around, and think he's on course till nightfall and the stars tell him otherwise, and he's lost a whole day goin' backwards. And sailors are really up the sticks if they don't know the stars' movements at night.

It had been a voyage of 24 days and nights on a schooner to get to a new coast. He had counted. So, he assumed it would be the same to get back, the grand sailor he was. At which point Gethsarade planned to be received with all the accolades he got in Hesperia. Then, he would unload his riches and buy out the old rat he used to rent from, and make that sod pay *him* to live. Then he would buy Bonto's Bend for running him out for wanting what's fair and improve the cuisine. Not getting paid, he laughed, the place of all destiny's beginning. Can't say anyone truly has anything if they haven't gone a while with nothing.

Yes, they say the sea puts things in perspective. The sea is simple. There's the deadly nature of it. It's so simple sailors can lose their minds if they don't pay attention and will float right off.

As for Gethsarade, he was only one lad on a big boat. He tried his best, but soon the food went bad, and he had to throw it overboard, and that alone was enough to make him think of going back. He wasn't sure how far out he was, or even how many times he had been turned around, but he sure was getting hungry. Fish, though fresh, never suited him.

So, one night, Gethsarade sat on his ship and knew he had to decide for certain. He didn't know how far he had to go, but in all likelihood he was a day or so behind, leaving him with the chance that if he turned around he might starve.

I'll never go back, he said to himself. He tried to imagine all the faces of envy in his future of fame and riches. *The life of the retired sea captain, full of intrigue and spicy meals and whatnot,* he thought. *Sounds like a fine life. Maybe I'll live like the Count of Mousey Christo, where the good guy wins everything in the end. If Amalie could see me now. Or, rather then. I mean, then as in the future.*

He got to correcting himself on all sorts of things, like one does when sitting under the moonbeams talking to themselves just to be strikin' up a conversation. Or maybe he was perhaps just losing his mind to starvation and solitude.

Then struck him like an apple off its tree: *he was never going to see her again.*

He stood up, and then realized he had no reason to stand up. He was the only one there. So, he sat back down, and then he realized he would never get splashed in the face by Tiburt or ridiculed by Gy. He stood again. *Someone's got to do something about this standing thing.* He sat back down. The thought about his money: *Amalie was probably going to marry some dumb bloke with so sense of style and didn't even own a decent sash or a beret. Probably would never hear any quality guitar music,* and then he stared up at the sky. Something he remembered Gy having said struck him. Something about the night sky. Gethsarade thought he remembered saying he would try to remember something about when the time was right.

The time must be right, he thought, because he was thinking of trying to think of it. *No. It wasn't the night sky, specifically. It was the twilight sky. Or maybe just the twilight. Or the feeling of it. Yes, that's it.*

221

He searched the emerging stars under the maroon and emerald sky, as it faded to indigo. He felt the feeling of having been through such trouble. The heat had pressed down on him all day, but the night brought troubles all its own. At the time one usually began to prepare for rest, he strained to see if clouds were on the horizon. He hoped there would be no red-sky morning, and he hoped the Great Nut under his pillow in the empty captain's quarters would not create any other red skies at evening time as well.

He hated the sea. "Puts things in perspective," Gy said and then added, "old friend." *Well, that was his perspective.* He had nothing to look forward to, except huge amounts of wealth and fame, the sort of one's dreams. *Amalie, sweet,* he thought. *This is all I worked for, and it's what I deserve.*

He would have tended to battening the hatches, and so on, and tied the boom line once, then again, and once more, laying out the line in a neat row along the topside knee-knockers. He would have about this time been lighting up a pipe or tuning his string-less guitar, but instead he just looked at the sky.

He couldn't bring himself to do anything just yet, though. He kept looking at the stars, waiting for some impossible sign.

Then something else hit him. If he needed a sign to show him, and he hadn't seen one in a while, then he was probably going the wrong way or needed to find a map, which someone had said once, that dog, Tiburt.

Gethsarade realized to his sudden glee, and then his sudden horror at the gravity of his mistake set in even more. He was not able to function, not because he was fearful of the other side, but because his heart was unable to accept the fear of uncertainty, or perhaps certainty rather of letting go of the day his heart was not in this journey homeward. Then it was not home anymore. He thought once more of the old Algarve de Porto, and of all it would be, trying not to be a fool so much as to think it could be the same. But how different would it be? The same fools would be there. No. He knew exactly what would happen.

He also knew why he stared at the sky and could not batten down the hatches, and it was also why he thought of his sweet Amalie and felt nothing—or rather, the same. It was the same. He had left, but he didn't let go. *Maybe that's why we don't realize what we've got until it's gone. We never think about what letting it go means, only the pain of holding on to it.*

I can't, he thought. *I won't.* He bowed his head and thought hard on the shame and exposure of telling everyone who he really was, a nobody, and the hard slap upon his cheek of Amalie's rose-scented palm. Her teary blue eyes. Her asking him why over and over. And the life of humiliation in some rent home, all alone, on the poor side of town, strumming his string-less guitar. *Doubtlessly everyone learning who I am would cost me everything I am sure to gain, just to see her again.*

He thought of running from the pain, he thought of it over and over and over until his mind went drunk with thoughts upon the waves at day and mad with them at night. He thought less and less of having the whole world captured in his palm and more and more of having his shanty in Promise's End, if now and then he could see his love on the floor of Persimmonia's, but she would refuse to look up at him playing or care. But he would see her. Better than Faro? Far better.

He absentmindedly went to turn the boat a bit, and found he already had, and he was not sure to what degree. He thought on it a bit more, went to batten a thing or two, and found he had battened them, and so he unbattened them again, then battened them all over. He went to the captain's quarter and, much to his surprise, he had drawn a path in drunken lines and absent circles back the way he had come, but it was so long ago, he had forgotten even that location.

Then he went to polish the Great Nut, only to find it ha been polished, wrapped, with a clean note tucked in the twine, describing his utter remorse and acceptance of his fate to come. Then he went to check compass again, and lo he had been turned around without even paying attention. *Stupid me, fool!*

But he thought then again of Amalie's face and forgot for the who-knows-how-many-eth time to turn it back.

Then, at one point he simply collapsed, fell onto the deck, and threw up into a bucket. He thought then and there, *I am done, finished. This is how I die.* But then his thoughts were distracted by the sound of faint laughter. "Just as I prophesied:

223

Hurdy gurdy, hooty burdy,
A palindrome, igniting I,
Once, thrice folly and a-fowl,
The feather is on the other try!"

Gethsarade could not remember if someone had once told him starvation brings odd visions, or if Tiburt was really there with him, talking.

"Alas, my life would have ended the way it began, and never figuring out what the hell you are saying, Tibby. Ah, wrong, old Tib! I'm still kicking!"

"Like a palindrome. Yes?"

"What? Nonsense!"

"The stuff of stars."

"What?"

"Nonsense."

"Nonsense to your nonsense!"

The vision of Tiburt was twice as annoying as the real thing.

"Wait, why are you here? You're not dead. I just left you. Are you dead?" said Gethsarade.

"Oh, don't worry about that, but you should probably hurry up and get back here."

"Why?"

Then his visage faded just as the others.

"Once again, frustrating and not helpful, Tiburt! What the hell? Oh, dear, I'm still crazy. Now I'm yelling at nothing at all!"

"Yes, yes." the new voice didn't quite register. It said something again. "What are you doing all the way out here yelling at nothing?"

Gethsarade thought he could ask the face in the water the same thing.

"I just, wait, I'm sorry...who are you?" asked Gethsarade. "Why, I'm you, of course!"

Gethsarade looked at the face of the one speaking searching for meaning in his words, for meaning itself was lost out there in the waves.

"My friend, yes, yes, I am Vincent and, as your friend, if you cannot figure out how you should act, remember me and what I did for you."

"But if you want me to be so brave, why did you leave me behind when I needed you to be brave for me? If I were your friend…"

He searched the face again, slowly, achingly. He realized he was looking down into a bucket, *what was someone doing in there?* But this sudden flash of awareness wasn't enough to stop the conversation.

The face said, "In those days, your mama cared for you and we spoke. She knew you wanted to earn a name as a hero. But she swore to protect you, and she asked me to spare you."

"She spoke to you?"

"Yes! She spoke to you, didn't she? She asked me to be courageous. Well, I could not deny her, realizing when she showed me the letter that you, my friend, were truly special. You were something I myself was always trying to be, someone with a real destiny. But you could not believe in yourself.

"So, you created me. When you needed someone to do for you what you could not do, I stood up to the cook. When you needed to get back at Bonto, there I was. When you needed to laugh in the face of Barrogan Black, I helped you. When you needed the courage to ask Amalie to a date with you, I gave just the nudge."

"You didn't need me, per se. You needed time. Time to find out who you are. It had to be the right time. I could not drag you off to fight a battle I knew I was going to lose. I simply could not do it. But you never even gave me a chance to decide.

"I took over for a moment, but things got complicated when you took this new well of confidence for granted. You started taking advantage. What would you do if I had decided to take you out of that trash heap Faro before it was time? Yes, you would have decided because you are a hero, Gethsarade."

"I'm no hero. I just play my little Lucinda and that's all I can do. Look, I just stole the town's treasure. I broke a town."

Once he heard his own voice again, he began to realize the voice he was hearing was his own, but different. And the face was his own, but different. It was happier.

"True, you are a master. But you could not see yourself, when you led a city of muck-slickers and milk-toasts into full-fledged battle. You led soldiers, in your mind, of course, but it was spectacular. You are greatness. Not me. You don't need me. You need to believe in yourself. I'm just flubbing things up now. You're the Captain." And just then, he began to fade.

"Will I ever see you again?" Gethsarade shouted into the bucket.

"If you need me and I hope you don't." Almost then, as if his old friend smiled, gave him a wink and a nod towards the setting sun, and the wisps that formed his mouth appeared to say to him, "Go on back then, old boy. We'll be here." The face disappeared once more and would not come back.

Gethsarade wept. "Now I'm mad, my mind is playing tricks on me. Really good ones!"

This alter ego, he thought, *this one wrecking everything, couldn't be trusted, could he?* Gy would not understand and Tiburt, of course, would not. Amalie would not. As a matter of fact, he would likely never see her again, even if he did go back, at least not but once. He didn't want to believe in his origin, he realized, because he didn't want to believe in destiny, not the reverse.

Never, ever, ever again, he thought, *again.* It was at this thought, it was almost as if the reflection upon the waters and some confusion with the phosphorescent gloom of the warm doldrum glaze interacted to produce a visage-like apparition in the surface of the deep.

But of all things to be produced by the mysterious reflections of the evening waters, he found the smile of Lady Ridroga. "Mama!" he cried.

"Do you remember, my love, what I asked you?"

"Yes, Mama." he said, not knowing what else to say.

"I asked you to find yourself."

"I know. It just kind of got away from me." But he instead pretended to be someone else because, to him, Gethsarade of Faro was a coward and a nobody. Look where that fool got himself. He was about to go live just another lie.

"My little hero." she said.

"Yes? Oh, mama, you're turned around, I'm over here, listen, listen to my voice, mama. *Oy, mi madre.*"

"Oh? Oh, my little hero, why are you over there? Never mind, you silly boy. Do you remember what I asked you?"

"Yes, mama."

"What was it again?"

"You asked me to find myself."

"Oh, yes. How's it going?"

"Not well, mi madre," he said. "Mama? Mama. Mama!"

"Yes, dear?"

"Never mind. I love you, Mama."

"I love you too, my little hero." With those words, she faded.

"Goodbye Mama."

When she was gone, he said out loud, "Well that was unproductive," but it caused him to snap to.

He realized he had come to the aft bow, and his heart was beating its way out of his chest, and, much to his surprise, he was staring at the setting sun, no, not the sun anymore, but the horizon—a sharp, straight golden line. It reflected the blaze of dusk in all directions, a line, a straight line, yet a circle. A circle in a line. Tears, warm tears were on his cheeks.

"Oh, so soon, much sooner than I expected for my life to be ended. But is this not what Tiburt said? It has all come about, full circle. A circle within a straight line, that's the impossible sign he gave. Oh well, I cannot fight anymore, it is the end." He held out his arms to receive the warmth of death.

But the only thing that happened was the bucket he was holding fell into the water with a dead plop. Also, after a moment, a bird pooped on him and flew off mockingly.

"Oh, my goodness. What a dunce I am! What have I done! I am sorry, mama!" he cried to the waters, for he knew finally for once in life where his heart was leading him, and as usual it was not where he was going.

"Magic, Tiburt," he laughed, patting his shoulder. Handkerchiefs were getting short in supply.

"Hey! Quiet up there! What are you talking about? What's with the bucket? You should not litter!"

It was Arfaxad.

"Arf! are you real?"

"Good question. I suppose I should know the answer to that if I could figure out how much of me was positively fake."

"Oh, no, here it goes." Gethsarade pawed his face, shook his head, but listened anyway,

"But to prove my fakeness would positively take all knowledge of the universe as evidence, wouldn't it?

"Of course, I should pick, so if I had to say, I'd say given the state of nature I am of all things far less likely to exist than anything else, so my powers of reason are reasoned out, if I can't trust in anything else being real, then I can't reasonably believe I'm saying these words right now, but obviously, even this statement cannot be true."

He laughed. "I mean if it were only between and universe and I, I'd be forced to say logically that no, I'm not, so I'd need a second opinion from someone as unlikely as me. What do you think?"

"Well, I could never make up what you just said or want to, nor was I able to make you stop talking, so you're real. Okay."

"Okay! Wow, I'm real. Cool!"

"Do you remember me, sir?"

"Of course, I remember you! Flying squirrels all the way out here are not something one sees often. You're that Not Vincent, the Great So Many Things. Right?'

"Aaagh!" shouted another shark whom Gethsarade presumed was his mate.

'What's wrong with her? If I said something rude, I apologize.'

"Oh, no, not at all. We're having babies!"

"What? Really? Right now?"

Gethsarade heard more screams and looked overboard, and he and the other shark that was exactly like him, except a girl had

228

lots of babies all whipping about in the water. Beautiful little tiny exact replicas of Arfaxad.

Gethsarade said, "Oh wow, what are the odds?"

Another one popped and Atraxia sighed in relief, at which point all of them promptly left to go endure their solitary shark lives.

"Aww. Goodbye my loves," they said, and the two parents held each other and watched.

"You're such a good father." Smooch. "You're the best shark mom ever," they kissed again.

They saw Gethsarade's look of slight concern, and they said, "Oh, don't you know? it takes a mass-multi-oceanic biosystem to raise a shark-child."

Then they asked, "Now that's over, so how are you doing?" and he was very ho-hum about it, explaining the whole situation, and begrudgingly revealing he was not, in fact, Vincent Poppaldi.

Arfaxad leaned over and said, "Told you." Gethsarade rolled his eyes.

He said, "But when I get where I'm going, to my destiny of wealth and fame as the Great Gethsarade of Faro de Algarve and buy the town and make them all listen to my music in every restaurant." Arfaxad laughed exceedingly at him, but for Atraxia for only a moment for she was still hurting.

"You've done a dumb thing. You think that's your destiny?"

He turned away as they were holding fins and talking about it. "Could you imagine, dear, letting our family go to be all alone in the world?"

"I'd rather die, love. I'd seriously just die," he said shaking his head.

Gethsarade turned away again with his wounded pride, but he could not ignore their incredibly illogical reasoning. Gethsarade asked Arfaxad and Atraxia if they happened to remember the rats they were left with when they last met, and Arf said, "Oh, this one with an absolutely massive noggin asked how he might get to the Western shore, or at least as close as possible, without risking getting beached. Very nice guy, humble. He told me I had beautiful eyebrows. Why? Wait, what do you think, am I some kind of monster? I wasn't going to just let them die. Wait, you wanted that to happen, didn't you? Oh, rats! Rats! I should have fangifully devoured them all!"

"No," replied Gethsarade with a sigh, "It's fine. I wouldn't have wanted you to kill them although it would certainly have made things a lot easier in retrospect."

"I suppose."

"Aren't you supposed to help me change my mind?" asked Gethsarade.

"No. I don't think so. No, you're good. You're probably right."

This angered Gethsarade even more, regardless that it made him painfully aware of how stupid he had been about everything. He was listening to an insane daddy shark for advice.

"Hey, buddy, could I ask you something?"

"You know it, nec-bro-nomicon."

"Whatever. Can you help me?"

Atraxia's poked her head out of the water and smiled.

"Forgive me, dear friends, for I know you are right, and I am only in such deep remorse of it all," said Gethsarade.

"Well, my little non-famous squirrel captain friend, seeing as we are in your debt for our love itself, I can think of only one thing to say: How may we be of service to you?"

"Well, I fear I may need some of your shark sense."

"Oh, how I dreamed of this night! We'll fix you up with a nice girl, the one down by Tally Reef. I know just the one. Don't mind she's a little overweight, as there is more to love!"

"But dear, she picks her nose."

"Don't worry, they're a perfect match, as like he said, I have shark sense." They commenced arguing.

"Friends!" shouted Gethsarade in attempt to mediate.

"If it wasn't for my excellent sense, we wouldn't be in shark-love, remember? It was my idea!"

"Well, you wouldn't even have had the very idea if I hadn't told you you're a shark!"

"Don't muddy the water!"

"Friends, I only mean I need a little help with direction. I am lost under the sun and stars for their turning."

230

But as it happened, they said, "The sea puts things in perspective. If there's one thing sharks know better than love and philosophy, it's directions!"

"Dear Lord of all gracious nuts, I hope so," he said, smiling.

"Where do you need to go?"

"Well I'm trying to get west or maybe east. I'm not sure which right now."

"I'll tell you. It's easy, just wait till sundown."

"What happens at sundown?"

"Well, sundown, of course! If you look up into the heavens, you will see a star just above the horizon."

"I've no interest in more magic talk! Please, just tell me how to make my way, as I need to get to somewhere, starting now."

"Oh, now, then. As I was saying, the sun rises in the east, takes a quick nap in the top of the sky at noon, and sets in the west, just the same as on land. So, if you keep track of the time of day, you can always know where you are and where you need to be based on the direction. For east, point yourself towards the sun in the morning and away from it in the evening. For west, vice versa. Simple geometry. Got it?"

"Okay, point myself right, so it's really that easy?"

"If it has to be, yes. Hey, I thought you were a captain, or something."

"I am. But a captain is nothing without his mates."

"Okay, whatever. I don't know what that means."

"I have to say, Arfaxad, you're the last being I should take advice from."

"But you're taking it." He smiled.

"Someday, friend, I'll see you again." and they waved him off, while he without another turn of his brow to mind a thought elsewise, he spun the rudder and pulled the ship about into the darkening of the sky.

"Fate!" he cried flinging his red shirt to the deck in abject frustration.

"I'll not once more in my days say these words: what are the odds. For I know now the moment I shall, I should be met with swine a-flight! Flying, bloody Dutch, furry, pigs eating beans and

231

carrying on about romance and words. Why, I don't know why anyone says things. It's just asking for trouble. I've lost my mind." Of course, all of this was in the most strictly discourteous dialect of Porto.

It wasn't fate. It wasn't the heavens playing a joke on him. It was family. It was blood. Blood.

By the stars that be, laughed he to the vespers of his mates, "Hurdy gurdy, hooty birdy, ho, old Tib! Wish you were here, now. I swear I shall free you, old rat. For blood it was that led me to the map, blood it was that wrote the very map that led me to find my love, and blood there again called out to me, and it had to be from the paw of my father to me and me alone. It's in the blood!

"It's in the blood! There is power in the blood!" he shouted.

"My father laughed in the face of certain death not because he had his confidence in the stars, but in blood! It was to me. It sounded like it was written to me because it was literally to me!" He strained himself not to repeat the words that had wreaked trouble on his head so often, and laughed before he cried once more saying, "What, prithee stars and sky, are the bloody odds, do you know? They are a probability of one! They are the certainty of blood. Do you, oh sky, do you know what else is in the blood of me? The blood of a hero. Not of a list-less wanderer anymore."

As the tears came to his eyes and as he shouted to the heavens, as it had finally all come together for him, "I found my family. I am found, by my blood, and I shall never betray nor leave it again."

With resolve, he leapt down onto the main deck and began with a new sense of sprit and vigor to lash up the bight and take in sails. *Wither ever this boat should go, there will be no further use for it,* he thought. *Someone else shall have the fortune. I shall wander no more.*

He ran to the hammock where underneath was a cloak carefully wrapped around the Great Nut of Wisdom. *I shall return this to its rightful owners.* He placed it in a rucksack, slung it around his back, and proceeded to the main deck once more to ensure the ship was being carried right by the wind, where he should never see and therefore face any old demons of temptation to board and wander.

Just then, the shores of Hesperia came into view. At first, they were like a glowing area on the horizon, then they darkened into fuzzy lumps, and then became in the day the fulfillment of all their sleepy glory.

This would mean I was sailing in a sodding circle the whole time! I was going to die in the middle of the ocean like an idiot. What are the odds? he thought as he clapped himself on the head.

He dug his nails into the wood of the helm. *Whatever life awaits me by going back to tell the truth and return the Great Nut to its rightful place, I must live by the truth.*

He grabbed the boom, swung out so the wind caught the sail, swung the ship into the bay, and weighed the anchor. He raced up to the officer's deck and leapt to the lines about him, launching himself over the bay at a height no spear or arrow would dare fly.

Just then, a gust at his back confirmed to him through every strain and pluck of his being's fiber, and he threw his paws up in the air and laughed into the sky at the victory of fate sure to come on the unwavering wind. *That I should be carried now up the mountain slope, what luck again! What else could follow such luck, after all?*

So, he sailed on into the misty-dark horizon. *But should it not be misty-bright?* He thought.

In fully realizing he was who he was, then he finally believed in his wings.

Back in Hesperia…

On the morning of the fire, when they finished tending to it at the base of the Hollow and were weary, someone shouted a second blaze had caught farther away where the trees began to clear.

Everyone filed after, worried the wind was creating an epidemic. Before they had the new fire out, they realized they had quietly been surrounded, and their resistance was pitiful. Barrogan and his new army won easily. He chained them and led them to their new prison. These were all the events of the morning of Gethsarade's departure, of course, and by the dark dawn of his second coming, everyone had all become accustomed to the new misery.

He took the path Amalie showed him back to the city over the treetops. His joy at returning turned to dismay as he vaulted once more up another herald branch and saw the city, nay the whole top of the mountain, now under a plume of black smoke.

What he thought was the marine mist to his fury he found to carry instead the scent of old ash as he closed in and, he whispered but one name to himself, *Barrogan Black,* as the rage of a beleaguered son rose in his chest.

His paws began to shake as the scent of rats wafted before his nose, and the weight of his calamity fell upon him.

Going up the normal way for it was unguarded, it seemed the town was empty of its inhabitants, and the pirats must have surprised and overcome the Eloran army and captured them, one and all.

"What have I done?" he gasped.

Black had taken over the Hollow and transformed it into the headquarters of his rule and a prison for all its former surviving inhabitants. He had accurately predicted the civilians would gather to the fire, all of them, if it were big enough, and try to put it out. The savages and Happenlings under his command captured them by funneling them in and holding them on the ground where they were put in chains and led to the trees they once used for progress.

Barrogan had correctly surmised that though the inhabitants' wings made them able to cast themselves vast distances, it unfortunately also made them unable to leap short distances quickly. This meant that, on the ground, they were helpless in escaping.

The place Black was holding them was not hard for Gethsarade to find. He only needed to follow the echoes of slave labor and howls of the tortured over the pleasured raging of the damned.

Down below, in the library of the Great Commons Hollow, the prisoners of Barrogan Black sat weeping.

"This is the end of all things," said Great Father Tadwick.

"I interject. Remember the prophecy. It is not over," Amalie interjected.

Great Father commanded her silence and held up his paw. "I must remember to be graceful. You don't know so much. I myself wrote that prophecy. And I rewrote it, and it was wrong, again. It was all wrong."

18: All Great Journeys

Amalie and Great Father sat together weeping in chains in the heart of a tree. Surrounding them were their loved ones and the regular townsfolks in the prison of the Great Commons Hollow, and the Sons of Sangareth sneered at them across the way, and back at them sneered the Guardians of Elorus, all in their own particular chains and nets, starving and waiting like the others to be picked off to be worked to death. The captors came for prisoners one after another. Great Father just looked down.

Amalie set about the business of comforting the others, soothing weeping babes, and shooting annoyed and superior glances over to the gaolers. As it goes with gaolers, this one pretended not to know anything.

After some time, he began to find her amusing and met her hateful stares with kissy faces and smiles. At this, she stopped and forced down a vomit, causing an uproar of chatter among the onlookers and children.

The guard, feeling pricked, started towards her, and this to her dismay at the hungry grin that had taken over his face and his eyes glistened with an evil, unrelenting gaze. To her relief, he was stopped by a paw on his shoulder.

"Oy, quit playin' with our dinner, go eat, and get back here to finish your shift." This was spoken by another rat, accompanied by several guards who were dropping off more of the captured, and these immediately got priority from Amalie and Great Father. Meanwhile, the following conversation ensued.

"Hey, why are we stuck here watchin' when everyone else gets to have all the fun pillaging? By the time I get out of here, all the fun will have been had."

"Black's orders," said the guard.

"Ain't that all? I been waitin' for this just as long as everyone else. I deserve my shot at the loot just like all them. Why am I stuck down here? It's not fair."

"I don't know mate. It's a mystery."

But then the new guard lost his sense of conversational civility towards the new help.

"Or maybe, I don't know, it could something to do with all your extra helpins of midrats or you stuffing your boots with other rats' baubles all the time when you think they're not looking?"

"I swear I ain't nevah done any such thing!"

"Sure, Guvvy, sure. Now get out of here and don't question your captain. He's the only reason you're alive, or any of us for that matter."

"Aye," the former watch left off grumbling to himself that he was going to get what was his or something or other.

But unbeknownst to the rest of them at the time, poor stupid Guvvy would not return, for shortly after having left to help himself to too much food, he turned a corner and was knocked right unconscious and dragged into an unused corner where no light would fall.

After a few more moments, another figure emerged wearing the stocked-up knickers of a chronically hungry kleptomaniac, and for a rat to possess an abnormal tendency to swipe things, well, that's bad.

Gethsarade took out one of the pirats with a club as he was walking out and then put on his shirt as a disguise.

Soon, he had followed the other one back to the hall where the prisoners were being held in what had been the library. He was horrified to find them there in chains like the Happenlings he now thought back on. He found Amalie weeping by her wounded Great Father.

She scolded him heavily the moment he lifted his hood, crying, "Who do you think you are showing up here? Traitor!"

She slapped him even harder than before, but this time, he grabbed her and held her to him while she sobbed.

"I would go anywhere with you if you asked. I think even if you had or hadn't ever told me who you are, I assumed I knew you based on the one I saw before me, not what I'd heard. If that's what you think, you don't know much about us girls. I might not have ever found out if you just never wanted to tell me. Great Father was right. You are naive."

"What is going on?" asked Great Father, coming over to them.

"You? Was this Barrogan Black's doing?" he asked.

Amalie's tail went straight and she raised her fists, about to make a scene, "This is your doing!"

Gethsarade put his paws up and said, "No, I am here to help."

She said, "How can you possibly help us! You did this!"

One of the guards saw him, and since one of the squirrels was yelling at him, and the guard could not see he had wings in the dark. Gethsarade thought quickly and tucked his tail in the bilge water to look like he had a rat's tail against the shadows, quietly thanking Tiburt for this bit of brilliance.

The guard threw Gethsarade the key and yelled, he was going to go take a pee, and to watch out for the lady one, a real fireball. Gethsarade said "Well, that was easy." As the guard disappeared. He began unlocking the cell doors, but stopped.

She asked, "What's wrong?"

He said, "We can't just go about without a plan. When the guard comes back, tell him there was a security alert and I had to leave and I will return, so distract him until then, as I need only a moment, please. Play along."

"How am I supposed to trust you'll come back?" said Amalie.

"I've done this before," he said.

The guard came back and yelled a lot and began beating on one of the prisoners.

At first, she did not want to listen to Gethsarade, but she only went along with him because she looked back to her grandfather for judgment in the situation, and he nodded.

Amalie gingerly walked up to the guard and smiled at him.

He stopped, and she said, "Please, the guard you gave the key to said he would return, so do not punish us for the actions of others."

"Fine," the guard relaxed and said, "It's alright; I got a spare." He sat down and said, "It's not like you useless maggots are going anywhere."

"What are you going to do with us?"

The guard simply said, "Oh, I don't know, this and that. I think the master plans to…."

"Master?" said Amalie. "So, the leader of your band prefers you to call him your master?"

"What's wrong? Everyone needs a master."

"A lot is wrong," she went on, "In our realm, no one has a master unless they earn one. There is my Great Father here, but his is a position of respect." The elder just stared ahead at the wall.

"What do you mean 'earn one'?" said the guard.

"I mean only those who have sinned in a matter deserving public impunity are rewarded with subjugation. It is called a reward because they earned it. What sin did you commit here among your equals that you have been awarded the disgrace of subjugation of even your so-called 'leader?' Or is there no such thing as freedom in your world?"

The guard thought for a moment, then struck her across the face. "You got no place to talk to me like that. Talking badly out of line about our captain to us is a crime worthy of death. So, feel grateful, little one. I award you with my grace in that I don't let your throat slip across my knife as you stand before me. Now go back to your pathetic and weak mates with your pathetic and weak ideas."

It seemed whatever Gethsarade was planning, he still needed more time. She got back up and slowly wiped her bloodied mouth.

"You want our riches, but know not how to use them for yourself, and dust shall claim them instead of your children. What wealth is that?"

He said, "Well it's a good thing I don't got no kids."

She said, "It's no wonder you do not understand the concept of joy. I warrant to you there is nothing more profitable than to build one's estate in a land of peace. You think you are strong because you take what you want. I warrant to you, sir, for all the strength of your arms, and of your master's whip, nothing can withstand the power of a single squirrel endowed with his or her rightful freedom, and the courage to do what's right, as perhaps you're the weak one, for you do not understand the concept of the difficulty of building and sustaining such a thing."

The squirrel raised his paw again, and she about fell down wincing, and he laughed. "Point taken. If freedom is so powerful, why are you all in chains?" He laughed again and went back to take a swig.

"Enjoy the rich flavors of our persimmon brew, my good sir, for your ignorance could never concoct it," Amalie taunted. She paused, looking around, "You shall never taste it again."

"Are you threatening me now, little weakling in bonds and shackles? I'll just make one of you do it," the guard said as his eyes went red.

"No, sir. I'm simply saying that is the price of ignorance and violence. It is a misfortune to have a lifetime built for a moment most fleeting and eternal punishment."

"Why do you not understand your place!" he screamed, then everyone heard a bonk sound. The guard stopped talking, his eyes glazed over, and he fell to the floor.

There was Gethsarade, standing behind him. He emerged from behind the shadows holding the pirat's sword.

"Because her place is truly on the highest throne in all the land, rat, and yours is prostrate at her feet, like so," he looked deeply into Amalie's eyes.

She looked back for a moment and said quietly, "Vincent! I never stopped believing in you." She threw her arms around him and Gethsarade bowed his head in shame.

Then she smacked him as customary. "Now, where the hell have you been?" she yelled.

"Shh. There are other guards. There is no time, I will tell you everything later. Only follow me. Now, does anyone know where the Guardians are being held?" he asked, and began unlocking the squirrels.

"No," said one of the squirrels after being freed, who then held back his paws. Gethsarade remembered his face from the bar. The squirrel said, "Why should we follow you? You disappeared right in the high moment we needed help."

"What is he talking about, Vincent?" asked another.

Gethsarade sighed. "He is right. I promise, I will explain everything, but if you want to live, we must act now."

The squirrel shut up, and Gethsarade breathed a sigh of relief.

"My name is not Vincent Poppaldi. My name is Gethsarade, child of the infamous Sangareth who threatened your walls just as you say, Great Father."

They gasped. Great Father muttered, "Worthless mongrel; why did you have to ruin it?"

Gethsarade held up his paws up to calm them. "I don't know how much of the stories are true or lost to interpretation, but I assure you on account of the fact I am giving you freedom now, I am not that squirrel. I am my own. See?"

They all stood facing one another but said nothing. So Gethsarade took the moment and handed Gy the sword after unlocking him and turned around.

"If you truly think I am here to do any one of you harm after what I know, then take my life, for I do not any longer wish to live if it means to live one more falsehood or deceit. No more."

They were not persuaded by the emotion in his voice, so Gethsarade closed his eyes, turned around with his paws in the air, and Gy put the point of the sword in his back. Gethsarade braced for the end. But Gy just pushed his shoulder so as to turn him around.

"Stop being such a bore. Lead on, sir. I won't kill you, for it is the trademark of those righteous in heart to give the benefit of the doubt. But, of course, you know my beliefs, don't you? Bare as the birth of morn." He eyed Gethsarade. "So, I'm keeping this here sword, see?"

"Seems fair," said Gethsarade. "I can only take a few, enough so no one will notice, and we need to maximize our effectiveness while minimizing our visibility. So, I'm taking you, Gy and Tiburt, to work your magic of distraction, and you two know this prison as well as I. Sorry about that."

Tiburt perked up.

"So, we must free the Guardians first, then we shall come back for you and free you all then; you must be prepared for battle. Onward, friends."

He motioned them to follow, but they were hesitant, and Gy brushed past and eyed them. The crowd followed Gy, and Gethsarade hurried up to the front so he could see.

"You lead, and I'll decide if they follow," Gy said to him out of the side of his mouth.

"Fine."

"Then, from this day, we are parted as friends forever, as your reward for leaving."

Gethsarade remained silent, cut to the core. They went about silently cutting ropes and unlocking chains. In the middle of it all, Tiburt crossed paths with Gethsarade. They stopped and needley-eyed one another.

"You are the greatest sorcerer of them all, and an evil one, for the magic you do," said Tiburt.

Gethsarade tried to defend himself, "My actions never were intended to harm anyone but myself. Please understand."

"And that," Tiburt said, "you understand, is why dark magic is dark, yes?"

"Please, I can't do the magic allegory all the time, just say it," said Gethsarade.

"It's not allegory. It's not the deception of others. You can deceive others to get them to do right, though it is considerably harder. But simply to deceive others is neither light nor dark.

"Darkness is the deception of one's self into thinking one's actions only affect one, while they manipulate the universe. Such a life and such a lie make you incapable of practicing light magic, and everything around you falls. It makes you stink."

Tiburt threw a bucket of water on Gethsarade. Everyone laughed.

"You know what light magic is?"

Gethsarade sighed, "What?"

"Forgiveness!" Tiburt turned to the crowd, and they began to nod, one by one.

"We forgive you. We forgive you for leaving, for betraying myself and the Sons of Sangareth, and basically lying to everyone and stealing the Great Nut of Elorus."

Suddenly, he was interrupted by lots of long and loud shouting.

"Tiburt, you idiot!" shouted Great Father above them all. "Can't you all just keep your mouth shut?"

"He stole the Great Nut?" someone yelled from the back. "Let's hang him!"

"No, you morons. We can all fly," said Great Father.

Tiburt cleared his throat, and opened his mouth to change the subject.

But Great Father beat him to it, "The Great Nut isn't real, folks. He didn't steal anything."

"I didn't?" said Gethsarade.

"No, you didn't. That thing was wood painted gold. How do you think you carried it? No one could carry it if it was real, are you kidding? Do you know how much gold weighs?" Clearly, Gethsarade did not.

"Why did he steal it, then?" said the idiot from the back.

Everyone looked at Gethsarade, who was looking at Great Father, who was looking at Gethsarade.

"Go ahead. They wouldn't believe me if I told them."

He crossed his arms and leaned over towards Great Father and gave him the eyebrows, and all the while Gethsarade kept his cool while processing his monumental idiocy.

Great Father was barely holding it together, when Amalie said, "Let me get this straight. You, Gethsarade Sangareth, not Vincent, stole the fake Great Nut, and that was when the bell started ringing, not because Barrogan Black stole it."

"Yes?"

"So Barrogan Black doesn't have it."

"And?"

"We could use it as a bargaining chip."

"But it's not real."

"He doesn't know that."

"It's possible," mumbled Great Father. "Where is it now?"

"Oh, it's down at the bay inside the ship."

To this there were many mumbled expletives and complaints.

"What? It's still heavy. I was going to get it later."

Amalie said, "You mean you thought you were going to come back here and confess your love and all your sins so everyone could think of you as the hero again, and then whisk me away with the treasure like a romance story?"

"Maybe."

"He's a cheat and a liar, so get rid of him!" said the wretch.

"You're not making this easy, Son of Sangareth. Like someone else I knew," said Great Father.

"Oh, coming from the one who sells his children for power," snapped Amalie.

"Says the one who sells out on her fiancée to serve the interests of her Pap," said Gy.

"Oh, yeah?" said Gethsarade, coming to Amalie's defense. "Well, says the one who… yeah awright, you're pretty honest, actually. But you still came here to help me do all this stuff. So, what if you're honest about being bad?"

Gy just looked down.

"Look, everyone. The facts are everyone has lied to everyone. Every single one of us has lied at some time or another, betrayed, done things, and pretended to be someone we're not to get what we want."

"Yeah, and? You literally did that more than anyone ever."

"Yes, thank you. My point is, now everything's on the table, so we don't have to pretend to be anyone other than who we are any more. I can be Gethsarade, and you, Tiburt, can just be a rat. And you, Great Father, can just be a conniving twit, and Amalie…."

He touched her arm. "I don't want you to be with me if you don't want to be."

She bowed her head for a long time.

"Amalie, it's alright, I know. I know you don't love me, and you're just following orders. He might do such a thing to you, but I couldn't. Yes, I held on to hope even up till now, but I could never force someone to live a lie like I've lived. I'm just a street musician from Porto. I mean, I am the son of Sangareth, but that's it—not some hero. So, I understand if we're done. I just want you to be happy, like I never was," he began to turn away.

"No. You don't understand."

She put her paw on his shoulder and he turned to face her again, not holding up hope any more.

"I do want to be with you. That's the one and only thing I do want. I love you."

"In spite of everything?"

"Yes, in spite of everything. I think I know who you really are now. The real you is who I want."

"But I'm not even a millionaire."

She laughed, "I know, that's a good thing."

They embraced. Tiburt and Gy cheered silently, and Great Father moved to break it up, saying something about not until the wedding, but Gy moved in front of him and said, "Sorry, no, you're still a douchebag." At this Great Father was offended, that is all.

Then Gethsarade felt himself become filled with a new energy, "We need to get out of here."

"A little help here, then?" said one of the Knights of Elorus.

"Sure," said Gethsarade, but then he thought about it, and went over to the cage containing the Sons of Sangareth.

"Whoa!" said the townsfolks, "But you can't let those Sons of Sangareth out! They will betray us all."

"Doubtful, tops." and when he let the Sons of Sangareth out, they jostled each other playfully and cheered.

Gethsarade said to the townsfolks, "Now you have your true and capable Guardians."

The Sons began to snarl at the Knights, "Fakers! Buffoons! How could you think you could do what we do?"

Then Gethsarade got between them, silenced them, and then went over to the cage containing the Knights and opened it, this time much to the chagrin of the Sons.

"Now you Guardians got your much-needed numbers to command. And here is enough to beat the horde together. Sound soundy?"

They all began to hiss and push one another, but Gethsarade silenced them again instead.

"Now you can all either fight it out here and then they come kill us and all of us die or you can fight together and give all of us half a chance at surviving this. I leave it up to you. I say, with your few and their many we are a thousand for Hesperia."

"The Sons of Sangareth would never endanger our beloved duty."

"Neither would the Knights of Elorus."

They shook paws.

"One, two, a thousand for Hesperia!" the crowd repeated over and over.

Great Father stood with mouth agape and muttered to himself in the midst of the onlookers still in chains,

"Holy crap. He did it. This was what I was trying to do all along."

Then he stood up and shouted, "I decree this moment, the sins of Gethsarade and his family are dispersed, washed clean, and they are no more. He has done the most difficult thing of all us by atoning for them. He has put up his own life, not for his own good, but for others, and showing his heart has truly changed from this course onward. I was unwilling to uncover my own faults, and that was my downfall. I could not unite you. Where I failed, he has succeeded. We should belabor this matter no more. Let us be a united squirreldom!"

"One, two, a thousand for Hesperia!" they all cheered.

Barrogan Black burst in just when things had got all nice and fuzzy feeling, and no one suspected the sudden plot turn.

"What's going on here?" he shouted. He drew his sword once he had surmised it all, and soon he was joined by all the others.

"Bloody heaven! You came back, liar of liars, faker of fakers. I'm so glad."

"Perhaps we shouldn't have been yelling our heads off and instead listened to the hero, aye!" shouted someone from the back.

Gethsarade took the moment. "Quite right. Quite right. Well, so much for a plan. Charge!"

Pirats began to flood the floor at Barrogan's clarion, and Gethsarade warned, "We need to get out in the open." He drew the sword of one pirat who was fighting another one and began swinging with all his might at anyone who charged him, while shouting commands to one party to slash the nets and another to follow him to the hold where the rest of the townfolk were.

"Free everyone!" he yelled to Tiburt and Gy, the latter who set about unlocking chains and severing ropes quickly as he could while batting off rats upon rats. The Knights shielded the Sons of Sangareth as they found their way into the air, flinging one another, and taking out rows at a time. The townsfolk joined the fray one by one.

The battle was heavily on, and Gethsarade threw down one pirat, and once he found a clear moment, he drew the oversized butcher blades he got courtesy of Mr. Cervello, setting off in a spin that took out a whole section of the line. Then he stood in front of Barrogan who smiled with his terrifying, blood-red teeth.

"Nice spin move. How will you fare at the true sport of swordplay in close-combat style?" teased Barrogan.

"Let's say, I've been practicing."

They clashed, and Gethsarade swung his giant blades with all his might at Barrogan Black's head, not wanting to take the chance at a drawn-out fight.

As it may be known to some, there are rats with some big teeth, but then there are also rats with teeth so strong they can bite through metal, for Barrogan, as it has been explained, was no ordinary river rat.

"You think I'm just some little squat rodent, but I am a Nutria, a king among rodents!" He exclaimed through blows upon Gethsarade's withering blocks.

"And our teeth are the sharpest, hardest teeth of all creatures anywhere! You have nothing against me!" Barrogan broke through Gethsarade's guard and sank his teeth straight into Gethsarade's blade, broke it off of its hilt, and caught a second, shattering it in Gethsarade's paw like a dry biscuit. The shards fell to the floor and Barrogan, a dwarf of a nutria, but still a nutria, with all the strength of one, bore down on Gethsarade and took in his mouth his entire shoulder and tossed him to the deck with his jaws.

The crowd looked on in horror as they fought, and in a moment as quick as a gopher's shadow, Barrogan Black had Gethsarade at the serious end of his own blade.

"You just don't get it," Barrogan held up his fist and the battle halted for it was won. The pirat commanders under Barrogan's employ called out, and the squirrels began to lay down their arms and kneel to the deck, their fresh capacity for bravery quickly exhausted.

To this Amalie cried, but could do nothing as the only one still fighting. She, too, was soon grabbed and held down next to Gethsarade.

"I don't get it, do I? Well, enlighten me," said Gethsarade, looking afresh for diversion.

"You and I...we are a lot alike."

"Well. You're not about to tell me you're my father. That just wouldn't work," he said through spasms of pain from his punctured torso.

"You definitely aren't any relation to any friend I've ever had, so I don't know what you're getting at to be honest."

"But what you don't know, is how I got the book, my boy. You see I'm old by now, quite enough to see the day of many a generation of victims. Before you were ever found upon some disgusting shore, I met someone who looked a lot like you. Yes, I recognized your face right away, son. You are the spit-and-shine of a sailor I pleasurably took the life of years ago. And he had a book, one I will burn now, with all the others. No, you're not like your father at all. You're an opportunist, like me. But you'll die, that you'll do like your father."

Gethsarade began to regret asking, for Barrogan went on to describe in detail how he killed everyone on the ship and found the book that explained how to find the treasure of the Golden Nut (in his interpretation, of course).

He thought he might have nodded off for a moment, but came back to catch Black saying, "...but the map only describes how to find the Nut according to where old Sangareth hid it, and it was never put there. That's when I realized what Sangareth meant when he laughed in my face and told me I would never find it right before I killed him. He encased the map within words, not directions, so to me it was useless. Nevertheless, you can all be sure, your hero Sangareth, though his son tried to bring you salvation. But I side with the opposition, for in trying to prevent your entire demise, he and this impostor became the actual vehicle for it. By bringing the book to me. This lout never came here to help you all, but to help me take everything!"

"You are on no one else's side, you sod! You know nothing of which you speak, and we all here as are one against you!" Great Father spat the words at Black, who began to seethe.

So Gethsarade, in the middle of all this boring talk, was thinking maybe Amalie was right in saying what was in the blood was in the blood.

He interrupted Barrogan. "Beg pardon. This is all very interesting, but I think you're a little off, Mister Black. You see, I've realized something through the last act of sacrifice. Sangareth was a hero after all, and his whole life turned out wrong, not because of some accident, but because of a single act of love, devotion, and sacrifice and, in this, he found himself."

He went on, "That squirrel you killed was not a poor sap. He understood loss and pain more than you ever could. You should have burned his ship, rather than taken it. Now, you will face your apocalypse at my paw."

"You know nothing of pain! Doubtless you always had the advantage in your adventuring. You were simply given everything, even now. Even forgiveness for your sins, which are doubtlessly innumerable. In your shoes, all of you would be dead. In my shoes, you would have been slaughtered by the first test, ages ago, and gone running back like the weakling you are to sleep upon your little parents' precious graves," he said this last part with a chuckle, until Gethsarade hocked and spat in his face.

"Pathetic," was all he said, and Barrogan reared back and slammed Gethsarade, screaming in agony, down upon the deck. Gethsarade lucked out, however, for it had worked. Black had put him down on the deck just close enough to the shackle and chain he had been trying to reach. He got it in his paw behind his back and waited for Barrogan to be distracted again. Fortunately, Amalie provided the needed fuse.

She spoke up, "You didn't kill any mean squirrel; instead, you took the life of a commander of Hesperia—one you will pay for."

Barrogan looked over, getting frustrated that his victims seemed to be impaired in some way from properly cowering before him. But the second he turned his gaze, he got whacked with a chain over the eyes, blinding him, and he bellowed out in agony.

"...And for the life of my father, Sangareth. I am not just some plinking musician," said Gethsarade. "I am not some withered pluck of an explorer. I am no scurvy sailor, lost accidentally at sea!"

As he shouted this, Gethsarade grabbed Black's paw, the one holding him down, and pushed out with all his might, allowing him to reach the other end of the chain. He whipped it around Black's neck and pulled even as Black still bellowed.

He was right. Black's weakness was also his strength. His giant black head kept him top heavy, and he crashed beside Gethsarade on the deck, dazing himself, and leaving him choking.

Gethsarade took the opportunity to leap onto his back in a grappling fashion and wrapped the chain around again, then tighter around his own arm for good measure, and soon Barrogan Black's head could not pull enough blood from his tiny body to hold oxygen and he went to the deck, lips dark blue, unable to fight at all.

Gethsarade looked around, and declared loudly, "I am Commander Gethsarade, Son of Sangareth of the Great Army of Hesperia! I am strong, I am..." and at last he leaned in to Black's ear and said with a whisper, "the hair of the dog that bit you!" he said with his eyes wide and a whisper. And he bonked Captain Black on the head knocking him out.

"And I am home." He turned to face them, and finding the smile of Amalie, a cheer went up from the crowd. "Your commander is defeated. Throw down your arms, all of you." The floor of the library shuddered with the clanking of swords.

But all was not well. Just then, there was a massive booming sound. The natives had felled a branch against the bottom entrance, successfully blocking it, but no one knew how. Then, Happenlings and savages, with teeth bared, and whip-whooping for crazy-head blood began pouring into the upper chamber onto the scene.

"Fools ye be, I am but a harbinger! Thar be thine apockalypse!" called out Black struggling up and still hacking.

"Fishes in a barrel, you are, all." The voice at the entrance called down, familiar to Gethsarade. His mind flashed back to the days on the ship. He realized it was that bloke, Scurrid, the Leader of the Happenlings.

"I will take my vittles now, Captain!" he jumped down into the fray at the bottom. Hesperia no longer stood at the advantage.

Gethsarade smelled smoke. "Get the high ground!" he yelled, but it was too late for some. Up at the upper entrance, and behind the squirrels and rats pouring in he could only see bright, burning red.

"He is burning us out!" The shrieks of terror began to rise higher, and the fight against the rats was abandoned to get all to the top of the chamber and out, if it were possible.

But still, enemies continued to pour in at such a rate that the squirrels of Hesperia, even the Guardians, were relegated to waiting until some opening in the flow, but it never came.

"Bah! You'll die!" cried Black. "Maybe I'll die too, but at least you all will!" And his laughing echoed all around.

The red hall began to fill in the darkness at its bottom with writhing, slithering rat tails and rotten teeth and jagged black claws, all one monstrous mass.

As the red light grew brighter in the night air and the darkness rose with the squirrels of Hesperia all at once desperately scrambling up the columns and sections of books, Black yelled for one of the rats to help him out of the ropes he was put in. Scurrid made no effort to command anyone to do so.

It was all the flying squirrels could do but to take to the heights of the hollow, where the rats and ground squirrels could not reach them. They all fell to the bottom like a waterfall, and as Hesperians waited for their chance to get out, the floor kept rising, full of writhing rats, and one of them, Barrogan in his insanity, thought to set and hold up torches, smoking out the squirrels while holding onto the rafters of the chamber at the same time.

As the smoke gathered in the upper lofts of the chamber, Hesperians began to cough and hack and slowly lose their strength and fall due to lack of air, kicking and then disappearing into the writhing fighters.

Amalie and Great Father coughed, holding on another, but their breathing became harder, and their claws began to fail them in holding on.

Gy was so large and muscular he could not do without air to breathe like the others, and he lost consciousness and fell before the rest.

Gethsarade watched him fall, and something arose within him. A fire, and he saw red, like no rage that had ever filled his mind. With a warrior's yell, he jumped down, drawing his choppers as he descended into the blackness, and forever went by for Amalie then. The rats rose, more squirrels fell, and still Gethsarade and Gy did not rise.

Tiburt wailed at the loss of Gy, and swearing he could not go on any more, submitted himself to death.

"Go down will I and not come up again, darkness for me!" But his neck caught, he looked up, and saw he was being held back by Great Father who had clung close by him.

"Fool of a magician, you'll only be killed and what will it mean for you, then? They die with honor. Let them."

Just then someone shouted, "The way is clearing out!" Great Father without any hesitation took Tiburt by the scruff and threw him straight through the opening, just as it stopped up again for squirrels now frantically escaping.

Tiburt immediately got up and started pulling left and right, still sobbing wildly, with black tears still streaming down his face, for Great Father and Amalie still were inside, no doubt helping all others escape before them.

Just Tiburt was about to lose hope, Amalie's face peeked through the doorway, and he grabbed her arm, pulling her out. He comforted her as she was coughing so badly she could barely lift herself. "There we go, up, up, now. Yes, breathe, love. Breathe, it's alright now."

"But the others are still inside, Great Father! Oh, my Gethsara...!" and she collapsed again into a fit of coughing. She remained behind with Tiburt, both because she could not stand or move, and because she intended to live or die by the side of her love.

As she recovered, as all others escaped from Library Tree and turned once in safety to watch in horror, as the smoke poured like Death's Black River from the opening and up to fill the sky, and as the flames rose up all around the tree in thick, red walls, the open door seemed as though it would give up no one else.

Through the pouring smoke straggled a paw, clutching the edge of the deck, and Amalie's breath went away again. But the paw disappeared, whomever it was, and the cane of Great Father struck out of the black piles of smoke instead, wedging sideways in the doorway, and out came Great Father's head then shoulders. Tiburt saw he was straining, so he ran over again and bent to help him. And as he pulled Great Father out of the piling glow at last, they gasped to see that in his other paw held onto Gethsarade's limp body, all bloody, nipped and gnashed by the untold horde of teeth and claws still screeching without escape in the darkness inside below.

Amalie came to them, "Is he alive?" she asked.

"I don't know," said Great Father in between hacks.

Just as it seemed all hope was lost, Gethsarade sputtered and coughed, and went into a fit, but alive to do it, so they all shouted in joy. They helped each other to the edge and threw Tiburt first to the other tree, for the boughway to it had given before them. There he turned to aid the rest of them, still wailing from the flames, biting at the haunches as they rose ever higher.

But just then he froze, for he saw behind the three of them still on the bough a shadow with a grotesquely enlarged head. For just a moment, he slid back in fright, and the others looked around at what he was so terrified at beyond even the hellish fires. The flames rose up between Tiburt and his friends, and that was his last vision of them to live with.

On the bough, they stood confused at why Tiburt suddenly drew back, till they heard a voice behind them. It sounded so damaged it was barely distinguishable from the rasping hisses and growls of the flames.

"That's right, take it all in," said Barrogan Black. His body had been burned all over, without a hair left anywhere but only singed masses and blackened clumps left of his skin. Yet his eyes still burned with their red stare. He was dead standing, smiling, smoke puffing out between his crimson teeth. It seemed they glowed in the night.

He had chewed his way out through the burning walls. Before Gethsarade could recover, the three rose up to meet the beast. But Great Father at his age and Amalie in her gentility were useless in combat, and though they gave their best battle cry, Black knocked the two of them both down and threw Gethsarade aside like a mill sack. Great Father fell unconscious with one swipe, his motionless face lay covered with blood. Black kicked Amalie to the side and failing quarter to ceremony sank his black blade into Great Father's torso, and it shined silver again and red out the other side. Great Father bellowed, and then nothing for evermore.

Amalie cried out and even the screaming heat could not abate her tears. Barrogan Black smiled and began to walk towards her as she tried to crawl away.

Gethsarade had taken a hard blow and, out of the grog still sloshing in his brain, he glanced up. Everything was a double blur. He shook his head, and things got a little clearer, but it looked like there were ghosts wavering between himself and the scene of Barrogan Black waving a sword at his love.

Then for just a moment, the ghosts seemed familiar, in fact one of them was wearing his clothes. But it was handsomer, and to Gethsarade's disbelief, the apparition smiled at him in a playful sort

254

of way, and motioned silently toward a narrow opening in the flames he had not seen before. He only had time to grab Amalie and fly out to survival, and riches and fame...and maybe Black would survive to terrorize them all forever. The other ghost he did not recognize, but it only watched him with a brow of steel. Gethsarade had only a moment to think.

But he could think, not of Amalie, or of fortune, but of his father Sangareth, and the champion of truth he was. But then, something tingled inside of him, and his head jerked up, but ah! The visions had gone. Nevertheless, he knew what must be done.

"Sorry, friend," he whispered to no one and pushed himself off the deck with everything he had left.

Amalie's unintended distraction had worked, and Black had forgotten about Gethsarade. As he raised his blade to strike, suddenly Gethsarade roared out of the smoke and tackled him from behind as hard as he could, and they both went off the bough to the platform below, where the fire had started.

Amalie rushed to her father's side, weeping, to behold his last breaths as Barrogan and Gethsarade battled it out for the final time.

Their cries of fury and anger were heard by all around the tree as Library Tree burned away till it crumbled and crashed to the forest floor, and they all wept in the darkness of the forest's silence.

"He saved us," the townsfolk said, "He was the hero..." And they watched and listened behind the wall of ember as the ochre of dawn rose in the throes of gasps and sobs, hoping their last of hopes would arise despite everything and all the odds.

But none did.

19: A Note on the Impossible

Somewhere out over the sea, a breeze blew and the *Tara Feen* stretched its sails, or as it is translated from the ancient Hesperian tongue, "Goldwing."

They had put Black's burnt heap of a body in a net as he began to come to, and aboard the *Tara Feen* he made out the faces of Amalie Tadwick, Great Father Herron Tadwick, and Gethsarade Sangareth, who did not arise out of the flames in accordance with the hopes of namesake or legend. Still, they had escaped out another secret way of only Great Father's knowing. Black's burned body was useless to him, and he grunted sorely, for his mouth had been tied shut as well.

"Do you know what we do with your kind?" asked Gethsarade to Barrogan Black, held out over the side of the ship by a yardarm as all watched the ceremony of his demise.

Black struggled furiously, but there was nothing he could do to escape his bonds in his weakened state. So he just sat in the net, cursing Gethsarade's name in the form of grunts and muffles.

Gethsarade leapt up onto the beam, strolled over to the edge where Barrogan hung. Gethsarade looked down at him in his newly found stately manner, and Barrogan kicked and writhed defiantly, with a muffled cry that was something like, "Just get it over with."

"I'll tell you…" and Gethsarade turned to the audience. "Friends! This criminal once told me the thing he hated more than anything…was musicians! Dear citizens, Guardians, and Sons of Sangareth, all. I'll tell you what we do with such injustice as this."

They all paused for his next words.

"Wait for it...," he held up a finger, and a few rolled their eyes impatiently. Amalie thought to herself, 'My love, always dramatic.'

"Wait...."

A droning was heard and seemed to draw nearer. It caused their ears to ache as it grew, and one of the townsfolk with more simple sensibilities cried, "I think I'm going to be sick from that awful noise!" They puzzled back and forth till someone gasped and pointed to the sky at an incoming parliament of Owls!

"We do this!" shouted Gethsarade, and he drew his sword, bringing it down fast and hard upon the rope holding up the net containing Barrogan Black, sending him down toward the sea. But Gethsarade had timed it correctly, and just then King Hootley Toohu and his entourage swooped down and scooped up the net, carrying Barrogan Black off to the soundtrack of their terrible hurdy gurdy playing.

The last anyone saw of Barrogan Black was the fear in his eyes at the realization the fate he would forever suffer was worse than fiery death.

Gethsarade exclaimed, "I hereby condemn thee, Barrogan Black, to listen to the sweet beats of the Owl Kingdom as their prisoner until the day you die!" Black screamed as his voice faded.

King Hootley himself landed on the deck with his guards who went ahead of him, though it was a tight fit on the quarterdeck.

"How goes it, good friend and supplier of audience to the King's Owlz. With a Z." He said this while his guards blared the hurdy gurdy behind him, much to everyone's dismay.

Gethsarade kept his smile. "It's going pretty well, old friend. I see you've been expanding your repertoire."

"Yes! We really appreciated the pointers you gave us after all!" The guard holding the instrument behind him rattled off with what must have been the most horrendous caricature of composition in history. Still, it was loads better than the never-ending, soul-splitting whine of awfulness. "Our lyricist, Boogle. Like it?"

"Do I?!"

"Wonderful! Maybe we can jam sometime. Spit some barz. Check out my new crew...." King Toohoo uttered a series of nonsense one could only assume to be a list of stag names so absolutely boorish and cliched that no self-respecting squirrel ought ever write them down. They all crossed their wings at the mention of each moniker.

"It's a great side hustle," the Owl King said.

"Cool, cool. Hey, it's been swell. We'll check back with you on that jam sesh later, sound sound?"

"Aye. Farewell, Gethsarade."

They were off.

All onboard cheered, though more or less also because the awful noise was gone.

Gethsarade checked the crowd, and the tide. "I know. I know. You should have heard it before. Right, now that's over, so let's get down to business. Bos'n!"

"Yes, Captain?" Tiburt said, popping up his head over the crowd by the aid of a line, though with some difficulty on a crutch.

"Turn the ship out to sea."

"Aye, Aye," Tiburt said. Then he hobbled off to yell at the crew some unintelligible commands he probably didn't know much about but hoped maybe they did.

"But how shall we teach the truth to Hesperia?" asked Amalie.

"I wouldn't worry, my dear," interjected Great Father, still limping from his wounds at the paws of Barrogan Black. Amalie took him by the paw and braced him as he sat down on a bit. "As far as Hesperia is concerned, you and I are dead, and we all died for truth, the truth that matters. Let it be. Let the book rest in its hiding place at Tadwick. We will rewrite all that has happened here and begin a new history."

"But it wouldn't be the truth, then." said Amalie.

"In a certain way, but I think knowledge and truth are different."

"I risked my life for the truth!" said Gethsarade.

"How was I supposed to know you were going to do that? What is real, my son, is truth, realer than any nugget or log, or book or shield, and is worth protecting. I think our fair town can handle the truth by itself, but perhaps Sangareth was right: the truth is necessarily hidden, revealed only to the willing. We should hold it, protect it. That is our sacred duty. To take it back now would remove the opportunity to have faith, and faith is the one thing arguably more important than truth."

"And what? Should we do service by telling it to no one? Is that not how it dies," replied Amalie.

"Truth cannot die, though any of us can. But I think it should be revealed once all is decided, whether they should believe or not believe, before they see. When Hesperia finally makes its choice, it will be ready and we will hear of it. Until then, I think the truth is safer with us."

"This stands against everything we have stood for!" cried Amalie.

"I know, dear. That is what it is to be wrong."

"While…," Gethsarade interrupted having done some thinking, "While I can understand the importance of truth, dear, I think Great Father is right. If I had known what I would have to go through to get here, when I wasn't ready, I don't think I would have gone through with it. Nor would you. Against all odds, it had to happen this way, *this way,* or I can't imagine our lives working out like this at all. What can happen will happen, so what must happen cannot be stopped. But it is true, Hesperia is not ready and won't be for a long time."

"But you saw how they came together…over you."

"After they stood at point of sword and after they had done all the evil they could. That is not willingness, that's nothing. Till then, they didn't want change, as they only wanted more of the same. In that respect, they only changed in alliance, not in nature. Until they do so on their own, I now think Great Father is right. This book is in better paws somewhere far away if only for now."

To this finally Amalie nodded, silent.

"A toast," he lifted a flask. "Till the dead arise…one, two, a thousand for Hesperia!"

"One, two, a thousand for Hesperia!" the ship's crew one and all declared the pledge to the sea and heavens above.

And our hero Gethsarade realized he had found his way indeed. Then after all, Amalie and Gethsarade had their wedding, but not the kind of wedding as is the usual kind here where the whole town gets together, and they all have big whirling, flying festival.

Rather, they had one quite grounded, bedecked, even, on the boards of the once lost ship, the *Tara Feen*. Tiburt was there, though nearly not, in bandages and missing his precious fake tail cover, for he no longer needed it. He could walk about as he pleased, for he found he could kiss an owl and like it, and there was no problem with that, because owls sometimes need fingers and squirrels sometimes need wings and rats sometimes need to be fluffy, and we all need to just be loved and understood.

It doesn't stop the truth from being important, because that *is* the truth. His new friend, the owl Lady Bookatooka, who was a little odd herself, circled high above the ship looking down. Then, with a wink, she took off to catch up with her parliament, into the night with their captives in tow.

When the priest, Tiburt, said, "Squirrel and wife," the newlywed couple kissed despite being all bandaged up and sore.

Everyone cheered, including all sharks, turtles, otters, and birds in attendance, on or around the ship.

Then Great Father said, "Hey, everyone stop! This isn't a party without some music. Gethsarade, take it away!"

To Gethsarade's surprise, they actually wanted to hear him play. And as he whipped out his instrument and they all began to dance and sing, Amalie, and Tiburt all thought to themselves, *Where did this dude even come from?*

In the fracas, someone threw up to Gethsarade an interesting looking victual, which he threw down his gullet without thinking. Then he stopped very suddenly and asked Amalie, "What did you say the reception meal was?" To which she replied, "Oh, it's fish sausage. I thought you'd like a sea dish. What do you think?"

He looked very annoyed for a moment. She put her paw on his shoulder, but he shrugged it off. "I'll have it all thrown out if you don't like it."

"No," he held up his paw. "It's delicious." He hiccupped. He wiped his brow, and that was the only hiccup of the day and they went back to dancing.

Gethsarade got the cheers he had always dreamed of, for being good was more important than ripping mad guitar skills. And as the clapping died down, Great Father lifted his head, for it had been weighed down while everyone else enjoyed themselves, as this is the tendency of leaders. He lifted his paw, and all went silent.

"Gethsarade, I applaud you. You are wiser truly than all my schemes. All I wanted was to bring our kind together, and I thought I needed to possess all power to do so, for we are a wretched and conniving bunch. But your scheme of not scheming, of being just plain truthful, could work after all, I think. Perhaps I should have listened to your father from the beginning, and all this would have been a trifle."

"All is well."

"No, I must tell you, for your new imperative demands it. You must hear of how the revolt really happened, a terrible secret…I made a judgment call about your father. Since then I questioned himself on so many occasions. Yet, I couldn't bear to tell anyone for the threat of disrupting the family name, and I eventually felt I had been wrong all these years. The day you returned to claim your father's rightful place of honor, I realized I needed to make things right. You complicated things with this pretending with this alter ego, but I see the purpose now.

"It was not because I needed to help you with a way out of your false claim to be an explorer and still not reveal your true identity. It was fate for me to see the pattern I had instilled in my own life of pretending, for all the sins I committed in allowing without thinking the good name of my friend to be defamed. He was simply of a different mind, not of different blood. We all here lied, and everyone pretends to be someone they are not. It was Sangareth, he alone did not, and that was what I so feared. You have proven truer a squirrel than all of us." He broke down and said, "Everything is my fault. Please forgive me. Please." and Gethsarade indeed did forgive him.

"All is well…Great Father," he said. "All is well."

261

And all, indeed, was for Gethsarade, crew, and company. For the rest of his days Gethsarade traveled the world and adventured with his beloved Amalie, and their legend together has yet to fade from the song of the sea nor the elegy of time.

Epilogue

In older days, no one wrote about anyone but the most important figures. Kings being naughty, lords and kits going out of line, those types. They were the only ones, of course, who could afford to have themselves written about, to spread word and fear of their name and glory and, of course, the power of their lands.

This, as you can tell, was not one of those tales. Go and read other books about us. They may hold more truth than this one, and sway you better on things.

But it is the hope of telling this story one can remember, there is no inconsistency to be found in sacrifice for others while also standing up for one's self, and no fault at all in one who is proud enough of where he or she came from, yet is still able to envision higher.

For we all come from trouble, but that does not make anyone. Only some take wing and choose to rise above, while others go on applauding themselves merely for their suffering. And you can believe you can't change, but you can never tell that to who you'll be tomorrow. There will always be imposters, opportunists, and those who think the right thing is the weak thing, but only because they've never done it. They will pass into the mist as soon as they can.

But the way to find your truest dream is not what many think. It is not a grand roaming down the dark halls of mystery. For one who is kind has learned all that the dark rows teach, and there is as much truth all around us now as there is out in the world. And one who searches is often not imprisoned by his or her circumstances but by their own mind and heart, while preserving the soul. Something as simple as warming a baby on the shore can save a life and in but one life is contained a whole world of truth.

ADDENDUM

Dear Readers,

The aforementioned ending is unconfirmed. You may take it if you like. One or more Rodentian scholars added to it later being more concerned with consistency of later tradition, we now think, than of accuracy.

Now, the regular opinion is that scholarly matters become less relevant over time. But sometimes it takes the passing of time and memory till we realize the real truth and how to tell it.

The real story is a bit of a flop plot-wise, so I couldn't blame anyone for believing whatever they will. But I think one of these endings to this story makes sense of Gethsarade's and assures us we are all heroes in our own way, which sounds good to other ears.

This ending is my account, and should be read only if you, dear readers, are willing. This ending lets our hero lie where he fell and be who he was. But then, I have all my life followed my reasonable mind, unlike those all whom I shan't see again, and they are remembered by me all the days as is my reasonability my punishment. Thus, I won't dare tell you what ending to take. The choice is yours. If you can stomach it, this is probably how it really went....

The ones inside the wall of fire that consumed Library Tree were Gethsarade, Amalie, Great Father Tadwick, Barrogan Black, and those who never escaped from inside the chamber, namely myself. It is true, I escaped by some miracle of both passing out and being presumed dead by the writhing horde, and then cushioned by their corpses, fools all. 'Tis death saved me.

The citizens who escaped heard the clang of the upper door (the last thing I remember), then all heard over the roar of flames Great Father Tadwick's gruff, booming voice and his secrets. Then various shouting was heard. No one saw the final fight between

Barrogan and Gethsarade at the bottom of the fire. They only heard, horrible, unreal screaming that faded too slowly away.

Some still say they hear it from time to time to this day. It may have been that Amalie had a moment or two to escape the flames, but was unwilling to abandon either of her loves. She finally relinquished her civic duties and there fell the House of Tadwick.

And listening, some souls on the outside attempted to even brave the flames to get back in to save those nobles who had first saved them. But the flames pushed them back every time. After so many tense moments, and much grievous alarm, the voices behind the wall of burning red choked and faded to nothing. The tear-streaked voice chimed like a bell in the night, "He saved us..." but nothing more was to be done, in truth.

They found the bodies of all within, but oddly not those I have named, who fought the last fight to save their home.

Sometime after the fight, I awoke, dug my way out of the bodies, and seeing the remnants of destruction, I wept aloud, for no face I knew was there. The fire was still dying in the first fall of the new winter's snow, putting out the flames with its calming gentility.

As the only known survivor of those from Hesperia who fell to the flames and smoke, I was later asked about the mysterious Scurrid unfound in the wreckage. I only then realized it must have been he who lit the flames from the outside, intending to consume everyone at once and take all Hesperia for himself without Barrogan Black, or any savage, or anyone at all to challenge him. So, when he realized he had failed and fair Hesperia remained, he skittered off like the true coward he had shown himself to be. We assume we'll never to see him again. Let us hope that holds.

There are more mysteries to this story we cannot account for, mainly, we know my good friend Tiburt was never seen again. Many are still beyond certain they saw him with their own eyes coughing up smoke, but that I think only once, and by night no one can say they saw him again before the last curtain of fire went up the Library Tree and went all the way down. It took a few to hold him back, and they remember the words they warned him with as he struggled to dive back into the fire, "The fire is too hot. You'll only be doubly killed." But then, he fought till none could hold his tiny body any more, and the last they saw was his tail going into the flames. No one saw him again. So that is the simplest conclusion given the facts we know.

Yet there is another mystery that might account for the reason so many take the traditional ending for the better. No one ever saw the ship *Tara Feen* again. Some have even gone to taking on wilder tales, such as our hero Gethsarade never coming back at all, and even fewer still assert Gethsarade was a figment, along with the *Tara Feen,* a fictional account created to support the political ambitions of fringe groups about the realm and to shovel away whoever it really was to blame for the fire.

Yet, legends continued to spread of a hero who traveled the world and did good. We heard often many more tales than could ever be recorded.

Gethsarade should have survived as he could fly, after all. But perhaps he knew there was only one way to make sure the dead stayed buried. He had watched Barrogan fall and rise and fall and rise. Perhaps we like to hear the story end with something better because we like things to conform to the pattern of a good legend about what we suppose our heroes to be like. For us, it is a mystery most black.

I submit, perhaps for Gethsarade, that he realized if he wanted to stop the Apocalypse, he was the last of hopes, and he had to walk into the light, bright and burning, if he truly wished to become his father's son. No hero dies on time or rests at happy funerals. My one regret is that my final words to him were not kinder.

Some only accept the meanest explanation for anything because they don't like to think there are things out there bigger, more imaginative, or more important than themselves. Or, conversely, to think the real meaning of things could be so messy.

I do not know how many hold onto this, for these things were not done in a corner. No doubt the lever of time's mill will keep that one turning a while, maybe longer.

Whatever many say, I can't say the truth is ever as simple as our small minds would like to believe, and I don't know if there will ever be an answer until perhaps the Savior of Hesperia should one day return yet again, for us all to take note. However, the grave stands empty. Let's hope the truth never fits our liking, and let us tell it anyway, let us keep hope, my friends, and let him come on the *Tara Feen,* flying on the clouds of heaven if he can!

And this time, we shall know the true name as a farmer knows his own nuts, and I won't be calling him any name but friend on that day. The truth is the epitaph of the brave, so bury these bones and lay them all over my own, if it pleases. Truly, I only know one thing for sure about all this: I miss my friend.

G. B.

The End.

Dear Readers,

I'd like first of all to thank you for giving my work your time. If you are reading this far, then I'd like to think it has been a worthwhile experience for you. If not, then please burn this book. Being a writer is so God-awful embarrassing that I'd rather there be no evidence if it can be helped. Just ask my mother in law. She thinks I should just be a stay-at-home dad. I had aspirations once.

That said, please shamelessly follow my Facebook page (facebook.com/mgclaybrook) so that I can give you free books because I can't pay people to buy them. I just give them away to anyone who will let me. No, I'm not drunk. Just honest. Make sure and join my **Official Fan Page** and accept my invitation to my secret super-fan list that I use as my team of Advance Copy Readers of my new releases. That way, you'll be one of the few and proud yipsters who know what's up before anyone has heard of it yet. Also, you may occasionally view some perspicacious caterwauling and vague threats of nominal interest to the public. I've been followed by the guy from CHIPS, once by Bill Gates for six and a half minutes, also Ron Perlman (@Perlmutations), which is obviously my greatest achievement in life. All these beautiful treasures I save for the elite, and by that, I mean people who actually like me. There are not a lot of them on purpose.

So please, know that your interest in my work is sincerely appreciated and, to be quite honest, I'd really like you to go on Amazon and write an honest review if it's all the same (disclaimer: you are under no obligation but be honest please) because Heaven low-key knows I need them. Like, I know I'm supposed to be all professional and obscure here, but let's face it, Amazon kinda sucks about this and I need money because I'm published on Amazon. The best way to support a writer, or any artist, is to talk about them, of course, and all that, yadda yadda, it's not about the money, but it's about the money, you know?

In all honesty, thank you for your support, and I hope you have found something to give you a little joy, or at least a few obscure new pop-culture references to look up for some cerebro-genic, quizzicularial stimulation.

Love,
M. C.

About the Author

Matthew Claybrook dreamt about writing until his family crushed his dreams when he was seven by saying writers are a dime a dozen. Just kidding, fam. He's over it. You were right.

Unfortunately, he later got lost on the way to college, then tried to become a rock star, like all self-respecting ex-military do. Then, he tried to start his own business as if that was even going to go well. It didn't. He then actually found his way to college.

It was awful. He struggled all the way through his B.S. in Theology and, yes, that's correctly stated, with only most of his family wondering why, even. After that, he and his wife both decided to have a kid and become teachers at the same time.

And so, after this long line of excellent decisions, Matthew decided to complete his run by becoming a writer, and he has never regretted it more than three times a day, on average. Currently, he is somewhere in fact suggesting coconuts migrate, and likely wearing white socks with black shoes just to keep people unsure about him. He hopes to one day to achieve the greatest status of all writers: to become one of those writers everyone praises but does not read.

If one were crazy, one might follow him at **facebook.com/mgclaybrook** and one might get suckered into more of his books. But don't worry if you don't really want to, as he's writing this jacked up on coffee, and his mother in law doesn't read them, either. I mean, like, he doesn't even know you. He'll be fine. I said, stop it. I'm not cr- I said he'll be fine.

This page left blank because I have nothing left to say.